Far From Mortal Realms

A Novel of Humans and Fae

Karen A. Wyle

DEDICATION

To my father, who always strove
To protect and rescue his children.

CHAPTER I

ADIRA barreled through her front door, then stopped in mid-stride to take a deep breath of the fresh spring air and let the sunshine warm her face. She could spare a moment to appreciate the morning before she hurried to the office and the pastries Dad would have waiting there. And the coffee, her favorite extra strength hazelnut – Dad made a point of providing it, even now that he felt it more prudent to drink decaf.

As she walked the few blocks between her home and the office, she played her usual guessing game. Would their law practice take her to some new Fair Folk realm today, and if it did, how would that realm compare to this peaceful New England town? Would it have tempests or calm skies, recognizable trees or carnivorous vines, fae resembling humans or more mindboggling creatures? And what puzzles would she and Dad be called upon to solve, what sly schemes to detect and thwart? How would they outwit the Fair Folk today?

* * * * *

Abe looked out the window at the water rippling and sparkling in the lake, savoring both the sight and the anticipation of Adira's arrival. He took a deep sniff of the coffee brewing for her and glanced over at the mammoth 19th-century grandfather clock in the hall. The handsome piece of furniture served a useful purpose, given that Fair Folk visitors sometimes enjoyed sending digital devices into fits. A year or so ago, one of their rare Fair Folk clients had paid for their services with special shielding against such mischief, allowing them to use and even update a desktop and laptop apiece, but Abe still half expected the shielding to fail.

Abe heard his daughter's firm tread mounting the front steps and grabbed two mugs, handing one to Adira as she flung open the front door. She seized it and followed close on his heels as he went to fill his own. As she dropped into one of the solid wooden chairs in the conference room and tipped it backward, he retrieved the tray he had brought from home, full almost to spilling over with the fruits of his Sunday baking, and set it on the table. She licked her lips, contemplated the cookies and muffins, and finally selected a brownie, biting away a quarter of it. He chuckled, picked up a fruit bar, and settled into his own chair, pulling a handwritten list out of his scuffed black briefcase. "Shall we plunge in?"

Adira grinned wryly. "What, no small talk? 'Have you seen the crocuses blooming, or the trout-lilies?' 'How did you sleep? Did you have pleasant dreams?'"

What with the bustle of getting ready for Adira's arrival, he had almost forgotten the dream he'd had before waking. Reminded, he sighed and said, "Rather a lovely one. We might even be able to market it, in fact. I've always wanted to try that." The fae couldn't dream, and many of them seemed fascinated by the very idea. Sometimes they bought human dreams and brought them to life as mini-realms. Not that he'd heard of it happening in the past few years.

"Anyway, I found myself in a graveyard, not long before dawn, with fog almost hiding the gravestones –"

Adira frowned. "I'm not sure we should be dealing with the sort of fae who'd relish a spectacle like that. Didn't you tell me about one of the Unseelie courts setting up a nightmare realm with a graveyard full of shrieking ghouls and lurking wolves, and fog that turned out to be quicksand?" Adira shuddered dramatically, perhaps to disguise a less theatrical and more genuine reaction. Abe remembered telling her about that realm when she was around nine, and then regretting it for the weeks during which it inspired nightmares.

"No, it wasn't like that at all! As I looked around, I saw deer, one after another, emerging from the fog. And then ghosts appeared from behind the stones, thrilled, slowly moving toward the deer – shy at first, but then clustering around them and stroking them. It was lovely, so peaceful . . . . If one of the Fair Folk is interested in it, I'd like to visit it again sometime. We could write that into the contract."

Adira shrugged. If so gentle a scene attracted her, she had no intention of letting her father see as much. "No dreams of any value for me – at least, none I'm willing to let anyone else handle." She looked Abe in the eye with a certain defiance, where another woman might have blushed. "Let's move on. What's our schedule for the day?"

Abe looked over at the clock again. "In a little more than half an hour, we have a dedicated gardener on a quest to capture the blue ribbon for his not-yet-prizewinning tomatoes. He's heard about a previous winner getting an assist from the Fair Folk and wants us to negotiate something similar."

Adira shook her head, setting her black hair bouncing. "What, didn't he hear about what happened afterward?"

Abe grimaced and replied, "As I recall, after that fellow's garden reached his roof in a giant tangle and lifted it free of the walls, he had the plants torn out – twice – and then paid even more for the fae to make them disappear. But perhaps our client is less up to date than we are on fae-related news. At least he has the good sense to hire us to get him reasonable terms. Any thoughts?"

Adira swallowed the final bite of her brownie and said, "We can see whether he grows anything that any of the Fair Folk – hold on, with whom are we negotiating, given how many different parties could provide this service?"

Abe smirked. "Your favorite middleman, or middle-fae I should say, has agreed to shop our client's offer around." He ducked as Adira grabbed a muffin and pretended to throw it at him. Adira had little patience for the preferred glamour and habits of the being who styled itself the Viscount of Bloomingshire, though both professional courtesy and simple self-preservation required her to show it the most exquisite politeness.

As he expected, Adira put aside her show of temper and focused on the problem at hand. "So. We can see whether any of . . . the *viscount*'s contacts would like some of the client's seeds or seedlings, whether of tomatoes or some other crop. Aren't tomatoes related to some poisonous plant? That might appeal. Or he could offer to grow some fae plants and provide opportunities for his neighbors to see them. That lets everyone involved show off. Of course, he'd have to make sure not to eat any, nor to let anyone else do so."

Abe chewed his lip. "We'd have to include a clause saying that whatever plants they provided wouldn't shape themselves into a faerie ring and transport our gardener or his guests anywhere. And we'll set reasonable growth limits, and exclude any dangerous or unsightly mutations. Anything else we'll have to watch out for?"

Adira tossed her head and said, "We'll give the final language a good going-over, of course, but I think our usual boilerplate will take care of the other hazards. Though I fully expect our dear middle-fae to suggest some of it is unnecessary – say, the clauses that protect us as well as our client."

"Do you, really, after the dozens of times he's dealt with us? Would you care to make a small wager?"

Adira waved away the offer, took a sniff of her muffin – carrot and ginger, worth the smelling, if he did say so – and said, "What's next?"

Abe sighed as he replied, "Ms. and Mr. Dellor – I don't know which one took the other's name. A job trickier than most, which is saying something. Apparently one of the more old-fashioned Fair Folk has taken a baby boy and left a changeling in its place." He paused and lifted his chin, struck by a sudden thought. "I wonder if the risk of a baby being traded for a changeling is the source of the prohibition against mentioning newborns to the fae? I'd always thought of it as one of their peculiar rules, but it may have human, and pragmatic, origins. But back to our potential clients. The parents want our help to get their baby back."

Adira, keeping her voice level with apparent effort, asked, "Have they already tried traditional self-help?" Such methods tended to skew toward making the fae infant's new environment hostile enough for it to flee, by such means as beating with birch rods. And whatever the results of such abuse may have been centuries ago, Fair Folk in the modern era would have their vengeance.

"I don't think so. They seem to be thinking along different lines. They have what *might* be a viable idea for providing adequate recompense."

Adira tapped her chin for a few seconds and then said, voice tight, "They want to exchange some other child for their baby. An orphan? Or a child removed from its parents by social services?"

"The latter. The child in question is two years old, but so neglected his weight is closer to that of a six-month-old. He has no relatives who would be a reliable improvement on his birth parents. The fae could restore him to health."

"And of course," Adira said savagely, "these clients have no interest in caring for *that* child."

Abe pushed his chair back and sat up straight. "Be fair, daughter. You have no children, but as the greatly loved child of two parents, you must have some conception of what these parents' own child means to them."

Adira's manner softened for a moment and then shifted toward stubbornness. "At any rate, whether I empathize adequately or no, I can at least be professional. But I believe I'm justified in considering the child's interest as well – the child to be *traded away*, that is. Assuming he becomes a healthy human child, what then? Does he somehow become one of the fae? Or is he trapped forever, a human among them, growing and changing as they remain unchanging, surrounded by beings with no fundamental understanding of his emotions and needs? And never able to have a family of his own?"

Abe pulled his chair forward again, planted his elbows on the table, and leaned toward her. "We must be very careful in discussing these aspects of the problem. Even other Fair Folk, let alone the being who has taken the baby, will be less than tolerant if we implicitly criticize an age-old practice of their people. I've seen what it's like to anger the fae, and I have no wish to see it again, or to expose you to it."

Adira tossed her chin at his daring to exhibit protective impulses. "That doesn't prevent us from bargaining for some protections for the child. For example, he could retain the right to rejoin the mortal community when he reaches his majority. And before that, we could require his . . . guardians to allow him access to human children on some regular basis. But will the clients allow us to set any such conditions?"

Abe let himself smile, if grimly. "Anticipating your objections, and having some of my own, I told the mother that we would only take the case if they gave us some rein to exercise our best judgment and fulfill our professional responsibilities. She'll get back to us and confirm the arrangement in the next day or two. Now, before we move on to this afternoon's schedule, has any new business come your way?"

Adira tapped her stylus on her laptop. "Something has – in a manner of speaking."

Abe studied his daughter. She had a look he associated with secrets and other news, and with problems she had solved without his assistance. "Please go on," he said, in fond expectation.

"I got a message – written, in mediocre calligraphy, and slipped through the mail slot of my door at home. It said it came from a fae of the Unseelie Court – it didn't specify Autumn or Winter – and that a mortal had tried to cheat another resident of that realm and then slandered the intended victim when the scheme fell through. The message appealed to us, as reputable representatives of mortals, to take some sort of action against the slanderer."

Abe was already shaking his head. "My goodness. 'A little learning is a dangerous thing.' We're supposed to believe, not just that any mortal would be such a fool – that, I suppose, is possible – but that any fae would condescend to ask a mortal to handle a grievance against another mortal? And that a fae victim of slander, particularly a member of one of the Unseelie Courts, would not have immediately wreaked vengeance on the slanderer in some appropriately final manner?"

Adira chuckled. "The note said the residents of that realm were attempting to take a low profile where mortals were concerned. As if such a concern would have outweighed the importance of deterring misbehaving mortals! Oh – here's the really ridiculous part. The message came in an envelope – with a return address! A fae, relying on the mortal postal service!"

Abe burst out laughing, which set Adira off. When they finally settled down, he asked her, "Did you reply to this optimistic con artist?"

"Oh, yes!" Adira said, with one final chortle. "I invited the author, and the injured party, to visit us at our office, where we could verify their status as bona fide Fair Folk and discuss their options. I don't suppose they'll think they can successfully bluff through *that* test."

Abe would have gone on to discuss the afternoon's appointments, but a familiar prickling up and down his spine, and the stirring of the hair on his arms, informed him that further discussion would have to be postponed. "Party manners, my dear," he announced. He shouldn't feel the need to remind Adira, but her mood this morning prompted him to do so. The imminent arrival of one of the Fair Folk required that they observe precautions such as refraining from using each other's true names, lest they give a fae power over them, and adopting properly deferential manners. The self-styled Viscount of Bloomingshire must be on their doorstep.

Early, of course. The fae's mischievous nature often led it to ignore expectations. Abe had hoped the eager gardener would arrive first, but Abe had already briefed him at length, and quizzed him twice, as to the necessary behavior. He would also make a point of sitting next to their client so he could step on the man's foot if necessary.

The viscount opened the front door, the doorbell chiming a lively tune unknown to its manufacturer, and bowed with a flourish, flinging a blue velvet cape wide to display a yellow and white striped waistcoat and an elaborately folded white neck cloth. As the fae straightened up, it grinned its unsettling, toothy grin, looked down its long, bony nose, and said, "My dear Alexander and Folke – your very humble servant." Its mocking expression showed its awareness that they dared not use their actual surnames for a practice specializing in dealings with the Fair Folk.

The frivolous thought that crossed Abe's mind almost made him snort, which would have risked giving offense.

He maintained his gravely polite expression while imagining what the viscount would have said about a firm name of "Tightrope and Walker." No image could better describe the skills and perils involved in dealing with the fae on a daily basis, the need to constantly maintain focus in order to avoid tumbling to disastrous depths.

While they awaited the gardener, Abe inquired whether the fae had heard about the recent substitution of a changeling for a local human baby. The viscount was smugly pleased to inform Abe that it had, in fact, heard of the affair. "So gauche, I would have thought, to cling to these antiquated customs, but I was not consulted."

In the conversation that followed, Abe was able to confirm his guess that the fae who had taken their client's baby hailed from the Autumn Court. That court was one of the four seasonal courts that had presumably inspired Scottish folklore. The Spring and Summer Courts more or less behaved according to the traditional descriptions of Seelie Courts, sometimes mischievous but generally as benign as any Fair Folk could be said to be, while the Autumn and Winter Courts inclined more toward the dangerous and hostile. Of the Unseelie Courts, Winter was more associated with clever cruelty, but it would be foolish to let down one's guard when dealing with Autumn. Clara, with her Scottish heritage and her study of same, would have been a useful on-scene consultant, but even if Clara had been more involved in their practice, Abe would never suggest she set foot there. He and Adira could manage on their own.

* * * * *

That afternoon

The first stage of the gardener's case left them with no more than the viscount's pledge to find an appropriate fae provider for the services they had negotiated. After both the client and the viscount had departed, it was time to head for the offices of a state politician who had had a close encounter with some violent demonstrators and now wanted the additional security fae powers could provide. It soon became evident that they would have to tread carefully in negotiating that contract: the man's pomposity was exactly what would tempt many Fair Folk into doing him some sort of mischief. His tendency to make condescending remarks to Adira, as not only junior but (she sensed) regrettably female, made her struggle with her unavoidable professional obligation to protect him thoroughly.

They drove home taking turns listing all the precautions they needed to take. When they reentered the office, Adira headed straight for the office filing room to recover from the morning, sitting at the worn and stained wooden desk and resting her head in her arms. But whatever paternal senses often alerted Dad to her distress apparently kicked in, and there he stood in the doorway, forehead wrinkled in concern.

Before he could offer some attempt at consolation or distraction, she forestalled him with a distraction of her own. "Why don't you text Mom about that dream, before you make any deals about it? You might have to keep it confidential afterward, and she'd like to hear it."

Dad's expression melted into the fond smile with which he greeted almost any mention of his wife. "I'll do that later, though by the time I get to it she may be asleep – unless I'm much mistaken about the local time in Cairo." Adira's mother had continued with the folklore research they had both pursued before Dad's unexpected detour into law, and was often several time zones away from Vermont.

Just as Adira was congratulating herself on her tactic, Dad added, "And I'll leave you to your reflections for another few minutes. I assume you'll go get some lunch. But then, when we go over this afternoon's agenda, I think you'll find it hard to resist cheering up." He came forward, kissed the top of her head, and left the room.

A few moments of clearing her mind with deep breathing, followed by an overstuffed cheese sandwich and root beer at one of her favorite sandwich shops, revived her sufficiently to face the afternoon, even if Dad's assessment of their afternoon tasks should prove misplaced. As they sat down to go over the list, he began by saying, "I've changed my mind. I'm going to save our second afternoon meeting for a surprise. I really think you'll enjoy it more that way." He laughed at her raised eyebrows and tilted head. "No, really! For now, how would you like to talk to some trees?"

"You mean dryads? Doesn't that rather depend on the particular dryads?"

Dad's grin made a welcome contrast to the fae version they'd both been enduring from the viscount that morning. "I don't, in fact, mean dryads. This particular grove of trees has no interest in mimicking either human form or the more common faerie configurations. They typically communicate via the shifting patterns of their leaves in sunlight – year-round leaves in, for the most part, year-round sunlight. Not even other fae can understand it. They would like to welcome some sort of flowering plants, such as are common in our own fields and forests – rather than any fae equivalents that would have their own possibly incompatible personalities. They wish us to advise them on the best choice and assist in obtaining the necessary starter crop."

Adira couldn't stop her eyes from going wide. "And in order to do this . . . ."

Dad actually rubbed his hands together. "In order that we may communicate with them conveniently, they will temporarily grant us the ability to understand their language of light and shadow."

How long would this job last? Oh, how tempting to drag her feet so it would last longer . . . . Putting aside that alluring vision, she said, "When are we going? Should we do any research beforehand, if you haven't already?"

Dad brandished a sheaf of notes. "I've done some, but we'll need more details before I can do any more. And we're meeting them in fifteen minutes. They've granted us permission to come directly, so we can use the portal without assistance."

The portal had been an indirect result of Adira's exasperation with the viscount's mannerisms, its sly digs at Dad and herself, and its tendency to hint at never-explained difficulties. It was still unclear how the viscount had been selected, or selected itself, to be their intermediary, but it had appeared years before Adira joined the practice and had often been their unavoidable gatekeeper. After nine months of experience with this unsatisfactory arrangement, Adira had been unwise enough to roll her eyes as their guide made its adieus after depositing them at a meeting with a Summer Court dignitary. That being could have punished them both for her discourtesy, but to their great good fortune, it had responded with amusement instead. After their successful negotiation over access rights to a waterfall on certain mortal private property, it had tossed Abe a bracelet set with what looked like rubies, saying with a wink, "Bury this behind your office at noon on Midsummer Day, and if you've made the necessary prior arrangements, you will be able to visit any fae realm without an escort."

Dad had bowed deeply, placed the bracelet on his wrist, and asked with only a trace of diffidence, "Is the viscount likely to inquire about this change?"

Their benefactor had laughed and said, "I will take pleasure in informing it myself. I will explain the change as serving my own future convenience, which is of course the truth. And I will instruct it not to importune you on the subject."

Whether the viscount's demeanor had become more menacing since then was difficult to say. But Adira would not think about that now, not when she was about to talk to trees, and help them find just the right flowers to surround them.

Several hours later, back at the office, Adira drifted somewhere between exhilaration and exhaustion. Even with the trees' grant of comprehension, keeping track of the sometimes minute changes in light patterns required constant attention. But how lovely were the patterns, and how subtly different the silent voices of the various trees!

After discussing in what ways the trees had become dissatisfied with their ageless copses and glens, and confirming that actual flowers were preferred to moss, they had settled on bluebells. Someone would need to plant the initial bulbs, and it remained to be decided whether these workers would be mortal or fae – which meant Adira and her father would not yet have to relinquish their knowledge of the language. As for the patience needed to let the bluebells spread, trees had patience aplenty, and it pleased them that the flowers would be connected by a system of roots.

What next? Could she go home and relax, with iced coffee this time? But wait, Dad had some sort of surprise up his sleeve. Maybe it could wait until tomorrow.

She turned to ask him, only to see him tapping his foot, the expression of glee on his face reminding her of childhood birthdays when she thought he might burst from the effort of keeping that year's secret. She suppressed a chuckle and followed as he led the way back to the portal.

It was always visible to them – and to Mom, maybe because she was a member of the family. Anyone else, or at least any other mortal, would see nothing there, and would walk through unaffected unless she or Dad intended them to do otherwise. What met Adira's eyes, as usual, was an oval ring hovering an inch or so above the ground, just big enough for her to step through without ducking. It sparkled in ever-shifting colors in her peripheral vision, more like mist when she looked at it head-on, and showed a changing series of vistas. Only when they came within a yard of it would that view change to their destination. But what greeted her this afternoon was not so much a sight as the sensation of wind, and fine sprays of water on the wind, and the smell of salt.

She stopped in her tracks, only to find Dad grabbing her hand and pulling her forward.

They were standing on what might be called a cliff, about hill-height. And they were facing the sea, that salty wind in their hair, with small waves rolling in and breaking on a beach of silvery sand and scattered shells.

Adira turned to her father. "Dad, who are we waiting for? Are they coming by boat?"

He laughed, not mocking her but as if delight had filled him to overflowing and come out as laughter. "Wait just a minute, sweetheart, and you'll see!"

She looked out at the horizon, breathing deep of the sea-scented air, and saw something emerging, or growing, or approaching. She couldn't make out any details – and then she could, because she saw the backlit, translucent jade of waves, waves rushing toward them, waves growing taller and taller, until she was sure she and Dad would be drenched or even swept off the cliff –

And then the waves stopped, suddenly, just behind their far smaller counterparts breaking on the beach. Two enormous standing waves faced them, topped with high white crests ruffling in the wind and shedding spray all around.

Her jaw dropped, confronted with grandeur; and then snapped shut again, as she imagined surfing those waves, and shut the thought down in case these formidable fae, for so these two waves must be, could somehow sense that desire.

Dad, beside her, spoke into the hiss of the small waves that mounted the shingle and drew back again. "Hello again, Your Majesties. As we discussed, I have brought my daughter, who is my equal partner in all that we do. Let me make her known to you as Valentina, which in one of our tongues means 'strong and powerful.'"

A rumble, not quite a roar, carried across the gulf between waves and cliff. "Welcome, counselors. Now that we have met both of you, make known to us the request of the mortal you represent."

This would be news to Adira as well. She took a step back, to convey that her father would do the talking. He glanced her way, nodded, and said, "Your Majesties, we represent a scientist, one who studies oceans. Ever since she learned that there is an ocean beyond the confines of the mortal world, she has longed to explore and study it as well. She seeks to know whether there are conditions under which you would give her leave to do so."

"Hmmmmm." Or so Adira would have rendered the somehow meditative rumble that emerged from the wave to her right. "And is our ocean so different from the oceans familiar to you and to this scientist?"

Dad smiled. "That, Your Majesty, is the question to be examined. I am aware of no previous study of the subject."

From the wave to Adira's left came a voice with lighter tones, bringing to mind the ceaseless wind and a seagull's cry. "How does this scientist propose to study our ocean?"

"The procedure," Abe replied, "would be the subject of future discussion between us, should you be open to the possibility of such a study taking place." Adira could imagine some of the precautions they would deem necessary.

Above all, it was essential that their client avoid direct contact with the ocean waters. For a mortal to touch a flower could be perilous, and eating or drinking anything found in Faerie would be worse. Adira could only imagine what might befall a mortal who immersed herself, unprotected, in an all-enveloping ocean.

Though these ocean fae might not welcome the idea of a metal and rubber submersible, or whatever vehicles or tools their client hoped to use, intruding on the waters which might be in some inextricable way their very substance.

The hiss and roar of Their Majesties' speech interrupted her musings. "We will allow you to meet with us again – either of you, now that we have met Valentina – to discuss the matter. You may return when summoned."

Dad said nothing in response, but bowed deeply, Adira following suit. As they both straightened up, the waves, fixed in place so long that Adira had forgotten to find it strange, rolled forward in unison and descended in a breathtaking crash of water and spray and foam before slowly receding back into the unbroken expanse beyond.

As they stepped through the portal onto the lawn behind their office, Adira asked her father, "Exactly how are they going to 'summon' us? I do hope they won't be sending the viscount."

"Never fear! But I think I'll keep their methods for one more surprise. You enjoyed this one, didn't you?"

Adira bumped her shoulder against him and gave him a side hug. "All right, I did at that. I'll wait and see. And now, I'm going home to my armchair, my footstool, and a drink.

See you in the morning!" She turned around, threw Dad a salute, and headed down the street.

* * * * *

Abe watched his daughter saunter down the block, remembering the days when the two of them would have locked up the office and returned together to the home where she grew up. It had been a joy having her back home for a while after her years away at law school, but he had been wise enough – if barely – to cherish it as a temporary blessing. Naturally a woman in her latter twenties wanted privacy and autonomy. Adira was, as far as Abe knew, between lovers, having ended a two-year relationship three months before, but she would hardly want Abe or Clara looking over her shoulder wondering if she'd met someone new.

Which didn't keep the house from feeling all too empty when Clara was away.

Where was Clara now? Somewhere near Cairo, wasn't it? He sat back and pictured her, striding briskly through a village street with a shockingly vivid sunset behind her. She might be awash in the local version of tea, and walking so fast in order to reach her rented room and empty her bladder. Then she'd read through what she'd written during the day in the notebook she carried – if she still carried one. If Abe thought her research might shed light on a problem he faced in his practice, she would transcribe her notes for him or, better, talk them over with him. It could not replace the daily give and take they used to have, digesting and analyzing what they had learned and what light it shed on their previous notions, arguing genially –

most of the time – over how the pieces fit together. But it was still a satisfying form of communion.

Of course, nothing could equal their shared excitement when the Fair Folk revealed themselves beyond question or cavil. Questions had immediately leaped to mind: why there, in one portion of Vermont, and would they make contact in other places? Why now, and for how long? Which legends could be adequately explained by past fae activity? Would more marvels – witches, trolls, unicorns – be next to appear?

Most of those questions remained unanswered, but other things became clear. He and Clara had, however illogically, felt vindicated when the Fair Folk proved willing to make bargains with humans, just as in many of the tales the two of them had collected. Nor were they surprised that those dealings often ended badly for the humans involved. Clara had been sad, or angry, or horrified, depending on the details . . . but she responded by doing everything she could to publicize the risks. His fellow mortals, his neighbors or those who could easily have been neighbors, too often refused to heed Clara's warnings. They plunged ahead with confidence, just as "marks" had always fallen prey to con artists, assuring themselves that they were different, too savvy to be fooled, or that they lived under a lucky star. Clara sighed, or swore, and kept trying.

Abe had found himself drawn to a different path. And Clara might call it knight-errantry, but he believed that in the end, she respected him for it.

At least he could call or text her. She might be asleep already, so it had better be text, more easily ignored until morning.

My dearest Clara,

How is your exploration of Cairo's environs going? Have you been able to get the old men talking, and to find your way in to see the old women? I particularly hope the men and the women told you some of the same tales, so you can compare their versions. You're off to Romania next, aren't you? And then home as planned, I hope, as I very much miss you, and I'm sure Adira would love to see you as well.

We had a busy day, challenging in some respects but rewarding in others. I got to see Adira awestruck, which as you know doesn't happen that often. I'll tell you the details when we actually talk. Preview hint: ocean fae!

Adira was the one to suggest I tell you about last night's dream, and I'm guessing she was (as so often) right. I think you'll like the sound of it. Please let me know, when convenient, whether you'd prefer I keep it private, or whether I should try to use it to bring in a little extra cash. It'll sound grim at first, but trust me, it was anything but.

You see, I found myself in a graveyard . . . .

CHAPTER 2

A DIRA had been eager to start work this morning, and now she had to waste time meeting with a county bar official. She'd seen it coming, of course, but it would be a nuisance even if she persuaded the man to be reasonable.

Mr. Fells had insisted, in his smoothly indirect way, on coming to the office, no doubt expecting to see crystal balls and dream-catchers and other supposedly supernatural paraphernalia. The firm's tidy and professional decorating scheme must have disappointed him, though he did cast a suspicious eye on the grandfather clock. Now they sat in the perfectly conventional, if small, conference room, Adira with her usual strong coffee, the visitor with what was probably a stale teabag steeping in his cup of hot water. She had struggled with the desire to deprive him of Abe's baked treats, but had reluctantly acknowledged that she might need to sweeten his temper. She had, at least, kept her favorite brownies and pumpkin muffins tucked safely away in an empty drawer of one of the file cabinets.

As Fells straightened his papers in front of him, Adira slid an additional stack across the table and said, "I don't know whether you've had the chance to review my father's bar file, but he makes a habit of obtaining a copy twice a year. It might answer some of the questions I would expect you to have."

Fells twitched an eyebrow. "I have, in fact, reviewed that file, although . . . what is the most recent update you have here?"

"The beginning of this month." Seeing his prim frown, she added, "Please take whatever time you need to look it over." Not that there was much to it, as their practice was in all key – and startling – respects the same as it had been for years. It would have been more efficient if they had sent the same official with whom Dad had repeatedly met and whom he had, over time, gradually mollified.

Fells leafed through the file, muttering, "More affidavits from clients. Which doesn't mean they weren't sold a load of . . . hmm, I wouldn't expect him to fall for . . . or her . . . ."

Adira gave him a tight smile. "Nor would you expect pretty much all the residents of this county and the surrounding region, going back more than twenty years now, to acknowledge the occasional presence of the Fair Folk. I believe your department's acceptance of that situation is well established by now."

"And you still don't know why your region of Vermont has been, ah, singled out?"

Adira shook her head. "Various Fair Folk have provided explanations, none very enlightening." The fae answering such questions had exercised to the fullest their talent for technically truthful yet fundamentally misleading statements. Not a few people elsewhere had relied on one of those explanations and tried to duplicate the conditions it suggested. At best, such efforts led nowhere.

Fells nodded grudgingly, took a fruit bar, and sipped his tea, though it was likely lukewarm by now. "As I understand it, your father obtained his law degree many years ago. Did he ever practice, ah, more conventional law, in any jurisdiction?"

"I don't think so. He and my mother met while he was in law school, and as soon as he graduated, they married and he joined her as a folklorist." And he'd been happy doing it – they'd both been happy – until the Fair Folk emerged.

Looking back, Adira could marvel at how her parents had made the change seem normal and natural. Instead of traveling with both parents, she would travel with her mother. Instead of working together, Mom would keep gathering and analyzing folktales, and Dad would deal with the reality that had inspired at least some of them. Mom would write down stories of magical beings and events, while Dad journeyed to witness them or protected his fellow humans from their dangers.

Dad's choice had seemed the more enticing. How many times, as a child, had she demanded to go with Dad to one or another Fair Folk realm, instead of only to Cyprus or Peru? But he had told her over and over that she would have to wait until she was older. Though they hadn't kept her waiting as long as many, less adventurous parents would have done.

Fell was shaking his head and making little grumpy noises, possibly at the eccentricity of a lawyer choosing not to practice law, even though Dad had eventually changed course. "Hmmm. If I may ask, how did your father – as I gather the firm predates your passing the bar – begin, ah, catering to the Fair Folk?"

Had it started with the time Dad absentmindedly walked into a fairy circle, then managed to talk his way out of spending the next decade or three watching some incomprehensible game played on a giant orange and purple checkerboard? No, that came later. "He became aware of several unfortunate incidents. For example, there was the owner of a new dry cleaning business – quite a nice fellow, apparently – who somehow met a fae from the Winter Court. They're the most likely to be malicious, which the owner hadn't heard. He didn't want to waste the opportunity, and asked for an enchantment to clean the most delicate fabrics without damaging them. When he asked what they would take in exchange, he should have known better than to accept the answer that it would be their pleasure, and that they had a use for the stains. Given what those fae take pleasure in, it was true, as it had to be . . . From that moment, every stain he removed, with the enchantment or without it, stained his skin and that of his customers, and nothing would remove those stains."

Fells seemed less than impressed. Now that she'd gone this far, she'd tell him the grimmer complete version of what had spurred Dad into action, and see how he liked the taste of it. "Then two horrendous encounters came to my father's attention. First, a man who taught creative writing wanted to write a best-selling novel and become famous. The fae arranged for him to get arrested for some gruesome crime that got lots of publicity, and a great many people bought his book out of morbid curiosity." Fells' eyes widened, and he gulped. Well, he'd asked for it. "And then someone went for that old favorite, wanting to live forever. He ended up permanently asleep, and from what family observers could tell, having frequent awful nightmares."

Maybe it had been a mistake to dwell on these details. She'd had a few of her own nightmares when she first joined the practice, and she'd been happy to see them fade with time. Too late now. "After more than a month of this, the man's wife got desperate and tried killing him – a mercy killing. But it didn't work. The man woke up just long enough to realize what was happening, and then fell asleep again, healing as he slept. The wife could only guess what new nightmare he had afterward." She'd ended up killing herself instead, but Fell had clearly heard enough. He looked somewhere between pale and green.

She retreated to a pedantic comment on Fells' original question. "Actually, it's rather rare for us to have Fair Folk as clients. We're more likely to represent – " Fells was unlikely to react well to words like *mortal* or *human*. "– the same sort of clients as any other attorney, when they seek some benefit from the Fair Folk. And those benefits can, if carefully negotiated, be quite valuable, obtainable in no other way."

Fells had recovered impressively well. At this last statement, he harrumphed and asked, "What did such people do before your father set up shop?"

Damn it, she'd just told him! "As you can imagine, Mr. Fells, they fared at least as poorly as lay people are wont to do when attempting to represent themselves. More so, usually, because the fae are by their nature expert at laying verbal traps – sometimes taking advantage of their unexpected rules, like not allowing people to thank them – and exploiting loopholes. It is our job to protect people from falling victim to such practices."

Fells abruptly leaned forward and planted his elbows on the table. "And yet, do you not, by your involvement, turn the tables in a problematic fashion? Are you and your father, trained and experienced attorneys, not dealing as a matter of course with unrepresented Fair Folk opponents?"

Adira suppressed a snort. She would have liked to introduce the man to some of the fae with whom she had negotiated and see how long he could maintain the illusion that they were defenseless against legal acumen. She gathered her patience and said, "Aside from the fact to which I have alluded, that the fae may properly be described as born with the equivalent of the skills you and I worked so hard to acquire, there is the simple fact that they do not include, in their numbers, any legal professionals. Perhaps through their encounters with lay communities, they have unfortunately picked up the popular notion that lawyers are dishonest and unreliable. And as you may have heard, one thing the Fair Folk do *not* tolerate, on pain of their most severe displeasure, is dishonesty."

It would not be a good moment to smile. But as often happened when she met with or discussed the fae, she was reminded of two quite different people: an ethics professor, young and earnest and skilled at inventing convoluted hypotheticals, and her maternal grandfather, the most uncompromising of Scottish Presbyterians, for whom a white lie or an evasion constituted as grievous a sin as a blatant and premeditated falsehood. Even she had to stay constantly alert to avoid the ambiguous language many lawyers found so useful, but she was better prepared than most for the perils of her chosen practice.

* * * * *

Tuesday's business began with two cases involving faerie circles: one the relatively common circumstance (in these environs) of someone having been caught in one and their families seeking their return, and the other more unusual. The client in the latter case, a woman in her late forties, actually *wanted* to step into a faerie circle and be taken out of the flow of mortal time.

"My husband's in prison, you see," the woman explained in a well modulated voice, with tolerable composure. "He's at the start of a ten-year term, and I'd rather not spend it without him. I could spend a week or a month with the Fair Folk while ten years pass here, couldn't I? So as long as you can make sure they bring me back once his sentence has run, that's what we're wanting."

Adira, as they'd agreed, confined her obvious role to taking notes. The client's intake information had suggested to Abe that she might find it easier to talk to someone nearer her own age. Adira seemed just as glad to let him take that role.

"I can certainly understand your feelings," Abe said gently. "Have you and your husband discussed how the different rates of time passing would affect the two of you? He'll have aged in the usual way when you get back, and you'll be essentially the same age as when you left. Would that bother him?"

The woman's eyes widened. "I hadn't thought of that. But – I wouldn't care. And as long as I convince him of that, he'd probably be just as happy to have me stay young."

So far, so good. Now for a more difficult subject. "If I may inquire, have you and your husband discussed how such an arrangement would affect him? He'd be spending those ten years without visits from you, and possibly with no communication between you. We might be able to arrange for you to be send letters to him, but at this initial stage, I can't guarantee it."

The woman's stoicism wavered, and she bit her lip as she replied, "His brothers and sister swear they'll visit often, and his mother's alive, though not well enough to make that trip. We know it'll be hard for him, but not as hard as knowing I'm on my own and struggling to make ends meet. He – he finds it hard to believe I'd be able to wait, without having to turn to someone else for support and comfort. Not that he doesn't trust me, but more that he doesn't trust himself to deserve my standing by him. And . . . I'm not altogether sure he *can* trust me to last so long." She broke down and sobbed into a crumpled tissue she had abstracted from her pocket.

Adira quietly slid a scrap of paper in Abe's direction. While their client tried to pull herself together, he read it quickly and buried it under the papers in front of him. *Music*, Adira had written. *She sounds like someone who can sing.* Moments later, the client wiped her eyes and sat up, saying in a still-unsteady voice, "I'm sorry. Where were we?"

Abe gave Adira a quick nod and said, "I was about to bring up the subject of compensation – what we lawyers call 'consideration.' What had you thought of offering in return for the service you seek?"

"I had hoped you would have some suggestions. I thought of something . . . ." To his surprise, the woman blushed. "I know I'm not a young woman, but some people say that the Fair Folk – that they want, that they brag to each other about . . . ."

Abe hastily put up his hand to stop her. "If you're referring to the possibility of intimate favors, we would strongly advise against it. Where physical contact with the fae is concerned, the rule of thumb is the less, the better. There are various other things you could offer, including, for example, music. Of course the fae have their own songs and instruments, but they crave anything new. Do you have any gifts of that kind?"

The woman sat up straight, her chin up and her eyes brighter. "As a matter of fact, I used to be a professional singer. I've stayed in practice, more or less, for my own pleasure and . . . for my husband's." She slumped down again. "He loves to hear me sing."

Abe reached out and covered her nearest hand with his own. "That could do very well. We'd have to negotiate the number of songs, and just what they could do with them. We'd also have to make sure you're free to record some music before you leave, for your husband to listen to while you're . . . away. Given how they value new music – we'd have to ascertain which songs in your repertoire are new to them – if you grant them broad usage rights, you could gain some additional concessions, such as just how quickly the years will pass for you."

A quick shudder went through the woman at the word "years," but she made no reply.

They ushered the client out and went over Adira's notes from the interview, Adira jotting down a few more that Abe considered worth including. The most important, they agreed, was that the Fair Folk enchant the woman so she would have no need of food, nor any tormenting desire for it. If she were to consume even a morsel of faerie food, her husband would regain his freedom only to find his wife imprisoned, unable to come home.

Then they began preparing for their second meeting with the senator seeking fae bodyguards. But before they had finished, prickling sensations alerted them both to an imminent interruption. Abe was about to get up and investigate when he heard a high-pitched yet pleasant peeping from the entryway near the door. He laughed and said to Adira, "It appears my next surprise has arrived. Please be so good as to call the senator and reschedule our appointment, and then meet me out front."

* * * * *

The senator's secretary did not receive the news of a postponement with equanimity, but Adira merely repeated that a short postponement was necessary and left her to deal with her petulant boss as best she could. If feathers needed smoothing, Dad could handle the job.

Adira hung up and made her way out front, even though she had a good idea what the supposed surprise must be. Their oceanic majesties had apparently sent a messenger, and it had sounded like some kind of shore-dwelling bird, possibly a sandpiper. Adira was fond of sandpipers, and she smiled as she approached, finding there were two birds rather than one.

And then the nearest sandpiper said, in its high, piping voice, "What a pleasure to see you again, Valentina."

Adira stared at the birds for at least five seconds – which was five seconds too long. One should never stare at the fae to begin with, as they preferred to have their glamours appreciated in a less vulgar manner. She dropped a curtsy and said, "My apologies, Your Majesty. We are honored to welcome you."

Dad patted her shoulder. "A quick recovery, my dear! Don't fret – I told Their Majesties that I had not informed you of the way in which they were likely to appear."

She gritted her teeth before she caught herself and donned a more appropriate expression. Dad probably hadn't meant to be condescending – and she should, by now, be past such naive mistakes. When would she stop underestimating how very different the Fair Folk were from mortals? To the ocean rulers, Greek god or tiny sea bird presumably made no more difference than one or another overelaborate costume worn by the Viscount of Bloomingshire. The comparison brought to mind a conversation many years ago with her father. She had been confused about how the Fair Folk, who supposedly lacked the power to lie and would harshly punish any lie told to them, could essentially lie about their looks with glamour. She still remembered his reply. "Because, little one, we are expected to know that glamour is their chosen seeming, sometimes their entertainment, but not their reality."

Meanwhile, Dad turned to Adira and asked, "For when did you reschedule that appointment?"

"I didn't actually do so. I simply dumped the problem in the secretary's lap. Presumably we'll receive a new date, most likely presented as a demand, but if it doesn't suit us we can fail to treat it as such."

Dad beamed. "Excellent! Then we can arrange for Their Majesties to meet our scientist tomorrow morning, as they have proposed."

Such a meeting was not as startling as the rest of the morning's events, but it was somewhat unusual. The Fair Folk tended to prefer as few meetings with the firm's clients as the proposed transaction allowed. But given the contemplated intimacy of this client's request, she could understand the rulers' insistence on scrutinizing the scientist before proceeding.

"Very good, then," said the sandpiper who had not yet spoken. "We will see you at the same spot as before. A good day to you!" And it spread its wings, except that suddenly those wings were larger, more than twice as long, and gray-black rather than brownish-white. What had been a sandpiper was now a seagull.

"Enough, my dear," said the other bird, still a sandpiper. "Let's be on our way and leave these good people to be about their business." And off they flew through the open doorway.

CHAPTER 3

IT HAD taken Abe and Adira several days to realize what was missing in the story of the changeling. The flood of fear and complaint and pleading from Ms. Dellor, the mother of the stolen boy, had included no details about the changeling left in his place. Was it, at least to appearances, a boy? Did it look like the human child? Feel human to the touch? Share any human habits? For that matter, how had the mother identified it as a changeling? Might she possibly be in error?

And what was happening to the changeling, if it was one, now?

Abe would have to follow up in person, to observe the baby firsthand. When he told Adira of his intention, she insisted on going as well. "We can compare notes afterward, in case one of us notices something the other didn't."

Abe called ahead, of course, and was mildly surprised – for no very good reason – to reach the father, with whom he had not yet spoken and whom the mother had seen no reason to mention. "Come over? Yeah, sure," the man said in a somehow absentminded manner. "Yeah, why not? Come see what we have going on. Meet the baby."

The curtains of the pleasant little house were drawn tight, as if to hide whatever was happening inside. The man who opened the door had a glass in his hand. From either the glass or the man came the rich caramel smell of whiskey. He stepped aside from the doorway, beckoned them in, and toasted to them as they entered. "Welcome! 'M in charge here, I s'poze. The missus went upstairs to lay down." He pointed a wavering arm toward the back of the house. "Been crying a lot, pour soul. Says it doesn't much matter what I do, the whatever-it-is can take care of itself."

They walked through a short entryway and came to what appeared to be a family room. Abe could see no trace of a baby – no playpen, no toys, no small blankets or spit-up rags. Following Abe's gaze with the exaggerated concentration of the inebriated, the man pointed to a doorway off to one side of the room. "His bedroom's in there. Well, the baby's bedroom, and that's where we've been keeping the, whatdyacallit, the changeling. You'll be wanting to take a look at it, so go on ahead. I'll just have a seat here and wait." Without waiting for any response, he half sat, half fell onto a well-stuffed sofa and took another sip of his drink.

In the bedroom they found everything missing from the earlier room, perfectly in order, like a showroom in a baby store or a magazine photograph. A white-painted wood crib stood against one wall, a blue and yellow checked quilt folded over one end, a blue and white Calder-style mobile hung above it and turning lazily in invisible air currents. A matching dresser with its knobs painted yellow faced it across the room. Half curtains in pale blue, with any cords tucked well out of reach, graced the matching windows on the wall between. A rocking chair, also in white wood, upholstered in white and yellow patterned fabric, sat opposite the crib next to the dresser, occupied at present by only a blue, oversized stuffed rabbit.

"Hidin' again." The slurred voice of the father, from the doorway behind her, made Abe start and Adira jump. "Dunno how it does that. M' wife noticed first. I didn't believe her 'til I saw it. Should've believed her, what with the other things."

From the crib came a ringing laugh, and then a baby appeared, standing and bouncing on its toes, as delighted as any baby playing peek-a-boo. It had silvery-white straight hair, more than any baby its age Abe could remember seeing. Its eyes were an unrelieved black, pupils and irises indistinguishable. And there was something else odd about it . . . . When the baby laughed again, he had it.

Teeth. The baby had a full set of perfect white teeth.

Abe tapped Adira on the shoulder and pointed. She moved closer to look and then turned back toward him. "It could be a mutation of some kind. And . . . we could have missed seeing the baby at first, from some trick of the light." Then she did a double-take and spun to face the crib again.

So quietly Abe could barely hear it, and then louder, its voice high and ringing like the sound a wet finger could coax from the rim of a wineglass, the baby was singing, singing words Abe could almost, but not quite, understand, a liquid language that drew him to step nearer and nearer to the crib.

And then from behind him, discordant and halting, came the sound of the father trying to sing along, first imitating the alien words and then adding his own. "Bay - bee - strange - little - bay - bee - are - you - my - bay - bee . . . ."

Abe turned away from Adira to hide the tears in his eyes.

Soon, of course, the changeling's attention shifted, looking at the shifting of light and shadow on the nursery wall. The father stumbled through half of another repetition of the song and then leaned against the wall with his eyes closed. Abe approached him, cleared his throat so as not to startle him, and asked, "Will you be all right here for now, while my daughter and I work on what to do next?"

The man nodded, almost losing his balance. "Be all right. Sure. Me and little singing Junior here. Be just fine."

Abe pulled a business card out of his jacket pocket and laid it on top of the dresser. He opened his mouth to mention it, then shrugged as the man started to snore, and instead pried him away from the wall and steered him, with difficulty, over to the rocking chair. Adira helped lower the man into the chair.

Should they just leave, with both parents – well, both coercively recruited foster parents – asleep? But just then he heard footsteps, with the rhythm of someone descending stairs. Adira, apprehending more quickly, left the room and went to meet Ms. Dellor, a tall thin woman whose current strength seemed barely sufficient to hold her upright. Abe held his breath until she reached the bottom of the stairs without mishap.

Adira and Ms. Dellor spoke briefly, Adira's professional manner modulated toward sympathy, and the woman trudged into the nursery, her shoulders tight and her spine hunched forward. Adira collected Abe and led him out the door. He looked back over his shoulder from the doorway, but could no longer see the nursery. Unless they were going to move in for the duration, there was no point in lingering. They left in silence.

* * * * *

Adira found Seanin McGann, the oceanographer, a delight, solid of build and cheerful in demeanor, with a blunt way of speaking leavened by self-deprecating humor. After their initial awe-inspiring appearance as waves, the ocean fae assumed a glamour much like the Greek god Poseidon and his less well-known wife, the Nereid Amphitrite. The cliff now included some large rocks shaped much like couches, so that the humans could sit in something like comfort while their hosts reclined in a suitably Greco-Roman fashion.

The preliminary negotiations took about an hour, and Adira was just explaining that they would write up a draft agreement when Dad muttered something under his breath. Adira looked at him, startled, as he rose and said, "We have enjoyed your hospitality and appreciate the reasonable manner in which you have discussed these terms. Now, I'm afraid that Valentina and I must be returning to our office. Ms. McGann, will you accompany us?"

In a very few minutes, the three of them were stepping back through the portal, with no opportunity for Dad to explain what had alerted – or alarmed – him. The answer, however, stood only a few steps from the portal, removing its monstrously high hat and flourishing it so the ostrich plumes rippled.

The dratted viscount, appearing with no notice or appointment.

Ms. McGann attended to the viscount's florid self-introduction with civility, but with none of the more individual qualities that usually characterized her speech. She must be wary of him, which only supported Adira's good opinion of her judgment. After she had left, heading for town, Dad invited the viscount into the office, politely of course, but without much more personal warmth than Ms. McGann had shown.

The viscount took the offered chair, throwing its long coattails behind it as it did so. It smirked at Adira and said, "Do pardon me, fair lady, and you, good sir, for my unheralded appearance, but I have become aware of an urgent situation in which your unequaled skills may be all that stand between a hapless mortal and a regrettable fate."

Adira fetched legal pads for Dad and for herself as Dad said, "We would of course like to hear about this situation. Please go on."

From the recesses of its cape, the viscount conjured a heavily gilded box of snuff and took a pinch. "I am perhaps being precipitate. Have you ever involved yourself in what we may call criminal trials among my people?"

A mere few minutes ago, Adira had been contemplating with pleasure and longing the idea of Dad's leftover baked goods, and then a big bowl of hot soup at the nearest coffee shop. Now her stomach cramped with something more like cold. "No, we haven't taken on any cases of that kind."

Dad cleared his throat. "Actually, not that long after I began this practice, I did handle such a matter. The details, of course, are confidential, and the memory is not one I often revisit." Adira glanced over at him to see his expression uncharacteristically bleak.

The viscount nodded. "Ah, I see. That would be before you and I began our association, would it not? I should apologize for reviving such unhappy recollections. Perhaps I should say no more of the unfortunate boy of whom I planned to speak."

Adira had never entirely trusted the viscount, and she trusted it even less now. She opened her mouth to concur, just as Dad said, "No, please go on." From his tone, he had similar reservations, but his professional conscience appeared more active, at the moment, than any sense of self-preservation.

The viscount sat back, with the air of one about to embark on an engrossing story. "Has either of you ever visited our realm of infinite ice?"

"I have, for one case," Dad replied. "It's a truly marvelous sight, with mountains like daggers and a frozen lake stretching off to the horizon, and icicles hanging from every surface, and the trees unbowed by those icicles, and the sunlight – when there is any – glinting off it all."

"Indeed, a lovely sight. It is equally lovely in moonlight – yes, day and night do follow each other there, much as in your environs. And there are also moonless nights, where only those with adequate vision may find their way unhindered. There is one other fact, unsurprising once one considers the matter, which you must understand. Fire of any kind is strictly – oh, most strictly – forbidden throughout this realm, with the sole and rare exception of certain ceremonial uses of which I must not speak. Can you, now, begin to guess what must have occurred to require your assistance?"

Adira looked intently at the viscount. "You mentioned a boy. He came there on some errand and then made a fire?"

The viscount examined its polished fingernails and sighed. "That is almost correct. This boy – sixteen years old, I believe – had no errand, and indeed, to hear him tell it, he had no idea he had crossed the boundary between a mortal and a faerie realm. He was wandering home from his sweetheart's house, no doubt filled with fond thoughts of her charms, and blundered into the ice realm. Naturally, since he did not belong there, he had no idea how to get where he *did* belong, and could scarcely see where he was in fact going. So he found a fallen branch – "

Surprising, that a branch had fallen from one of those *unbowed trees*.

"– and, using some supplies he had with him, contrived to turn it into a torch, the better to find his way. Naturally, he attracted attention, and has been detained pending the administrative proceeding that will see him consigned to the ice."

Dad scribbled a few notes, possibly to buy time, before he asked quietly, "Please explain just what that entails."

The viscount produced a tight-lipped smile. "My dear counselor, the phrase is both literal and descriptive. He will be immersed in the lake, pursuant to a spell that will prevent him from drowning or from requiring sustenance, with a patch above him enchanted to remain clear so that he may contemplate the world he will never be allowed to reenter. This clear area of ice will also allow passersby to see him, and whatever anguished expression he may have, and so be reminded of the price of such folly."

Adira had little occasion to regret her vivid visual imagination, but she did at this moment. In fact, she jumped to her feet, excused herself in brief and incoherent fashion, and rushed from the room, walking as fast as she could to the bathroom in case she had to vomit. Staring into the mirror only reminded her of that boy, who might soon be staring up at a sheet of impenetrable glass . . . .

She retched into the sink, glad now that she had little in her stomach to bring up, before washing her face, tidying her hair, and returning to the conference room. Resuming her seat, she apologized and asked, "Have I missed any further explanation?"

Dad reached over and stroked her hand. "No, we waited for you to return. Will you be all right?"

"Of course. Please go on, Lord Bloomingshire."

The viscount's eyes glinted at her in a disturbing fashion. "How clever of you to remember my title! You use it so seldom, I was not sure you would. . . . The procedure is normally quite abbreviated. However, when so informed, this lad cried out in distress that surely he would be allowed to explain himself, or to have someone on the order of a lawyer to speak for him. Amazing, what notions the young pick up. . . . The authorities, aware of my role as an intermediary, made the matter known to me, while indicating that they were not prepared to wait for long. I accordingly hastened to lay the case before you."

Dad pushed his chair back. "May my daughter and I confer before giving you an answer? I promise we will spend as little time as possible."

"But of course, dear sir, of course! I have brought myself the means to pass the time." The snuff box had at some point vanished, but the viscount now produced a small book in similar fashion. Adira would have liked to read the title, but the print was small enough that she would have had to lean over and squint, which would doubtless be considered impolite. She followed Dad out of the conference room to, it turned out, the file room, and closed the door behind them.

Dad leaned against a file cabinet, arms crossed, frowning. "I don't like this at all. But I don't know that I can see my way clear to refusing."

Adira found herself wanting to cry, which she could not remember doing in at least a year. "I think I like it even less. I have the feeling we're being set up, though I don't know why."

Dad winced. "You may well be right. But the basic facts must be as our visitor stated. The viscount may well be withholding details, and could even be doing so with the intent of misleading, but it cannot actually state an untruth."

Adira looked around as if some avenue to escape might be hidden among the cabinets and boxes. "What do you think it *isn't* saying? Are these ice fae just trying to give the boy the fright of his life, before letting him off the hook?"

Dad's manner brightened for a moment before he slumped back against the cabinet and said, "I'm afraid not. My impression of them, from my brief experience and from passing comments, is that they tend to be inflexible. I would guess that the prohibition against fire is one of their most fundamental laws."

Adira swallowed and asked him, "What do you see as the hazards here, for us?"

Dad sighed deeply. "My dear, I simply don't know. But they could be substantial. We would be perfectly justified in declining this case. That would, in fact, be the most prudent course."

And she would then be able to look forward to nights spent dreaming of that sixteen-year-old boy, screaming soundlessly up through the ice, or simply staring upward in horror and disbelief, hoping against hope for a rescue that would never come. "I only wish I could let myself decline. Can you?"

They returned to the conference room, apologized for the length of their absence, and sat back down. Adira spoke for them, saying, "Lord Bloomingshire, we appreciate your bringing this matter to us, and we will do whatever we can for the boy. What shall we call him?"

The viscount beamed at them. "I am so glad! As for the lad's name, I believe he was so incautious as to provide his real one. He is called Tom."

"We'll need a couple of hours," Dad said, "to grab something to eat and to clear our schedules for – how long is this proceeding likely to take? You said, if I recall, that their usual procedure is expeditious. How much additional time are they prepared to allow?"

"An excellent question! But alas, not one I am sufficiently well briefed to answer with certainty. I suggest," said the viscount, with its unsettling grin, "that you reschedule other commitments for as long a time as possible."

CHAPTER 4

ADIRA hadn't realized how grateful she had been for the return of spring, until she found herself once again plunged so deep into winter.

The portal brought them to a wilderness of bare trees stretching in every direction, their branches coated in ice to the very tips. Her father's earlier description suggested that he had visited on a sunnier day; the ice did not glint or glimmer in what muted light came through. The air seemed dry, and yet the cold seeped into her as if borne by damp currents.

Two ice fae met them at the portal, their skin – if it was skin – resembling silvery bark. She could see nothing, amongst the lines of the bark, that looked like eyes, though the fae did have what appeared to be mouths. Not that they seemed to have anything to say to the visiting mortals. Was she imagining the hostility she felt radiating from them, some combination of disdain and aversion? She had no way to know, though she wasn't given to pessimistic flights of fancy.

Where was their client? As soon as she asked herself that question, a boy appeared between the fae, trembling, eyes wide with panic. The fae seized and held his arms, tight enough that they must be hurting him. Still without speaking, they pivoted to the right, dragging the boy with them, and started walking, long strides covering the ground swiftly, the clusters of roots that served as their feet piercing the crust of snow. Adira and her father lurched into motion to catch up.

* * * * *

Abe could have told Adira more details of his only professional involvement with Fair Folk crimes and penalties. She was, after all, his partner. But she had not been his partner yet at the time, and that gave him cover for a reticence that – he now realized – arose not from his professional responsibilities, but from reluctance to discourage her from joining his practice in the future. That choice seemed unforgivably irresponsible in hindsight.

Adira had once witnessed the wrath with which the fae responded to violations of the rules and etiquette they demanded. Abe had managed to apologize abjectly enough to defuse that confrontation, a result Abe sometimes thought of as his most successful negotiation. Adira had been impressed, and reassured by his skill. Had he let her, had she let herself, become complacent?

He should have tried to dissuade her from joining him on this mission, or simply refused to take on a client on an emergency basis. Adira had, after all, been right – the viscount had found a way to bypass the protections built into their usual contracts, manipulating them into taking on this case without those safeguards. But it was too late now to decline.

The two fae led them to a sort of cave, icicles hanging from its entrance and frost patterns covering its walls in an simpler semblance of tapestry, and wordlessly pointed to its interior. The three of them sat on cold stone benches at a small, roughly hewn stone table, Tom across from Abe and Adira and reaching out to clutch Adira's hands. He could have been inspired by her undoubted attractiveness, his sweetheart notwithstanding, but from his pallor and Adira's warm, gentle expression, it seemed more likely that he was viewing her as a sort of maternal surrogate, or at least an adopted aunt. And he was confiding in her, in a panicked babble. "I didn't know! I was distracted, and I got lost, I couldn't see anything I knew, there wasn't any moon . . . and it kept getting colder, and my hands and feet were going numb . . . and then I saw a flicker of light and thought it was from someone's window, or even my pa coming out to look for me . . . ." He choked back a sob.

A light, on a moonless night in the realm of the ice fae. What might explain it? Some ceremony or revel of which Abe was ignorant?

Or a light kindled for Tom's benefit, as a lure?

"So I went toward it, and I thought everything would be all right, and then it just – disappeared. And I was left in the dark, still lost. And then I stumbled over a branch, and I remembered that I had matches with me, and I could maybe make a torch to see where I was. I figured the weight of ice must've brought it down, though there wasn't any ice left on it." He let out something between a sob and a laugh. "I thought I was lucky to find it, that fortune was being kind to me."

Neither fortune nor fate may have set it in his path.

The boy had grown a little calmer as he told his tale, but now his eyes went wide enough to show the whites, darting back and forth like those of a horse about to bolt.

"They told me what they mean to do to me. Put me in the lake and seal the ice over me, and leave me there, forever, while my parents and my girl and everyone looks for me and doesn't find me, and maybe thinks I ran away, and none of them can help me . . . . Can you help me? Can you stop them?"

Adira looked him in the eye and said firmly, "That's our job."

Abe hoped to God they would find some way to do it.

It was difficult to track the time of this realm, or to know how that time tracked with that of their own world. But the light reaching them inside the cave grew dimmer, to the point where there was almost none. Not long afterward, their exhausted client slumped against the wall behind him and fell asleep, his hands finally releasing Adira's and falling away.

Neither Abe nor his daughter had found that merciful escape.

A few minutes later, Adira interrupted the chill silence of the cave to say, quietly, "Let's talk about something else, something other than this place and this case."

The right topic might lift both their spirits, which could only help their client. "Of course," Abe said. "Did you have a subject in mind?"

It appeared she had not got that far. She blinked twice before saying, with a faint trace of a smile, "I'm open to suggestions."

Abe looked around at the walls of the cave. He had been in bleaker places, but not many . . . which inspired him to ask, "What are some of your favorites, of the realms you've visited?"

As he'd hoped, the question eased the tension in her eyes and forehead. Adira tapped her chin slowly with one finger, once and again, and finally answered, "One of them may surprise you, because it wasn't unearthly or dramatic. I really liked the realm with all the different sizes and types of farms – the hills with sheep and lambs that came up to me and let me bury my hands in their wool, and the vineyards with arbors and grapes cascading down, and the old-fashioned dairy farm." She laughed. "I remember they let me try to milk a cow, and I was pretty impressed with myself for managing it until I realized those cows could actually milk themselves, just squeezing the milk out into the pail."

Adira's fond memories of that realm made Abe treasure it in retrospect. At the time, he had wished forlornly that Clara were there with them, comparing the Fair Folk's version of pastoral living with the various folklore portrayals of it, hypothesizing about which had influenced which.

A gust of wind outside the cave made ice-clad branches clatter together. It pulled Adira out of her reverie, and her expression grew gloomy. "That feels very far away, now." She lifted her chin and sat up straighter. "But enough of that old news. Tell me about some realms I haven't seen, whether you've seen them yourself or not."

Abe rummaged through his memory. What would most appeal to her? Why not the realm he had described to her so long ago, and which had made her look at him as if he were a magician conjuring wonders? Swallowing a lump in his throat, he said, "There's one I know I told you about, one of the first Fair Folk realms I visited – the Kingdom of Clouds." Her face immediately brightened;

for a moment, he thought she might clap her hands, as she used to when he described it. "You remember that one, right enough! If you have business there, the rulers enchant you to be able to float in and out and around all the castles and mountain ranges, and close enough to admire the dragons and elephants and such – though not close enough for them to grab you."

Adira laughed. "I remember how you used to say it. 'But if you get close enough, they could . . . GRAB you!' I loved it. And I still wanted to try to ride one of the dragons, or lasso a cloud elephant."

Such a bold child she had been . . . and his tales had fired her imagination, and led her to follow in his footsteps. They, he, had brought her here. And it was too late for regrets on that score.

"There's a realm whose inhabitants were obsessed with food and feasting. They've got any food you can imagine, and some you probably can't – though of course I couldn't try any of it. And along somewhat similar lines, there's a realm inspired by various human festivals. Part of it is like a Renaissance Faire, with the resident fae taking turns being the king or queen of the revels, and the actual rulers playing whatever parts appeal to them at that moment. Their jousts would be bloodcurdling if the injuries were permanent! And, let me think . . . oh, I'd love to see this one! It's mostly one lovely scene after another, natural landscapes in different seasons and moods as well as different kinds of architecture, but all looking as if painted by some Impressionist master. And there's one that's all volcanoes, with the Fair Folk huge obsidian giants."

Adira was leaning forward, listening eagerly.

"And maybe the one I most want to visit, though I can't imagine what the fae there might need from us, and last I heard they weren't interested in mere tourism. It's essentially interstellar space, complete with all sizes and types of planets, and nebulae glowing in more colors than mortals can usually see, and galaxies in the distance. Some of the fae there are no bigger than dust, glowing and traveling in clouds. Others look like clusters of ice and join together to dance around planets like rings . . . ."

And that was all he could remember. He was tempted to invent some other realms, just to prolong Adira's escape from the reality around them. But to do so within a faerie realm might be treated as lying.

No one had yet arrived to brief them on what amended procedure the ice fae intended to employ, and if they simply waited, it might be the viscount who brought that information. Abe was increasingly disinclined to allow that fae to be his sole source of information. He therefore left Adira in charge of Tom, with what encouraging words he could muster, and ventured forth cautiously to find an ice fae and attempt a few questions. He did not go far, fearing to make some fatal blunder of his own, and thus had no real chance to warm himself with motion. In spite of the winter gear in which he had wrapped himself, he was chilled to the point of shivering before he spied a fae whose appearance, more ornate than that of the first two fae – diamond-shaped icicles where buttons would be, and a lacy snowflake collar – might indicate higher rank. Abe took one step toward it, bowed low, and asked, "Is it permitted for me to speak to you?"

The fae showed white, pointed teeth in a smile and spoke in a voice like jagged ice scratching across a chalkboard. "You should hope it is, as you have done so. And in fact, if you are the – lawyer, is that the word? – who has undertaken to speak for the vandal who carried a torch in our realm, then you have permission, for the time being. You had some purpose in addressing me?"

Abe made note of the fae's description of Tom, put it aside, and answered, "I do. We would like to know, and indeed need to know, how matters are to proceed. Where, and how, and to whom will we be allowed to make our plea for the boy?"

"Why, now, of course. Collect your partner and your client, and come with me."

* * * * *

Adira had almost had to drag Tom out of the cave, and his footsteps still dragged. Dad walked close behind them as if prepared to herd Tom along. The fae led them through a forest planted thick with what looked like birch trees, snow resting on their ice-encased branches. The earlier haze must have dissipated or otherwise vanished, for tonight, unlike the fateful night in question, there was a moon shining through the trees, and here and there Adira could see stars glimmering where leaves would have obscured them. Dad was mumbling to himself the way he sometimes did before meetings, when there were points he wanted to make sure to remember.

And then they were suddenly out of the forest, and the lake stretched in front of them, frozen ripples along its nearest edge and flat frosted ice beyond. Tom stumbled and moaned. Adira hadn't realized she could hear Dad breathing until his breaths stopped for several seconds, then resumed with a quiet gasp.

Off to the right, about ten yards away, stood three tall ice fae, wearing what must have been crowns, though they looked like branches broken off from the trees and fashioned into headdresses. On the upper points of the branches, diamond-like chunks of ice had been fastened, like those their escort wore, but larger and shining with their own light. Beyond and behind the three, a cluster of other beings had gathered, ice fae and a few other creatures: two foxes in winter pelts, one snow-white dove, three incongruous crows – and two white seal pups.

Surely seals were salt water creatures, not fresh? Dad tapped her shoulder to draw her attention and mouthed the words, *Their Majesties*. For whatever reason, the rulers of the ocean realm had come to observe.

The tallest of the crowned fae, standing between the other two, struck the ground with a tall white branch it held like a rod of office. "We begin," it announced in a voice somewhere between a creak and a shriek. "We will first hear from the accused, and then from his advocates. Accused mortal, step forward."

If they had had more time, and if they had known what was coming, she and Dad would have discussed the pros and cons of having Tom speak. Trial lawyers were often wary, for good reason, of having a defendant testify and possibly give the prosecution useful ammunition. Here, they had no choice – and it would probably work well enough. Tom's youthful demeanor, his terror, and the details he would relate might well do more good than harm.

Tom told his tale again, in much the same words and even less coherently. When he had repeated half his sentences and finally stammered to a halt, the crowned figure to the tallest one's left stepped forward and held up a scorched stick of wood. "Is this the torch you lit?"

Tom stared at the piece of wood, panting, his breath making little clouds. "It – it may be, but I wasn't looking at it – I was trying to see where I was."

The branch vanished as the fae said in its eerie voice, "So you did light a torch."

"I – I – I didn't know – I'm so sorry, I'm so awfully sorry, I wish I'd never done it! I wish I'd frozen to death and gone to heaven, instead of ending up in the lake forever and never dying and never going home and never seeing anyone I love again and – " He dropped to his knees, arms outstretched in desperation. "Oh, please, please don't do it! I didn't *know!*"

In some dispassionate corner of her mind, far from the pity and anger and fear that filled the rest, Adira heard the drone of her criminal law professor, repeating once again, *Ignorance of the law is no excuse.* But it might be different here – though she'd seen no sign of such a merciful difference.

The tallest fae held up its long pale hand, nails glinting in the moonlight, and said, "And now the advocates may speak."

While the two of them had never before handled anything like a trial, they were used to working together in negotiations. When Adira first joined the practice, they had decided in advance who would handle what issues, but these days they just as often took turns in a less rigid manner, reading each other's signals so that the flow (she hoped) appeared seamless. Now it was Dad who cleared his throat and spoke first. "Respected judges, we ask you to consider how this boy came to make the mistake he so deeply regrets. There are two circumstances that may strike you as both surprising and significant."

A familiar and increasingly detested drawl interrupted him, saying, "But really, does it matter what excuses a careless mortal asserts for breaking the most vital and sacred law of this realm? Are not the facts all that matter?"

As Adira clenched her fists, Dad turned toward the viscount, standing a few feet behind the three crowned fae, and bowed. "Good evening, Lord Bloomingshire. If the rulers of this realm will permit, we will explain why it is precisely the facts, and not any excuses, which I seek to call to their attention."

The crowned fae turned in unison toward the viscount with stares Adira thought could almost pierce him bodily. "You have served us by bringing these advocates to our attention, and to our realm. Serve us now by silence." The viscount bowed its head, but not before Adira spied a flicker of chagrin crossing its face.

Adira took up the narrative. "Lords of this realm, you have heard the accused relate what befell him that fateful night. Traveling from one spot to another in his country, he lost his way. There was no reason to predict he would, for presumably the first time in his short life, cross into your domain. And yet, wandering and alone, something drew him to do so – a light, where no light could be expected. A light which, in his confusion and trouble, he understandably hoped meant succor – a shelter from the elements he was not, as you are, made to withstand, or even better, the presence of his beloved father.

"I ask you, lords, what was this light? How did it appear, and lead him on a path he should never have trod? And why did it vanish once he had entered your lands?"

Adira resisted the urge to look in the viscount's direction as Dad began speaking again. "That is the first unexplained circumstance, the first anomalous fact, confronting us. The second is the branch he found – stumbled upon, in fact, lying directly in his path. A branch that, from its condition, was not brought down by ice." Dad pointed up and back at the forest from which they had emerged, now a glittering maze of tree limbs. "A branch somehow fallen where no other branches fall, with no ice encasing it, ideal for the purpose for which he used it – to provide a light, in place of the light he had followed and which had suddenly forsaken him."

Adira knew what needed to be said next, but it would probably be more effective from her father. She let him be the one to say, "We offer no explanations. My daughter and I seek only to clarify what events occurred. In this proceeding, if we understand its purpose, it matters far less how this light and this branch appeared than the simple fact that the accused brought neither into your realm, and could understandably have believed them available to him or even intended for him."

Dad looked at Adira, and she back at him. She could think of nothing worthwhile to add, and neither, it seemed, could he.

With no one speaking, the silence, punctuated only by barely audible, random creaking from the ice of the lake, was profound. A breeze came off the water as if seeking the trees beyond, further chilling those vulnerable to cold. Adira moved nearer to Tom and took his hands in both hers, rubbing to bring at least a little warmth to his thin fingers.

The leader turned his attention to Tom, looking him up and down. If what passed for its face gave any clue to the fae's thoughts, Adira lacked the key with which to decipher it. After a long minute, the fae turned away from Tom and said, "Advocates, if you contest the penalty of unending entombment in ice, what alternate penalty do you propose?"

Tom whimpered like a mortally injured dog. Trying her best to ignore the dreadful sound, Adira looked over at Dad and asked, "May my father and I speak to each other privately for a moment?"

The three crowned fae inclined their upper bodies in what might be an affirmative, again in unison. Adira waited to be sure she understood, then let go of Tom's hands and moved a few steps back toward the trees, Dad following. They conferred in whispers for as long as they dared, which might have been three minutes, and then rejoined Tom. Dad was the one to speak. "We propose that rather than serving only as a silent example, primarily to those who dwell here and have no need of it, this mortal be given the task of traveling to the various mortal lands from which the inhabitants might possibly stray into your realm, warning them that if they find themselves in unknown or unfamiliar territory, they must on no account produce any form of fire, and must use other means to find their way or to seek assistance."

The leader turned from one side to the other and back again, in what might have been its equivalent of shaking its head. "We have been informed that among the common characteristics of your kind are intense curiosity and a perverse desire to challenge limitations as proof of their daring. It is too likely that such a warning will only make mortals more likely to seek our realm, and then to kindle a flame, perhaps in the futile hope of escaping back to their own lands to boast of the achievement."

If the viscount could have been expected to guess their proposal, or if it had contrived to overhear them discuss it, it might have been the one to prejudice the rulers against the idea. Adira ground her teeth, caught herself, and stopped, saying, "If this particular form of service to you is unacceptable, it is only one of the possible ways in which the mortal could make himself useful and atone for his unwitting transgression. You will know far better than we do what those alternatives could be."

The three crowned fae abruptly shifted to cluster together, so close they might almost have been a tree with three trunks, their branching crowns tapping together. Adira had lost feeling in her toes, and dared not shuffle about or stamp her feet to awaken them. Beside her, Dad blew on his hands and then buried them in his pockets. Adira followed suit. Tom stood as stock-still as if already frozen, the tears on his lashes and cheeks already turned to ice.

Finally, the three separated and stood in a line again. The tallest, still in the center, spoke alone. "The traditional penalty is fixed and may not be avoided. This mortal will be placed in the lake, and the ice sealed over him."

Tom screamed, a high, shrieking sound terribly similar to the voice of the ice fae. The ruler put out its palm, like a birch without its bark, and spoke over him. "He will not, however, remain there forever. After the sun and moon have risen and set twelve times, he will be removed and thawed, to serve us in what ways we will have determined.

If he serves us well, we will consider whether he may eventually be returned to his own realm."

Tom fell silent and stood trembling. Adira and Dad looked at each other, conferring without words, before Dad said in a toneless voice, "We have no counteroffer."

Fae did not lie. Was there any ambiguity in the sentence pronounced? She saw none, but wanted reassurance nonetheless. She was trying to think of a way to request it when Tom burst out, staring at her, "Please be there when they let me out! Please say you'll be there!"

Adira tried and failed to call forth an encouraging expression. Giving up, she said to the fae, "I hope you will allow us to do as our client requests."

Behind them, Adira saw the viscount smile, with a sly satisfaction she could not explain, as the three crowned fae said in their eerie unison, "You may be there, indeed."

Tom still looked at her wild-eyed, but his voice was calmer, and sadder, as he said, "And please tell my family where I am – this place, not the lake – and that I can't come home yet, but will come as soon as I can. They'll tell my girl. They're on Little Riverside Road in Kirkstone County – anyone there can let you know how to find them."

"Of course," Dad said in the same tone he had used years ago when Adira awakened from a nightmare and needed comforting. The fae made no comment.

"And tell them – they'll want to help, but they can't, and they'd only get themselves in trouble trying, and couldn't afford – " Tom stopped short, and his voice wavered and went higher with his dismay. "I didn't even think! I owe you money for representing me – "

The sheer decency of the lad, to think of that, and to care about it, at a time like this. Heartsick, Adira held up her hand to stop Tom from saying any more. "You and your family don't owe us a penny."

Adira could not remember anything in her life she had less wanted to do than to watch the fae drag Tom to the ice, cast the spell that would let him survive in the lake, force him into the water, and seal the ice over his upturned, terrified face.

But she went with her client and held his hand until they pried his clutching fingers loose, and listened as he started to scream again, and then listened as the fae waved a wand of ice at him and stole his voice away. And she stood as close to the edge of the lake as they would let her, as if her presence there, and Dad's at her side, would make Tom any less afraid.

And then, when the ice closed over him and held him fast, she threw herself into her father's arms and sobbed.

Dad murmured in her ear, "Let's go home." She nodded, stepped back, dug a tissue out of her pocket, and looked around, only to realize there was no portal waiting. It had been the viscount, she now recalled, who had brought them here.

The crowned fae had not done the work of carrying out Tom's sentence, but they had observed it. She bowed to them and asked, "Will you provide us with the portal, or should we seek Lord Bloomingshire's assistance?"

The tallest of the fae turned back and forth as it had done before. "That is not what happens now. It appears you did not understand what it meant to intrude on our realm and advocate for a miscreant mortal."

The viscount stepped forward, its expression somehow combining smug satisfaction and ferocity. "From the moment you set foot here, your fates were inextricably intertwined with that of your client." It looked toward the lake and paused, as if to savor their shock, before going on. "It appears that the rulers of this place have declined to apply that principle in its most literal form, or you would already be beside the young offender beneath the ice. But you may not so blithely leave him, and this realm, behind. Here you will stay."

* * * * *

Abe had maintained his self-control only with difficulty as Tom was dragged to the lake and thrust under the ice. The image of Adira at Tom's age, of Adira in the icy hands of inhuman and implacable beings, kept imposing itself over what was actually happening. To his shame, it had been a relief when Tom's cries were silenced, and when the deed was done and he could turn away.

The viscount's announcement was so close to his dreadful imaginings that at first he could not parse it out, and thought Adira, or both of them, were to be next into the lake. By the time he understood the actual threat facing them, Adira was already speaking. "Lord Bloomingshire, I hope you will forgive me if I address the lords of this realm, since as you have acknowledged, they appear to have mitigated the rigor of their law at least to some extent."

The viscount said nothing, though its savage smile faded to something like its usual smirk. Abe was caught between dismay and pride as Adira turned without missing a beat and said to the crowned fae, "My lords, you have extended our client mercy beyond your usual practice. I do not claim to know the origin of the law you speak of enforcing, but would I be incorrect, as well as presumptuous, in saying that it may not have been intended to bring you into indefinite contact with mortals, and that such contact may be unwelcome?"

Two of the rulers turned slightly to look at each other before the shorter of them said, "We would have little contact with you if you were placed beneath the ice. However, we consider it possible that we will find uses for mortals such as yourselves."

Abe knew Adira well enough to see her react to this renewed threat, but he thought, and hoped, the ice fae could not discern it. Adira paused only long enough to take one breath before going on. "I hope I will not offend you further if I ask you to consider even greater forbearance. I request that you consider the impact which requiring us to stay here indefinitely would have on many people, fae as well as mortals, who have not in any way aggrieved or injured you."

Should he break in? No, Adira was doing at least as well as he could.

"Our case load is such that a number of negotiations, of importance to one or both of the contracting parties, are currently in progress. While I may not, due to my professional obligations of confidentiality, discuss their details, they concern the health, the career, or various future plans of those involved." She paused as if unsure how to proceed and then added, "In fact, I believe two of the fae involved, and most exalted fae at that, are present here." She looked toward the seal pups, who had stayed throughout the proceedings – except that they were now adult seals, at least as large as adult seals would be.

It had been risky for Adira to mention them without express permission, but the seals morphed into the regal divine figures Abe had seen once before. The ice fae, the three crowned figures and all the others watching, bowed to them before turning their attention back to Adira. She went on smoothly, "As far as I am aware, there is no other professional practice prepared to take our place." She looked over at Abe for confirmation, and he nodded.

As he did so, he caught sight of the viscount again, and what he saw threw him back into his earlier distress. The viscount was looking not at him but at Adira, and from its position behind the crowned fae, it was not troubling to conceal his malevolent glare. Whatever its role in this situation – and Abe was more than ever convinced that it had set the scene in motion – Adira appeared to be its particular target.

Why Adira? Abe had only to ask himself that question before his heart sank. As a child, Adira had been passionately outspoken, proudly showing and defending her emotions and reactions. She had learned to rein herself in, and in particular, to present a professional and reassuring countenance to their clients – but the viscount was no client. Useful as it often made itself, Adira had taken less trouble than she might to completely conceal her amusement and even contempt at the way it aped the fashions of a bygone era. Abe had, at times, defended the viscount's preferences, suggesting that they were intended to amuse both itself and those before whom it appeared with such glamours, but Adira had never been convinced.

And now the viscount intended to have its revenge. And no fae, understanding the circumstances, would much condemn that purpose. To disrespect any Fair Folk was to invite retribution.

Abe should have seen it coming, remonstrated more firmly with his daughter, warned her more convincingly. Now that it was too late to protect her in advance, how could he protect her when disaster already loomed?

And even as he stood there wasting time in self-recrimination, the rulers spoke in their horrific chorus. "You should not disdain the prospect of staying in our realm. There could be less agreeable prospects. The rulers of the Dungeon Realm indulge in what some fae would call torture."

Adira, admirably self-contained until now, went pale. She must not have heard of that realm before, or perhaps had only heard of the mortals who sought one of the few visitor passes made available, most of them probably assuming that everything so vividly presented was imaginary. Adira's reaction showed to him, and doubtless to the fae, that she was ignorant of the limitation under which the Dungeon Realm operated. Abe did know, and would have admired the cleverness of the rulers' phrasing, so effectively misleading without being false, if he were less furious at the attempted manipulation.

He spoke before Adira could. "My lords, I am ignorant of what rules we may have broken to merit such a fate. We were, I thought, invited here. And as to the Dungeon Realm, have the rules changed so much, and so recently? It was my understanding that while actual fae are sent there for punishment, and suffer the torments visitors see, it is forbidden for mortals to be inmates as opposed to visitors."

Abe's momentary fear that the rules had indeed changed was swept away in the cold wind that blew from the crowned fae, accompanied by a tangible sense of chagrin.

The viscount, concealing any disappointment that Abe had not been intimidated into silence, stepped forward to where the crowned fae could see it. Its face now showed only deference as it asked, "Exalted lords, may I offer a thought that occurs to me in response to the younger mortal's earlier argument?"

The three of them gestured in what must be assent, and the viscount said, not indulging in any of its more flamboyant mannerisms, "It would not require both of these mortals to tend to the clients to which the advocate refers, or, if that proved too challenging, to bring their matters to an expeditious close. Should you decide to be so gracious as to release one of them despite your law, you surely need not release both."

The leaders remained silent and immobile for at least a minute, while Abe held his breath and Adira might have done the same. Then they replied, "The suggestion has merit."

The viscount allowed itself a quick flicker of a smile before saying, "I rejoice to have met with your approval. If I may add one more detail for you to consider, it is only reasonable to assume that the elder of these two, with years more experience, would be best suited to perform such duties."

That finally jarred Abe out of his paralysis. Hoping he needed no special permission to speak, he said, "My lords, my partner has ample experience and is excellent at dealing with both mortals and fae. As a member of a younger generation, she is more attuned to new developments that may affect our practice. If only one of us may leave today, I urge that it be she."

The viscount stepped back again, once more out of view of at least the central crowned fae, and gave him a nod of exaggerated approval. Only then did Abe realize that in his haste to counter the viscount's narrative, he had appeared to concede the fundamental point that the ice fae were justified in holding one of them prisoner. He opened his mouth to backtrack, to somehow undo his error, but the three fae waved at him in their unnerving coordinated fashion, almost certainly commanding his silence. Together they said, "It is decided. Lord Bloomingshire will escort the elder home. The younger will remain."

Desperate now, Abe blurted out, "My lords – please!" But the viscount strode up to him, grabbed his arm, and tugged him away from Adira, allowing him not even a moment for a farewell or a word of encouragement. He could just glimpse her shocked, blank expression as the viscount manifested the portal and shoved him through.

* * * * *

Just like that, Dad was gone, and she had had no chance to comfort him, to tell him she'd be all right, that she'd find a way to be all right. In moments he would be back at their office, or wandering distraught around town . . . . Was he calling Mom right now, to tell her the news? Or wondering frantically how to keep it from her?

Movement nearby recalled her attention to her surroundings. The three crowned fae had vanished while she was lost in distraction, and the rest of the fae were dispersing. The ocean fae were nowhere to be seen. Only one of the ice fae lingered nearby. It might be the courier who had escorted Dad and her earlier. At least it was someone who might answer her questions, once she figured out what those questions were.

To start with, where was she to be kept? And would they offer her food she dared not eat, or simply enchant away her need for food?

The fae waved a branchlike hand for her attention and said, "Come." She followed, saying nothing. She had better wait and ask only the questions events did not answer.

The fae led her back through the trees, but not all the way to the icy cave where they had started. Instead it stopped in the middle of a cluster of trees that leaned together toward the top, their branches woven tightly overhead. The weave might not be enough to keep snow out, but once a little snow had fallen, what fell on the branches might act as a sort of mat to keep more from coming in.

There would be no fire to warm her. But as she wondered how she would avoid hypothermia, the fae picked up a handful of snow and threw it over her head. She did not suddenly feel warm; what happened felt far less natural, as if the very idea of cold had somehow been removed from her mind and almost from her memory. She shivered nonetheless, from the uncanniness of it.

She would presumably find out soon enough whether they would wipe away the thought of food as well. In the meantime, another question came to mind. "Must I stay in this . . . shelter? And if not, where am I allowed to go?"

"Where else would you go?"

Adira struggled for an answer. What came to mind first was, *anywhere. I must go somewhere.* She tried to explain. "Mortals like me need to move from place to place, more than I can within this cluster of trees, in order to remain healthy. And it is bad for us to go for long periods without seeing other living beings." She almost said that humans used such isolation as a punishment, but remembered that her own fate might be considered close enough to punishment that this would be thought particularly appropriate.

The fae said nothing. Adira had the impression that if it had been human, it would have shrugged its shoulders. Instead, it slid backward out of the shelter and left.

Before Adira's outlook could become truly bleak, she remembered that if her fate was to echo Tom's in some respects, there could well be tasks for her to perform. That would give her some occupation, some variety in her days. Perhaps, if she thought about it, and as she came to know this realm better, she could even propose ways in which she could be useful. Was there anything that more familiar realms might want to trade for, in this wilderness of ice? Was there anything its residents might perhaps want, or be brought to want, from the human world?

But she would think of nothing like that tonight. She had no idea what time it was, or would be in a place where one counted time. All she knew was that she was suddenly, utterly exhausted, and that for now, she had nothing better to do than sleep.

She curled up on the ground beneath the trees and awaited that escape, since it might be all too long before she could make any other.

* * * * *

From the dark of a winter's night, Abe found himself thrust back into a spring afternoon. If only it meant he could live the last few hours over again, and differently! But reach as desperately as he might, he could not grab them and pull them back.

Abe would have to tell Clara what had befallen their daughter. But not yet. For now, Clara was in blissful ignorance, rather than suspense or terror. And Abe had no idea how to tell her what had happened, how he had failed to see disaster coming and then failed to stop it, how a mincing mockery of a human being had played him for a fool. . . .

At least he and Adira had helped Tom. Even if Tom would not have needed help had the viscount not used him as a tool, he was not, at least, condemned to spend eternity in a frozen hell of a prison. The viscount would probably have been perfectly happy to let that happen, and Abe and Adira had prevented it.

He had to tell Clara. She might even see some way to help Adira. She knew so many folk tales, far more than Abe by now, and the fae were nothing if not creatures out of folk tales. Somewhere in a notebook, jotted down in her precise handwriting, Clara might have the key to Adira's rescue.

But before she could set to work digging through her notes and sources for that possible treasure, she would have to know what happened, and deal with her initial shock and horror and sorrow. He would be inflicting all that on his beloved wife.

He could not bear to tell Clara.

He had to tell Clara.

But he could wait. She might already be asleep. And he could, if he hurried, perform one other duty first. He could carry out Tom's instruction to bring news to his family. If

Tom had not made that request, Abe would have wanted to give them some news anyway, despite his professional obligation to keep anything he learned representing Tom in confidence. He could picture all too easily what the family must be suffering, not knowing where Tom was or why he was missing – and now that Abe, too, was a parent bereft for some unknowable length of time, it would have been almost impossible to stay silent.

And after dealing with the fae, it was a relief to be free to shape the truth, to spare Tom's family and girlfriend some small portion of what he and Clara were condemned to suffer.

Tom's mother answered the phone so quickly she must have been stationed over it for hours. Her voice, choked to a whisper, somehow mingled hope and dread. He told them he had news of Tom which Tom has asked him to convey, and arranged to come over immediately. Unable to whisk himself there Fair Folk style, he drove as fast as he dared to shorten their interval of suspense.

When he knocked, a girl who looked to be in her latter teens answered the door. She looked nothing like Tom, but until they were introduced he could not be sure of her identity. Her tight grip on his arm, as she led him inside, could have signaled the concern of a family member, but something about the mother's whispered thank-you supported Abe's guess that this was the girlfriend Tom had visited before his fateful trip homeward.

Tom's parents pushed back their kitchen chairs as Abe approached, but had no room in their thoughts for introductions. The boy and girl at the table, maybe thirteen and eight respectively, did not get up, but simply stared at him as he approached. Taking the one empty chair, he started with what mattered most. "First, let me assure you that I saw Tom only hours ago, and that he was alive and unharmed." The final word caught in his throat. "He lost his way in the woods and stumbled into Fair Folk territory, and is now in their . . . keeping." A kinder word than *custody*, let alone whatever words he might have found for Tom's state by the time Abe had left him.

The older girl was biting her lip, but let it go to say plaintively, "How could he get lost? He's gone home at night dozens of times – " She stopped abruptly, as if disclosing facts previously kept secret. But no one at the table cared, now, how often Tom had visited his girlfriend at night, nor how long he had stayed there or what they had done together.

Tom's father slammed a fist on the table, startling the little girl to the point that she cried out. The mother hushed her as the father said, his voice husky, "It was a dark night. I should have gone to find him."

Tom's brother had a determined, almost excited expression Abe knew and distrusted. The boy leaned toward Abe and asked, "Where are they keeping him?"

Abe looked the boy in the eye and said, "You can't go there, not without the consent of the rulers of that realm, which they wouldn't give. Please believe me that any attempt to trespass would only hurt Tom, as well as the trespasser."

"But won't they hurt him anyway if we leave him there?" the boy answered, spitting the words at Abe and glaring as if Abe was the primary obstacle in his way.

It would be so easy for Abe to lose all credibility. He said solemnly, "I won't pretend Tom is happy in his confinement, but I don't believe him to be in pain, or likely to be. I have also been promised, as his representative, that the conditions of his confinement will improve within a few days, though he will not be allowed to come home that soon."

The little girl piped up for the first time. "The Fair Folk make bargains, don't they?"

Abe peered more closely at her. He had not expected her to do anything beside listen, quietly or noisily, and he now reproached himself, imagining what Adira would have said at his reflexively discounting a child. He said gravely, "Yes, they do. But it's often dangerous to make such a bargain."

"But isn't that what you do? Help people bargain, so things don't go wrong?"

He didn't know whether to smile or sigh. "That's one of the things I do, but if what someone wants to do, the bargain they want to make, is too dangerous, then I refuse."

The child stuck her lower lip out, an expression so like one Adira would have shown him at that age that he had to hang on hard to his composure. "Well, I want to make a bargain, and you have to let me do it!"

Her father tapped her hand, hard enough to serve as a warning. "You mustn't treat our guest that way. But if you say you're sorry and are more polite, I'll let you tell him what you hope he can do for us."

"I'm sorry," the girl muttered, and then looked at him with renewed boldness. "I like to sew. I can make clothes for them. I make clothes for my dolls all the time."

Abe suppressed a smile. Apparently, the notion of fae as tiny creatures, doll-sized or smaller, remained widespread. In fact, he had once seen a passing mention of a Flower Garden Realm where the flowers were mostly the size of sunflowers and the faeries tiny enough to hide in their petals. The contrast between that image and the ice realm made him shiver, and he hoped the family failed to notice it. He replied, "The fae come in many sizes and shapes, but most of them are two-thirds my size or larger. It would take you a long time to make even one outfit. Still, I can convey your offer."

Tom's mother had gone pale, or paler, during this exchange. She cleared her throat twice and said, still hoarse, "I'll trade myself for Tom. Ask them to take me instead."

Her husband threw up his arm in front of her as if to shield her. "No, me. I'll go, if they send Tom home."

The woman took hold of his arm and gently pushed it down and away. "Love, your work keeps the family fed and housed. It would take a long time for me to find anyone willing to pay me for the things I know how to do."

Tom's brother jumped to his feet and said, "I can work! I can take care of you and my sister!" Then he looked at his father. "I don't want you to go. But if you have to, I can take care of us."

Abe could not let this contest of sacrifice go on. "We're all getting ahead of ourselves. I have yet to learn whether there's anything the rulers of that realm will take in exchange for releasing Tom. I'll find that out as soon as I can – though it may not be as soon as we would all prefer. If they're open to any such bargain, I'll let you know." Though if Tom, when he came out of the ice, opposed it, Abe would not be able to pursue it.

The silence that followed his words had nothing of peace in it. After it had become painful for him and probably for them all, the mother, who had slumped in her chair, pulled herself straight again and said, "Let me get you some tea."

Abe doubted he could swallow even a mouthful, and his endurance was nearing its breaking point. "Thank you, but no. I'd best be going. I'll call you as soon as I have any word."

He waited until six in the morning his time, after an almost sleepless night that left him more exhausted than simply staying awake would have done. That way, the news would not be the first thing to confront Clara in the morning, nor the ruin of her own sleep at night. It would have been easier to text, the first time texting had ever been easier, so he called.

"Darling! So early for you to call! How is the firm chugging along? How is Adira?"

He told her.

Clara was determined to fly home as soon as the complicated and cumbersome arrangements could be made. Abe lacked the strength to resist the thought of her company in misery. After they hung up, Abe went on a hunt in the kitchen. He had not had a drink in years, not so much pursuant to any resolution as to avoid the acid reflex that inevitably followed; but somewhere in a cabinet or lurking in the back of the refrigerator, there must be alcohol of some kind.

He found two bottles of Guinness. That was a better discovery than he deserved – by rights, he should be drinking something abominable like peppermint schnapps. But he popped the cap off the first, took both bottles to the living room, and found a recording of Irish folk tunes.

Maybe he'd think better drunk than sober. And if not, at least he would be drunk.

CHAPTER 5

ADIRA had done plenty of camping as a child, with one or both parents, in various exotic places and then closer to home. Waking up on the ground was nothing new, and she had even found shelter in a dead tree trunk once or twice. When she awoke to ground beneath her and thin blue sunlight filtering in from above, it took a moment for the pleased anticipation of a new morning in a forest to shiver and shatter in the memory of where she was, and why, and with what uncertain and fearsome prospects.

She tried to hold panic at bay by finding some plan she could form, or at least some task she could do. Then she realized that she did, in fact, have a place to go and a promise to redeem. The thought chilled her as the air around her could no longer do. But she climbed out of the cluster of trees and made her way, dragging her feet and clenching her fists, to the edge of the lake.

It was easy to find the spot, the only clear patch in all the expanse of ice. Treading carefully, she approached the edge, brushed away the thin layer of snow on the ground, and knelt where she could, if she leaned forward, see Tom's upturned face.

He had apparently given up screaming. His mouth was closed, his eyes wide open. Was he conscious and aware?

She hoped not, and then had to abandon that hope as his eyes, moving in slow motion, shifted toward her. When his eyelids relaxed slightly, she knew where she had to spend the next twelve – or was it eleven, now? — days.

Tom's eyes drifted closed every hour or so. Adira couldn't tell whether he was napping or whether his movements had been slowed so much that what she saw was a blink. When his eyes closed for whatever reason, she got up and walked around to stretch her legs and to have something, anything, else to look at. She walked to the edge of the forest and back, and a little ways around the lake in each direction, and then resumed her vigil.

The first night after she returned to the lake, she tried to sleep there, but the shore was too rocky for her to overcome the discomfort. Finally admitting defeat, she tried to estimate the angle of Tom's gaze, followed it to a spot on the shore, took off her scarf, and arranged it in the shape of a heart.

Then she returned to the cluster of trees and confronted the possibility that she would lose track of the days and fail to be waiting when Tom emerged. There was little snow inside, and even if she drew a line there for the first night and day, her movements while she slept might erase it. She knew better than to try to make any mark on one of the trees. In the end, she bit one of her fingernails to make a ragged edge and scratched a line on the inside of her arm.

On the second day, Adira awakened to sunshine, eye-watering and harsh and giving no warmth as she made her way to the lake. When she had sat or knelt or paced for what might have been six hours, or perhaps eight, the courier appeared at her side. She wrenched her eyes away from Tom's face and waited to learn the fae's errand.

She had spoken to none of them in days, so its voice, as if nails on a blackboard could reach out and squeeze her nerves, rattled her anew. "The lords have a task for you."

Adira glanced at Tom, whose eyes were ever so slowly opening, and then back at the fae. "Is it an errand that would take many days? I must be here when Tom is released from the ice. And I would . . . very much rather stay where he can see me, as much as I can, until that time."

"There is no knowing how long it may take. What you want is of little importance."

At least he hadn't said *of no importance*. "Please tell their lordships that I will undertake their errand, with all my will and with all my strength, once Tom comes out."

A pause, and then: "They are calling you now, not in ten days. You have an obligation to fulfill."

Adira took a deep breath, which only reminded her that she could no longer taste the air or feel the cold of it, and replied, "If they are willing to release Tom, at least until I can return, I will undertake this errand right away."

No pause this time. "Or they could put you under the ice until the twelve days are up."

Adira made herself keep breathing, without biting her lip or gasping or letting her eyes tear up. "They could. I will wait here to see whether they do."

She looked back at Tom. When next she glanced aside, the fae was gone.

Nothing happened for the rest of that day. No one came to seize her and thrust her under the ice. No one came to demand that she comply with the lords' demand. When she needed sleep too much to resist, she went back to the shelter and scratched another line on her arm.

The next day, after what might have been four hours or six, Adira noticed movement to her right – something white. Turning away from Tom just enough to see, she found two harp seal pups frolicking by her side. She smiled, and it felt as if she had not smiled in years and had forgotten how. Then she scrambled to her feet and bowed. "Your Majesties."

The pup nearest her stopped tussling with the other, and spoke in a voice uncannily like a cross between a human and a kitten. "They will not put you under the ice. At least not yet."

She could hardly hold herself upright. It was all she could do to refrain from the thanks that Fair Folk etiquette forbade. Instead, she bowed her head and said, "I am greatly relieved by this news, and appreciate whatever you may have done to induce them to spare me."

The pup neither affirmed nor denied the assumption. The other pup said, in an even higher voice, "Your father may ask to come see you, but we doubt it will be allowed."

Adira gulped and nodded. She rubbed her eyes, and when she took her hand away, the pups were gone. She sat back down at the edge of the lake and looked toward Tom. His eyes were open. She could not tell whether he had seen.

On the fourth day, when Adira first reached the lake, she looked in and saw tears frozen on Tom's cheeks. For the rest of that day, whenever she got up to stretch her legs, she returned to find new tears, but she could never catch him in the act of crying.

On the fifth day, she broke down in wrenching, noisy sobs – until she found herself silenced. It appeared that the ice fae found the sound of her grief an annoyance.

On the sixth day, one of the crowned fae appeared, flanked by two fae that looked particularly strong. It watched her watching Tom for a minute or so and then said, "You must begin the task we require of you."

Adira made herself breathe evenly and replied, "This is the sixth day since Tom was consigned to the lake. Tomorrow will be the seventh day. Seven is a powerful number, is it not? Even more so than twelve?"

The two strong fae stepped closer.

Panting now, Adira spoke faster, saying, "If you release Tom on the seventh day, will not justice be sufficiently served? I have been here throughout the daylight hours. I swear to you I have seen him suffering. As a mortal, I can assure you he will never dare to offend you again. If you release him tomorrow, I will immediately set about the task you have for me, and I will perform it with all my wits and strength and endurance until I complete it, or until I succumb to the death awaiting all mortals. Will you accept these terms?"

To her considerable shock, the crowned fae broke into what must have been laughter for a few seconds, though that laughter was a more fearsome sound than even its speech. Then it said, "The negotiator returns."

All three fae turned and vanished.

On the seventh day, nothing happened as the sun climbed in the pale sky, and reached its zenith, and began to descend. When the sky took on the dimmest flush of color, the same three fae appeared, or at least fae that looked the same to her untutored eyes. The thorned fae said to the others, "Break the ice."

Adira waited for the two strong fae to seize her. But instead, they reached in and pulled Tom free.

At first, he hung between them like a statue. But then he started to breathe, and when the fae let go of him, he stood on his feet. His eyes blinked once, then again, and he focused on Adira, standing close enough to touch him. She was preparing to embrace him when he gasped, opened and closed his mouth, and said in a voice too much like an ice fae's, "You've gone white!" Adira looked down at her arm. She had been doing so every day, to mark the days, but only now did she realize that she had gone as pale as the winter sky.

She bit her lip, stepped up to Tom, and pulled him into her arms. He began to shiver, and then to cry again, real tears, tears that soaked into her clothes. She held him until he stopped shaking, gently let go, and turned to the fae. "What is my task? I'm ready."

Even though Tom had come out of the ice only a few minutes before, he would have followed Adira as she went to learn her assigned task, but his guards led him away into the trees. Adira tried to turn around and look after him, but one of the strong fae grabbed Adira's arm and jerked her forward.

The three fae led Adira on a long trek around the lake. No matter how long they walked, the other shore seemed to grow no nearer, but when they had walked until moonrise, a structure of ice appeared before them. Turrets all around it bore spires much like the fae's crown, and the windows were shaped like the crown's ice diamonds and did not so much reflect as amplify the rays of moonlight.

A door in the lowest level opened as they approached. The floor within was smooth as glass or ice, and Adira had to step most carefully to avoid slipping. She had already been weary before that effort, and when they entered a room with a grand throne and a humble stool, she sank onto the stool without waiting for permission. Second thoughts followed immediately, and she looked around for any fae poised to punish her for her temerity, but only the crowned fae was present, and climbed up to sit on the throne without comment.

Adira slipped from the stool and sank to her knees, head bowed. The fae gave its creaking, shrieking laugh once more and said, "Get back on the stool. You will listen better facing me as I tell you your task."

She got to her feet and sat on the stool again, hands clasped, waiting. The fae let her wait for perhaps a minute before saying, "One of our young people is missing."

She had not thought, somehow, of young people here, or how they came to be born. But she must not let such musings distract her now.

"It happens sometimes that our young show less than the appropriate appreciation of our customs and traditions. This young fae has gone from undesirable attitude to prohibited deed. It has left our realm without permission, and from what clues it left behind, it may have assumed some glamour as disguise."

Adira could not help betraying surprise. Did not all fae use glamour? Was any variation in the ice fae's appearance, beyond rank or height, forbidden them?

"You are likely to know more about other realms, both fae and mortal, than we do. You must use that knowledge to surmise where this young person may have gone. When you find it, you must bring it home."

This time, Adira was able to avoid showing her shock at the notion that she, in her few years of life, had learned more and seen more of faerie realms than these ageless rulers. The rebellious youngster's escapade must be not simply rare but unheard-of. Rather than comment, she asked, "If this fae does not wish to return, how may I compel it?"

"We will send an escort with you. If the youngster resists, that fae will be able to do what is necessary."

And no doubt this escort would also keep an eye on Adira, to make sure she made no attempt to break her word – suicidally foolish as that would be.

As if to make doubly sure, the fae lord added, "Your former client, though he has been released from the ice, will stand as surety for your diligence and obedience. If you give us reason to return him to the lake, he will not emerge from it as long as the lake and this realm endure."

She did not need her knowledge that fae kept their promises to believe it.

What else did she need to know? "How am I to travel?"

"Your escort will provide the necessary portals."

Adira failed to see how a fae properly obedient to this realm's culture would be capable of locating multiple other realms, but the ruler could not be lying to her. Nor could it have invented the mission as some sort of trap for her. Her escort must, then, have either the necessary knowledge or some magic that made up for it.

The thought of being somewhere warm struck her with sudden longing, so that she asked, "Will the enchantments cast on me, against cold and hunger, remain effective?"

The fae made an impatient gesture. "You know better than to eat. Whether you feel hunger is of little importance. When you return, you will regain your immunity to cold. Have done with all these questions!"

Too late, then, to ask what she most wanted to know. If she returned to her own land, just long enough to see her parents, would she be seized and carried back here, to see Tom condemned by her rash conduct?

As she stood and bowed once more, her escort appeared at her side. It waved its hand, created a portal wreathed in ice, and said, "We go. Where?"

Adira had no idea where to start her search. While she tried to come up with some guiding hypothesis, it occurred to her that she had other business which might be best addressed first. "Before we go," she asked, "do you know whether Lord Bloomingshire is by any chance at hand?"

That fae itself appeared not three feet away and greeted her with its usual flourish. "My dear . . . *Valentina*, how good of you to inquire after me!"

Before she could hesitate, let alone reconsider, Adira dropped to her knees. "My lord, before I begin my task, I must beg your pardon for having offended you."

The viscount, now holding a quizzing glass, raised it and peered down at her through it. "And how, do you suppose, have you offended me?"

A dangerous question – if Adira guessed wrong, she might suggest to the fae some additional grievance it should have against her. But she had had time, in these last seven days, to examine memories and her conscience, and knew at least one way she had fallen short of both her professional responsibility and more fundamental courtesy. Hedging as much as she dared, she replied, "My lord, I fear I have at times given the appearance of carelessness as to the respect I should at all times have made sure to show you. If so – "

The fae threw the quizzing glass into nothingness and glared at her. "If so, you say. My dear girl, can you possibly doubt it?"

Adira bowed her head almost to the ground. "It was a grievous error, my lord, and I greatly regret it. I would regret it even if you had not brought home to me how seriously I displeased you."

The viscount tossed its head. "Very well, then. You have begged my pardon. I will consider granting it. Have you anything more to say before you attend to your errand?"

It had been years since Adira had knelt so long, and things were beginning to ache. She did her best to ignore the fact and said quietly, "While you make that decision, I would ask you, despite how little I deserve any favors from you, to confine any further punishment, any further expression of animus, to me alone. Neither my father, I hope, nor young Tom has committed the same fault as I. Please, I beg you – " She would have bet a tidy sum that he enjoyed that word on her lips. "I beg you not to inflict further suffering on them as a lesson to me."

The viscount relaxed into its habitual smirk. "I will consider that request, as well. You had best get underway, or you will incur a more royal displeasure than mine."

Adira bowed to the point of prostrating herself, climbed clumsily to her feet, and walked toward the portal, her escort following a short step behind. Only when she reached the portal did she realize she had not yet decided on a destination. Would the young fae be more likely to start with a realm somewhat similar to its own, or would it immediately fling itself into somewhere widely different?

The fae's home was cold, forested, with an enormous body of water. What would be most unlike it?

She turned and asked her escort, "Can you take me to a desert realm? A realm where there is no water in sight, and few if any trees, and a great deal of sand?"

Stepping through the portal, Adira found herself in a landscape as different from the ice realm as she could have imagined. Sand, mostly flat but here and there dotted with dunes, spread before her under a vividly purple sky. Other than the dunes, she saw nothing in any direction except the sand, the sky, and far off, one lone tree, black as if scorched by the sun, with only three branches and no sign it had ever borne a leaf.

Perhaps more to the point, she saw no animals, let alone recognizable people.

She could not see the sun, but she felt it blaze down from the purple sky. Her skin already prickled with it. Her immunity to cold, even if she had retained it, might offer no protection against heat. She sighed, feeling the thirsty dryness of the air as she did so, and started trudging toward the tree. She must at least make sure her quarry had not taken that form.

At one moment, a few strides seemed to take her halfway to the tree, but no matter how she hurried, it grew no closer as she became more exhausted and overheated. Finally she looked at her guide, who had kept pace with her and showed no signs of effort or distress. "Do you have a way to get to the tree, other than whatever we've been doing?"

The fae clicked its fingers together with a loud tapping noise, and the tree abruptly stood in front of them. That left the question of how to tell whether it was in fact a tree, or an immobile fae in a particularly bleak glamour. It seemed increasingly unlikely that a young fae seeking adventure would have come to this desolate place – it was not, after all, as if the ice realm was so densely populated that solitude itself would assume overwhelming importance. But she bowed and said, "Good fae, will you be so kind as to speak to me?"

Nothing happened, except that a breeze ruffled her shirt and quickly grew into a wind. It did nothing to cool her, but instead buffeted her with the heated air and increasing quantities of sharp-edged sand. She looked around for any other change – and saw, amazed, that the sky had become as blue as an earthly sky, dotted with familiar-seeming wisps of white cloud, while the sand, formerly ranging from off-white to beige to tan, had turned a vivid scarlet, interrupted at one point by a thin and blazingly white salt lick stretching to a range of mountains in the distance.

The one thing unchanged in this new vista was that nothing appeared to inhabit it. No tree, this time, and no shrubs, not even a tumbleweed, and nothing that looked or acted like an animal. It was possible that something burrowed underground, or that the mountains had more life than she could see – indeed, why else would this realm exist at all? But she could spend anything from hours to eternity looking for signs of such life, and how long would the ice rulers be patient?

She turned to the fae standing silent beside her and asked, "Can you bring the portal to us, without our having to find it and return to it?"

The fae inclined its upper body in what might be its equivalent of a nod.

But where next? Nowhere lifeless, and still not too similar to the ice, but possibly with the water this realm lacked . . . .

The idea that came to her had the seduction of the familiar and, at least formerly, welcoming. "Please take me to the ocean realm. And if there is more than one, I seek the one where I have been before, where the rulers sometimes assume the glamour of giant waves."

There she stood on the cliff, or one much like it, as what seemed the same odors wafted to her on the same or a similar breeze. And rather than dead silence or barren wind, she could hear bird calls, from the peep of pipers to the haunting caw of gulls, and catch glimpses in the surging waves of what looked like fish.

Would it be rude to call to Their Majesties? She would wait a little while, at least, though not so long that taking the initiative would look like impatience. In the meantime, she could relish the moisture in the air, and the salty scent. She had barely long enough to make that decision before the two giant waves approached and made it unnecessary.

She bowed low, noticing out of the corner of her eye that her escort did the same. "Your Majesties, I hope you will excuse my coming without an invitation. May I introduce . . . ." Belatedly, it occurred to her that she had no idea what to call the fae beside her. She gestured to it, and after an awkward pause, it said what might be its name in a creaking whisper. "This honorable fae has been assigned to escort me."

Her escort leaned its entire body forward. The waves rippled slightly as if in a minimal acknowledgment.

"May I ask, Your Majesties, if you are aware of each creature – or at least, any unfamiliar creature – that enters your waters, or flies above them, or walks along your shores?"

The crests of the waves bent lower and straightened up again.

"I seek a fae who has embraced wanderlust, my lords. It hails from the ice realm where I last saw you." Adira paused to fight back the waves of grief and fear that accompanied that memory. "It was in my thoughts that this fae might wish to visit a different sort of watery realm, and to assume a form very different from that which, if I understand its customs, it would have inhabited for all its life previously. If you are willing to tell me, have you noticed any new arrival that might have been this traveler?"

One wave remained in place, but the other rolled toward the shore, not crashing but gently depositing on the sand what appeared to be a manta ray. The wave still standing tall spoke in the roaring, rumbling voice she had almost forgotten. "A being with this appearance slid into our waters from another realm, diving and dancing and playing with abandon, and then began to move more slowly and vanished. It may be the fae you seek."

Adira found herself trembling. She fought to steady her voice as she asked, "How long ago, Your Majesty, did the being leave your waters?"

The manta ray melted into an onrushing wave and grew back to its towering stature. "We do not measure time as you do, I believe. But our days and nights pass not unlike yours, and this happened today."

Not until she received this report, for which she had hardly dared to hope, had Adira realized how little it would help her to learn as much. Only brilliant guessing greatly assisted by luck would bring her to the right place at the right time. But she bowed again and said, "It is gracious of you to share this information, Your Majesties. Before I go, may I ask if you will try to tell me, somehow, if the visitor returns again?"

The queenly form of Amphitrite suddenly stood on the shore. "If it returns, we will visit the ice realm and see if you are present. If not, we will inform the rulers." It paused for a moment in which the sound of the waves soothed Adira's overstrained nerves, and then said, "When we next see your father, we will tell him of your visit here."

"My father! Have you spoken to him since . . . since he had to leave me? Has my mother joined him? Are they well?"

The queen regarded Adira with an almost human compassion. "You ask me more than I know."

The moment of hope, immediately withdrawn, made it hard for Adira to keep her composure. She fought for it while considering where to search next. Desert, ocean . . . .

What about the realm of the feasts? Would the youngster be ready for the company of its own kind – if it saw all fae as its kind – and in quantity? But in such a crowd, how would she identify it?

Some realm with fae, then, but not so many of them.

Perhaps the fae, used to being one of the youngest, would appreciate the chance to be one of the oldest instead. Adira dimly recalled hearing of a realm where young fae from many lands came to study the many Fair Folk realms, sometimes by mingling with their inhabitants. She bowed one more time to the ocean rulers and said to her escort, "Please take me to the School Realm."

CHAPTER 6

A S ABE lay in bed watching daylight outline the slats of his window shades, an idea came to him that jolted him fully awake. Clara would be home in a few days, and once she arrived, they would look through all their collected folk tales. But in the meantime, what about his and Adira's case files? A loophole found and defeated, a precaution written into a contract, might trigger some insight and provide an approach he'd failed to consider.

It wasn't even as strong as a hope. If he had ever encountered anything close to the rule that had ambushed them, yoking the fate of attorney and client, he would surely have found it disturbing enough to remember it. But looking through his files would give him something to do.

He sat up, groaned, waited for his head to stop pounding, and got up to rinse away the sour residue of the night before.

Most of the Fair Folk with whom Abe dealt had some degree of distaste for computer printouts, preferring either his reasonably legible handwriting or their own calligraphic productions. This gave him an excuse to hang onto physical file cabinets full of folders, rather than relying utterly on hard drives and remote backups. Only in the last year or so had his back begun to complain when he spent too long leafing through file drawers.

He could start with the Fair Folk who were least accepting of strangers. There was the realm where the fae lived in something like burrows, socializing through underground tunnels and venturing to the surface only when essential. How long ago had it been? He called over his shoulder, "Adira, when did we – " and stopped, mouth hanging open before he shut it, stumbled out of the file room, and slumped down in the nearest chair.

The disorienting, gutted feeling reminded him of how he used to get almost to the phone to call his mother before he remembered she was dead. Gone. Dead and gone.

And then he recoiled from the thought, because Adira was gone, but not dead. She couldn't be. Someone would have told him. Would it be the viscount, solemn for once, or smirking to the last? Or one of the ice fae, telling him their debt was discharged, or demanding he return in her place?

He made a fist and slammed it into his other hand. He had to learn not to think of such things.

But that left simply missing her. Missing the tromp of her feet pacing back and forth, or the perking of coffee he hadn't started to brew, or her whistling a tune he'd never heard except for her whistling it.

Her face, as she looked into his office, not quite standing in his doorway, and asked some question about a case, or about their baked goods supply.

Her mischievous pleasure when she'd talked him into going to some new lunch spot and watched his double-take at the taste or texture of whatever he'd ordered.

The pride that filled him when she found some new angle in a case that had stymied them both.

He needed Adira to tell him the best way to get Adira back. Which was impossible, and the paradox suddenly infuriated him. He jumped to his feet and looked around for something to throw, or to smash. He picked up a paperweight, a squat abstract thing made of pewter, heavy enough to put a hole in his office wall.

What would Adira say, if she saw the hole? Would she drag him outside and make him take one deep breath after another, or would she sit him back down and rub his shoulders, prying into his knotted muscles with her long strong fingers?

Abe gripped the paperweight until his fingers ached, threw it down on his desk instead, and went to finish looking through his files.

Leafing through his archives reminded him of his duty to his present clients. Two cups of coffee, the real thing, got Abe to the point where he could reread Adira's notes about Enola Aline, the woman who wanted to go through a faerie circle until her husband came out of prison. The first sight of Adira's handwriting in the file brought him close to breaking down, but he bit his lip until it bled, letting the sting of it distract him, and he made it through.

Under current circumstances, the idea of a human, and especially a woman, willingly putting herself in the Fair Folk's power revolted him to the point of nausea – though that might have been the coffee, or the remains of his hangover. Should he call Ms. Aline and urge her to think again? He could think of no arguments likely to dissuade her unless he told her what had happened to Adira. And that would be a breach of attorney-client confidentiality as to Tom, as well as almost inevitably sending the story into the stream of public discourse, with results ranging from professionally damaging to more profoundly disastrous.

At least, at very least, he would narrow the list of realms to which he would make his inquiries. And if the list ended up so short he found no takers for the bargain . . . well, he'd worry about that if and when he had to.

Abe's attempt to find a faerie circle for Ms. Aline ran up against a limiting factor: access. He could not bring himself to contact the viscount, even if such contact were likely to be fruitful. Ms. Aline's musical abilities would have made the Faire and Festival Realm a promising destination: she would have been able to provide value by teaching the fae musicians new songs, and possibly entertaining visitors as well. But his prior dealings with that realm had left no loose ends that would let him reach it by portal, though he made the attempt.

Thus thwarted, Abe turned to the Farm Realm, whose memory Adira had cherished. It was known for its easy hospitality, and one of the dairy farmers had found Adira endearing enough to suggest a return visit at their convenience. The invitation had, he thought, included him, though he would have to find some truthful yet untroubling excuse for Adira's absence. The familiarity and bucolic peace of the place would make for an easy transition for his client, if nothing else. And if it soothed his own spirit, so much the better, for Ms. Aline as well as himself.

He had no particular reason to think that realm required singers, but he bulled ahead, reciting her musical gifts with as much confidence and enthusiasm as he could muster. To his relief, the shepherds of the realm turned out to have a tradition of singing to the sheep, and were intrigued by the idea of expanding their repertoire.

The ruler, styled the mayor, required that he produce his client for inspection. Abe had prepared Ms. Aline for this likelihood, preparation that included agreeing on a suitable alias for her to provide to the Fair Folk, and was able to meet with her in less than an hour. He led his client in practice at responding to her new name and then took her to her interview.

She made an obvious effort to overcome her low spirits and sang quite well enough to please the mayor, who invited her to make herself at home while the final negotiations took place. As she sat in a wicker chair on the mayor's front porch, Abe bargained for all the requirements he and Adira had worked out together, and finally wrote the deal down with a goose-feather quill pen.

As a final step, the mayor provided him with the location of a faerie circle he could reach by portal, and which the mayor guaranteed would convey Ms. Aline back to the realm with minimal delay. With the courteous farewell that of necessity replaced thanks, Abe retrieved his client from the front porch, where she sat softly singing the lilting melody of a centuries-old tune, and led her through his portal.

Back at the office, he served her the spread of delicacies he had prepared: red and green grapes, triangles of good bread and spreadable cheeses, delicately decorated chocolate truffles. She would soon be bidding such satisfactions farewell, but she could enjoy them one more time before beginning that fast.

Ms. Aline, subdued in mood, had little to say, but she appeared to appreciate both the food and the gesture. That left Abe to endure, and conceal, his piercing wish that he could share such a repast with his daughter. Had her captors even given her the same dreary relief from hunger Abe had won for his client? He could only hope so, and hope was hard to muster.

When Ms. Aline had eaten as much as she cared to, Abe offered her what remained. She started to decline, then paused. "I'll be visiting my husband one more time, before I . . . before I go. I want to say goodbye –" She visibly pushed back a sob, and gave Abe a small unsteady smile. "And to tell him what a gentle refuge you've found for me. Maybe the guard will be kind, this time, and let me give him something too small to hide a weapon in. A truffle, or a berry."

Abe doubted any guard would be so lacking in suspicion. His client might be contemplating a bribe, in which case he hoped she was cautious and skillful at it. "Good luck, Ms. Aline. I'll see you back here tomorrow, and we'll go to the circle together."

Morning came, a gray and rainy morning that might make his client welcome the thought of sunlit green hills and sheep with sun-warmed wool. She looked underslept when she appeared, carrying a suitcase just large enough for a few changes of clothes and other essentials, and declined coffee, though she took one of the muffins Abe had baked the night before. He hadn't baked much without Adira to devour the results, and he found it both gratifying and disorienting to watch someone else consuming baked goods in the office.

When she had finished the muffin down to the crumbs, he gestured toward the back door and asked gently, "Shall we?"

She gulped, picked up her suitcase, and followed him to the back yard and the portal hanging and glinting there. She took a deep sniff when they stepped out into a field of fragrant flowers, with a circle of taller flowers surrounding a small clear space. Abe led her into it, and they appeared in the lush grass of a meadow, surrounded by mildly inquisitive cows. Abe patted her hand and said, "Keep an eye out for cow pats, though whether they appear has more to do with the whim of the farmer than with the cattle themselves."

Eyes wide, Ms. Aline murmured, "I'll do my best to keep the farmer happy with me. Maybe it has a favorite song I can sing, to it or its cattle."

The mayor strode toward them, with a confident stride suggesting the farmer would make sure no cow pats sullied the mayoral path. "Welcome, Ms. Asher! I've arranged a pleasant cottage for you, just over the hill. Once you've settled in, I'll introduce you to the shepherds and the sheep."

Abe watched them ascend the hill before turning back to the portal. When he first met his client, he would never have expected to envy her. Now he thought with longing of her certainty that her wait would come to an end.

A few days later

The phone call jerked Abe from an unscheduled nap. Just as well, since he'd need to leave for the airport to pick up Clara in a couple of hours. He answered, and at first could make no sense of the slurred voice on the other end. Then he recognized it, but still couldn't understand the mumbling. He asked, "I'm sorry, but would you please repeat that?"

The father of the stolen baby made a choking noise, probably a sob, and said, "Come get thi' thing! My wife, she says she'll find a way to kill it otherwise, and then the faeries will probably kill her and me and maybe our own baby too – get it out of here! Now, tonight!"

That was all Abe needed. But he was at least as well aware of how badly things could go as this drunk, distraught father. "I'll be there in a few minutes. Go tell your wife, and stay with her until I arrive." But – he could hardly leave the fae child alone at his house or office, nor take it to the airport . . . . "If I got your wife out of the house for a while, could you manage with the changeling until I got back?"

The woman awaiting him could have been plucked from a 19th century madhouse. The remains of some sort of complex hairdo only made the wisps and hanks of hair that had escaped it look more chaotic. Her reddened eyes, wide and staring, stood out beside the stark pallor of her face. Her husband stood beside her, holding her hand gingerly, as if it might suddenly scratch or strike.

Ms. Dellor had looked distraught in their first call, and shocked, and angry, but her deterioration since then left Abe speechless and, for a moment, paralyzed. Other images tried to crowd into his mind – Clara, months from now, if they hadn't been able to bring Adira home, and Adira, after whatever the ice fae might do to her . . . . His convulsive rejection of those visions gave him an energy he converted into motion, approaching the woman and holding out his hand. When she didn't move, her husband took her arm and moved it toward Abe. That seemed to wake her up, and her hand darted forward to grab Abe's and pull him toward her. She stared at him for a moment and then hissed, "Are you here to take it away?"

Abe gulped. "Almost. I need a couple of hours or so to get ready, but until then, I'd like to take *you* away, for a, a respite. Then I'll bring you back and take the changeling away at the same time. Would that be all right with you?"

She turned her unnerving glare on her husband, who looked at his feet and shuffled them, and then jerked her eyes back to Abe. "I don't want to see that thing when I come back. And I want the bedding in the crib – burned. And anything it touched scrubbed clean."

Abe would have liked to see the fae infant, to offer it some friendly gesture amidst this implacable hostility. After all, it hadn't chosen – had it? – to take the place of this woman's child. He put the feeling aside and said, in as reassuring a tone as he could muster, "You can make sure of all that later. Shall we go?"

Back at his house, he steered Ms. Dellor to an armchair and thought wistfully of coffee. If he made some for himself, his guest might demand her own, and the stimulant might make her harder to handle. Though his other idea, a stiff drink, might be worse, and if it put her to sleep, he would have to rouse her all too soon. He had no interest in decaf, nor the energy to prepare both that and the more potent brew. Coffee it would be, then. He made it, appreciating the gradually intensifying odor even more than usual, and poured mugs for both of them before returning to the living room and hovering near her. "Coffee?"

She turned her head slowly, looked at both Abe and the coffee as if she had never before seen either, and slowly lifted her hand toward the second mug.

Abe's coffee gave him a moment's escape from the tangle of fears and troubles his life had become. Ms. Dellor's may not have accomplished as much, but it did seem to bring her partway back from whatever haunted dimension she had been inhabiting. She drank steadily, drained the last drop, and started to get up before Abe sprang to attention and took the mug from her. She even made a faint attempt at a smile and said, "That was good. Thank you."

By the time Abe took the mugs to the kitchen, rinsed them, and came back, she had fallen asleep in the chair. He would have to wake her after all, but at least he could change into fresh clothes to meet Clara at the airport.

"It just felt so, so alien." Ms. Dellor had still been taciturn, or dazed, when he woke her up and steered her to the car, but now that they were underway she was talking nonstop, staring out the window at the headlights going the other way and muttering so he had to strain to hear. "I'd carried my own baby in me and that felt so natural, so right. And now, in my boy's place, was this *thing*, and even though I hadn't carried it, I felt somehow as if I had, as if I'd had this alien creature inside me, like something out of a horror movie. I wanted to scream whenever I saw it or heard it."

She had said the same thing twice already. He answered more or less the way he had before. "That must have been awful. As soon as we pick up my wife at the airport, we'll go to your house and I'll take the changeling. You and your husband will be free of it."

"That's good. That's very good. Thank you so much." A brief pause, and then, once more, "It's not as bad for him. Maybe because he didn't carry our baby like I did. Sometimes he's even curious about it. He'd better not try to stop you taking it!"

"It'll be all right. He's the one who called me to come get it."

Ms. Dellor fell silent for maybe a mile. Then she took a deep breath as if prepared to launch back into her refrain. But she bit her lip, turned to look at him, and said, "Then what? What'll you do with it? What can you do with it?"

Abe suppressed a sigh. "I'll see if the fae who have your baby will take the changeling back, along with the child you're already . . . offering to them. A free bonus, as it were." And if they weren't interested, or were actively opposed to the idea, he'd try to find someone else. Some other Fair Folk, or even a fellow mortal without the same antipathy. Perhaps a childless couple, a couple who'd given up on having their own baby and hadn't been able to adopt – though depending on the reason for that inability, they might not offer the best haven for the faerie child.

Echoing his thoughts, the woman said, very low and quiet, "I don't . . . I don't want it hurt." She added, her voice a little louder, "I don't want it going to someone who'll just, just exploit it, to a freak show or something."

Abe freed a hand from the steering wheel just long enough to pat her hand. "No, I wouldn't do that." Even if he could countenance such a thing, he strongly suspected that the same Fair Folk who might disdain the idea of welcoming the child would take serious exception to a scheme that would treat any fae with less than the respect they viewed as their due.

* * * * *

The flight attendant approached Clara's row with her cumbersome cart and asked, "Would you like a beverage?"

Clara had brought her own bottle of water on board. She could order something alcoholic, but the occasion was all wrong. She had sometimes shared a bottle of wine with Abe, or more recently Adira, to celebrate an achievement or to toast the beginning of a new adventure. Both ideas were grotesquely unlike what now faced her. And while she would, on rare occasions, take a small glass of sherry to quiet her mind at night, it would take far too much alcohol to slow a mind racing in circles.

The flight attendant's smile had become a trifle fixed. Clara shook her head and, after a pause for any more explicit refusal, the cart rumbled away.

Clara reclined her seat as much as she could without inconveniencing the passenger behind her and looked out the window. They were a little ways above a layer of cumulus clouds. The sight brought to mind the idea of liminal spaces, transitions from one place to another, belonging to neither. It was a familiar concept, with so many tales of Faerie taking place in liminal spaces – on riverbanks or shorelines, or in mists. And here she was, suspended between the solid Earth and the darkness of space.

Then there were liminal times, like midnight, the cusp between one day and another. The Celtic tradition of handfasting required a year and a day before it became binding, with that extra day a sort of day outside the normal flow and tally of time. At this moment, one time zone lay behind and another ahead, and yet the former claimed to be ahead of the latter. Here, poised between, no time had hold of her, and no task. She had left her work miles and hours in her wake; and she could do nothing fruitful at this moment about the overwhelming problem of rescuing Adira from where her work and her father had taken her.

A throb of anger threatened the peace that had begun to fill her. She pushed it aside, watched the sky and the clouds pass, and relaxed.

The smooth voice from the loudspeaker roused her, warning, "We will be descending momentarily . . . ." As if on cue, pressure built in her ears. As she reached for her water bottle, she saw the clouds beneath the plane approach, and in moments, they were passing through fog.

From liminal space to the everyday. And yet, she was descending from the ideal of Faery to where she would have to face, and combat, its fearsome reality.

* * * * *

As he made the turn for the airport, Abe hoped Clara's flight would be on time – and only then realized that he had almost forgotten Adira's plight, and Clara's likely distress at it, for several hours. To realize this respite was to feel it end. His stomach churned, and he swallowed the sour bile that surged up into his throat.

Traversing the lobby, Abe noticed the array of fast food options and detoured toward one that sold milkshakes. The thick creamy cold of a milkshake would soothe his throat, if not his stomach, and there were no lines this late in the evening. He asked Ms. Dellor quietly, "Would you like something?"

She looked at him as if she had forgotten whatever language he was speaking. Slowly, tears welled up in her eyes and trickled down her face. He suppressed a sigh and steered her to a vacant table. "Will you sit here for just a minute?" He put a hand on her shoulder and pressed down lightly. She followed his suggestion, the verbal or the nonverbal, and he hustled back to the counter, looking over his shoulder every few seconds to make sure she hadn't run off. His hand shook as he pulled out a bill, waved away the change, grabbed his milkshakes, and almost-ran to the table, setting the milkshakes down and looking around for the nearest of the stores that sold drugs and souvenirs and snacks.

He had just time to identify, snatch up, and buy headache and reflux pills, fidgeting from foot to foot while he waited to pay. He opened the water bottle he'd bought along with them just as the speakers announced Clara's flight arriving. He gulped down the pills and ran back to where he'd left his client, who sat dozing in front of the barely touched milkshake he'd bought her. He tapped her shoulder, as gently as his nerves would allow, and helped her up. "I'd like to wait over there, off to the side where the passengers come through."

Clara was one of the first to appear, practically shoving her way through her fellow passengers. Her eyes passed over him at first, presumably due to the woman standing next to him, and then snapped back to meet his. She was vibrating with some combination of tension and jet lag and spared only one more glance for his companion, grabbing him and hugging him so hard he might end up with bruises.

She pulled back, studied his face, and said in a tight voice, "No news, then." At his confirming silence, she turned toward Ms. Dellor and forced a small smile. "I'm Clara, Abe's wife and a folklorist. Are you in some way involved in our . . . situation?"

Ms. Dellor looked back and forth between Abe and Clara, obviously trying to comprehend. Abe hurriedly filled Clara in on events, Clara's face showing sympathy, then a painful empathy, and finally, the beginnings of fascination. Ms. Dellor, watching this muttered monologue and Clara's reactions, waited until Abe had finished and asked, dully but with a faint trace of reviving energy, "What news? What situation?"

Clara reached out and took her hand. "You and I have something in common. We are both mothers who have, for the time being, lost children to the fae. Our daughter is a prisoner of the ice fae, while your son is in the Autumn Court."

Ms. Dellor looked first appalled and then ashamed, as if she had no right to let her grief overwhelm her when Clara was relatively composed. Abe, not clear of his own motives, added, "But our daughter is an adult, my partner in our practice." Clara stiffened, and Abe quit while he was behind.

Clara rode in the back seat with Ms. Dellor on the way back to her house. They spoke quietly, but from what Abe could hear, Ms. Dellor wanted to know more about Adira. Perhaps it made her feel somehow closer to her own lost babe to hear about another woman's child, as long as that other woman was similarly deprived.

Ms. Dellor grew more agitated as they got closer, and Abe was about to attempt some reassurance when Clara preempted him. "We'll take the changeling with us right away. You don't even have to look at it, if you don't want to. Is there a back door to the house?"

They arranged the logistics of the exchange, finishing just as Abe pulled into the driveway. The front door opened to show Mr. Dellor standing there looking lost, the more so as Ms. Dellor ran around behind the house, fumbling in her purse for her keys. Clara walked straight up to him and said, "Thank you so much for making things easier on your wife. I'm looking forward to getting to know your little guest. I've been studying stories of the Fair Folk for years, but since I'm not part of Abe's firm, I almost never meet any."

The man rocked back a little on his heels. "You . . . want th' faerie?"

Clara smiled and put a gentle hand on his arm. "Just for now, until we find the right home for it. But I'm glad for the chance to take care of it and learn about it for a little while. Why don't you take me to it?"

Abe followed Clara and Mr. Dellor into the nursery. The changeling was standing up in its crib, its black eyes searching the room. When it saw Clara it pointed at her and smiled, its teeth gleaming. Then it pivoted to face the night light, or something in its vicinity, pointed at that, and laughed its lilting laugh.

Clara pointed at the light as well and said, "Hello, little one! Do you think the light is pretty?" The changeling turned back to her, its eyes wide. Could it somehow understand her?

Clara held out her hands. "May I pick you up? We'd like to bring you to our home for a visit. Would you like that?"

The changeling looked around the room again. Clara said gently, "If you're seeking the couple who've been looking after you, I'm afraid the woman isn't feeling well, but you could say goodbye to the man."

As if on cue, Mr. Dellor cleared his throat from the doorway. Clara beckoned to him, and he slowly approached the crib. The man drew a deep, shaky breath and mumbled, "I'm sorry. Should've been more . . . hosp'bi-ble. Hos-pit-ble. Not your fault, is't?"

The infant reached out its hands toward the man. He looked around, eyes wide, jaw dropping, before taking the little hands and giving them a squeeze. Then he fled out of the room, and Abe could hear sobs as the footsteps died away.

It was Clara who remembered the need for a car seat, and Abe who went looking for one. In the end, he had Clara take the changeling outside before he tracked down the mother. It didn't surprise him that the mention of the car seat reduced her to floods of tears and some barely comprehensible reminiscences. "We brought him home . . . he was tiny, we had to readjust . . . I tucked him . . . sky-blue blanket . . . oh, my *baby*!"

When Abe wearily emerged with the car seat, Clara was holding the changeling as it pointed at one star after another, babbling in its clear chime of a voice and sweeping its hand across the sky as if it could see falling stars invisible to mortals. Its toothy smile disappeared as Abe approached, opened the back door, and struggled to find the right straps and positioning to install the seat. As he made his third attempt, the changeling started to laugh again. It kept laughing as Clara gently strapped it in, and all the way home.

CHAPTER 7

MOST of the time, Clara was able to resist the urge to feel ashamed. She had been given a unique opportunity to study a changeling, a fae infant (or so it appeared), at close quarters – and yes, it had happened only because she had come home early, and *that* had happened because her daughter was in danger, but she had not created that danger. Adira would be no better off if Clara ignored the changeling or held it at a distance. Adira, with her keen, rational mind and energetic curiosity, would understand.

And what a fascinating study it was!

The many legends she had read and heard concerned identifying a changeling and getting rid of one. It had hurt her heart to imagine just how often the identification was nonsense, and the prescribed remedies – beating with birch rods seemed to be the most common, though a gruesome minority involved hot ovens – were inflicted on innocent and helpless mortal babies. Probably, the rise of rational scholarship had coincided with the fae's gradual loss of interest in swapping one of their own for a human. At any rate, there were fewer accounts that followed a changeling over time, and among those few, the ones that showed the changeling mimicking a human growth pattern could easily be a matter of false labeling.

They had no way to know how old the changeling had been when it first appeared, or even whether it had been an infant at all. It was, however, clear that it grew faster than a human infant would. And its eye color kept changing, though the changes hadn't yet persisted for more than a second and were usually swifter, a flickering back and forth between black and blue and silver and a sunny yellow. Was that the beginning of glamour ability, or something else? If glamour, it suggested that at least some glamour was innate, rather than learned behavior – unless the changeling was actually old enough to have learned it before arriving.

The changeling seemed to find Abe amusing, or at least liked to give that impression. It would point and laugh when he came into the spare bedroom for which they had hastily rented a crib. Abe had told her about its singing, but it never sang for, or to, him. It saved that display – that communication? – for Clara. Sometimes, she attempted to sing along with it, as Abe said the missing baby's father had done. It would spend up to five minutes or so on such duets before it returned to its usual preoccupation of watching the light and shadows on the wall.

Nothing she observed had any direct application to Adira's plight. But when it came to research, she had long since learned that connections could reveal themselves over time. And in the meantime, it was the most potent distraction she could imagine. There were times when she even relaxed enough to nap.

She was, of course, more often miserable, in any of several flavors of misery. But that, at least, she shared with Abe.

* * * * *

Clara sat at her computer in the home office she and Abe sometimes shared, but when Abe glanced over at her, the screen showed the same page on the same site he had seen when he walked into the room ten minutes before.

Abe left the room quietly, made some of Clara's favorite orange and cranberry tea, and brought it in, to find that Clara had emerged from her trance and was scrolling through a new page. He tapped her on the shoulder and set the tea on the desk, asking, "Did you find something new?"

"I wouldn't say *found* something. I'm checking my memory on something. I was musing about why changelings turn up. The most common traditional explanation is that they, or the fae who send them, crave human milk – though I don't see how the fae back in Fair Folk territory would get hold of it, after the human infant digests whatever's in its stomach. Anyway, do you happen to know whether Ms. Dellor was nursing her baby or using formula?"

"Hmmm. She didn't mention either. But she, ah, strikes me as someone who airs any complaint, and she didn't mention any of the effects of suddenly ceasing to nurse an infant."

Clara nodded. "At any rate, our guest hasn't acted as if it was being deprived, or wanted anything in particular. So what else could induce the fae to make the exchange, beyond pure mischief? What does a human baby have to offer them?"

Her familiar earnest curiosity brought a smile from wherever smiles had been hiding. He gazed at her, drinking in her presence, and said, "My love, maybe some fae are more like you than we suppose, and love to learn and study. We study them – why shouldn't they study us? Possibly some of what seems everyday and insignificant to us is more intriguing to them. Or we may have undiscovered depths, which they seek to plumb."

Clara cocked her head, considering the notion. After a few moments, however, her interest seemed to fade, and the tension to reappear in her face. Hoping to hold it off, Abe asked, "Speaking of studying the unfamiliar, how is the changeling doing, from what you can tell?"

She accepted the change of subject readily enough, replying, "It seems contented, though I don't know whether I could tell if it was bored. It likes to watch the shadows on the wall, which I suppose could mean it's desperate for something to do. Oh, and its eyes keep changing color, just for a second or less. I hope that doesn't mean some sort of health problem. I've wondered if it's an early stage of manipulating glamour." She pursed her lips. "If it's learning how to do that, it could get harder to keep it secret, especially if it keeps growing so fast. It won't be long before it could hop out of the room and assume some other form to go for a walk – or even put on wings and fly out the window, if I ever open it."

"I guess we should keep the window closed." Abe did a double-take. "Wait a minute. Did you say the changeling likes to watch changing shadows? And that it makes its eyes flicker? How often have you seen this?"

"The eye color change, maybe three times a day. Watching shadows, almost every time I'm in there."

"Let's go look."

The changeling was standing in the crib and looking at the wall when they walked in. As usual, it pointed at Abe and let out its ringing chime of a laugh. Then it looked back at the wall, where the shadows of the tree outside were shifting about as a breeze blew. Abe studied its face. He could be imagining things, but the fae's expression struck him as wistful.

Abe stood next to the crib and faced the same direction as the changeling. As he had surmised, the shifting shadows reminded him of the language he had learned in the forest realm, and which had not yet been taken from him. He couldn't read any actual meaning in them – but then, even if the tree outside his house somehow possessed the power of language, it was unlikely to be the same language.

The changeling laughed again, but this time, it pointed not at Abe but at the shadows on the wall.

Abe turned toward the child just in time to see its eyes flicker from black to silver to black again, and then to a deep green, and then to a subdued shade of violet. Abe stared, and the fae stared back for a long moment before it laughed again and shut its eyes.

It could easily be a coincidence. It probably was. But what if it wasn't?

Abe walked slowly back to where Clara was working and asked, "Want to hear a wild idea?"

Clara listened, first puzzled and then intrigued, to his tale of the forest realm and its language of shifting shadows, and his gut feeling that the changeling had some connection to it. When he was done, she wrinkled her forehead and said, "But the fae there are just like trees, aren't they? They don't look human, or move around, or – do they even have eyes?"

"Not that I could see. It's not that they do what the changeling is doing. I just – I feel as if it's trying to tell me something, or that it's homesick, or both. Just in case it does somehow come from that realm, it's worth a try at getting it home. If that's where it comes from, its own people didn't give it up – some member of the Autumn Court must have lured or stolen it away. I can keep negotiating with that Court about getting the human baby back, and do a favor for the forest realm at the same time."

It might not fall within any current contract, but it could certainly count as casting bread upon the waters. It might somehow, someday, redound to his benefit. Or it might not – but reuniting a child with those who cared about it would at least bring a brief balm to his own soul.

He had not yet finished filling the forest floor with bluebells. He hoped his portal would take him there until the forest rulers considered the job completed.

On the short walk to the office and the portal behind it, he still had enough time to realize just how tricky this inquiry was going to be. He would be appearing for a different reason than authorized, in order to ask whether the forest fae had been unable to keep, or perhaps to keep track of, one of their offspring, and whether their offspring started out as mobile humanoids, and, if the changeling did indeed come from their realm, whether they had realized they had a grave grievance against their brethren in the Autumn Court . . . . By the time he crossed the portal, he was sweating more than the soft and temperate climate of the realm could justify.

Rather than seek out the tree with whom he usually dealt, he approached the largest tree he could find nearby, standing in a spot with more fallen leaves and exposed earth than grass. He bowed low before it, and quickly straightened up so he could see the light-and-shadow patterns that were its speech. He introduced himself, summarized his previous dealings with the Fair Folk here, and said diffidently, "Today, however, I come on a different errand, and hope you will deem my appearance justified. If I have overstepped, I beg your forgiveness and pardon."

The tree's branches swayed slowly, the leaves' movement similarly deliberate and giving Abe the impression of a sonorous voice. "The unexpected may be intriguing or vexing, depending on the details. Please continue."

Heartened by the *please*, Abe went on. "In connection with an unrelated matter, I became acquainted with a changeling that had been exchanged with a mortal baby. Due to the privilege already granted me of understanding your language, I gave more attention than I otherwise would to certain habits of this changeling, namely its intense interest in the shadows of leaves on walls, and its occasional tendency to change its eye color in a quick sequence that reminded me of the flickering of such shadows. I could not actually read meaning into either habit, and furthermore, I have been informed, and have some corroborating evidence, that the Fair Folk who made this substitution hail from . . . another realm. Nor can I understand how any fae coming from your realm could be made to resemble, to even a limited extent, a mortal infant – but I am aware of how little I know about the operations of glamour and the history of your own realm. I came seeking enlightenment, and, conceivably, to be of some service."

A wind blew over him, and the sudden rustle of leaves and the creaking of branches made him realize he had been addressing a larger audience. Looking around, he could catch fragments of their conversation, though not enough to piece together into meaning. Then the solemn speech of the large tree claimed his attention. "You did right to come to us in spite of your uncertainty. In return, I will explain that not all the Fair Folk in this realm share this form. There are others who also make up part of our community. Their young take another customary form, and they use glamour in ways we do not. We speak with them freely. It is possible that this changeling might be one of these, though we doubt it consented to such a role." Abe might have imagined hearing the faint rumble of thunder behind the words.

"We cannot know," the tree went on, "whether this changeling belongs here unless we see it. Will you bring it here?"

"Of course," Abe said, bowing again. Then, imagining the changeling's possible reaction to Abe attempting to pick it up and carry it, he added, "Things may go more easily if I may bring my wife Clara as well. The changeling has established a certain rapport with her."

The great tree's leaves rustled softly as if the tree were muttering to itself. Finally it said, "We are not presently inclined to extend the language ability we have loaned to you. But she may come."

It would be no use arguing. Abe could only hope Clara wouldn't feel too deprived, telling himself that the need for her to keep an eye on the changeling would have made it hard for her to follow the shifting shadows in any event.

Abe returned home to find Clara playing a game of patty-cake with the changeling. She glanced at him, brought the game to a conclusion, stroked the changeling's silver hair, and got up to give Abe a welcoming kiss. The changeling, meanwhile, returned to studying the shadows on the wall. Abe led Clara out of the room and gave her a short account of what had happened and what would happen next.

Clara took a deep breath and said, with a sort of nervous excitement, "Well, I always wondered when I'd end up seeing one of the faerie realms, and I guess the time has come! But – I won't understand what these, these trees are saying. Will I understand what you're saying to them?"

"Yes, love. I'll be speaking plain old everyday English." He paused. "I don't know how it works, how they can understand me. For all I know, I'm *not* really speaking English, and I just can't tell that their magic has changed how I speak. Huh." He shrugged off the intriguing yet unsettling idea. "Are you ready to do this?"

Clara stood up and said, "I'll go get our guest."

It seemed prudent to drive back to the office rather than walk. Clara carried the changeling, singing in an animated babble, to the car, holding it with a tenderness Abe found both endearing and disturbing, and once again buckled it into the car seat. In almost no time, they were out of the car again and heading around behind the building.

They reached the portal, and Clara's breathing grew rapid and shallow. She'd seen it before, but she'd never stepped through it. The changeling suddenly shrieked, reaching out toward the shimmering shape and bouncing in Clara's arms. Abe gulped, put an arm around Clara, and took them through.

The changeling's noise stopped as suddenly as if the infant had vanished. Abe swiveled to look and saw that it was looking at the treetops, leaning its head so far back that Clara had to adjust her hold, its eyes wide and changing colors every fraction of a second. A murmur from the trees swelled to an indecipherable visual clamoring, moving like ripples in a pond to include more and more of the trees, their green branches waving as if in an impossible confluence of winds.

One voice, if Abe could call it such, commanded the others to subside and then spoke directly to him. "Please ask your wife to set the child on its feet."

Abe cleared his throat to draw Clara's attention and said softly, "They want you to put the changeling down, on its feet."

Clara looked around warily at the trees, still waving their branches though not as wildly. Abe stroked the arm encircling the child. "I don't know exactly what they have in mind, but they won't hurt it." He was almost certain . . . .

Clara set the changeling gently down on the soft decayed leaves of the forest floor. It bent down and picked up a handful of the crumbly brown stuff, tossed it in the air, and laughed as the particles floated back down.

"Take the child by the hand," the tree instructed Abe, "and lead it to the sapling you see about ten of your strides in front of you." Abe bent low enough to grasp the changeling's hand. He had not, he realized suddenly, touched it before. He expected it to be cold to the touch, but its hand was warmer than his own. The changeling laughed again, but did nothing to resist. The rustling of leaves fell away entirely, as if the entire forest were holding its breath.

Abe moved them toward the sapling, which stood among a cluster of much larger trees, and saw on its lowest branch a large red squirrel. The squirrel started chattering, in a notably musical way, as they approached. Distracted by this first sign of animal life, it took Abe several seconds to realize that the squirrel was speaking – that he could understand it. No, not speaking but singing, a song of welcome.

And the changeling answered, its habitual song taking on the rhythm of the squirrel's.

The squirrel suddenly transformed into a squirrel-sized copy of the changeling, gave itself silvery translucent wings, and made them disappear again before resuming squirrel form. From above, the rustling resumed and grew ever louder. Abe looked up to see the immense trees saying in unison, "You were right. The changeling belongs here. How it was taken and sent into your world is a question for another day, and need not concern you."

Abe retreated to where Clara had been standing silently, taking in as much of the scene as she could fathom. Now she murmured, "Is it staying here, then?" He nodded. She walked over to where the changeling and squirrel were continuing their animated musical conversation and knelt by the changeling's side, saying, "Goodbye, little one." Abe could hear the tears blurring her voice.

The changeling turned toward her, its song becoming a chant reminiscent of human language, and grabbed her hand, tugging her to her feet and then toward Abe. It shoved her hand toward Abe's, let go, and then started running in circles around them, drawing the circle smaller and smaller before stopping abruptly and looking into their faces. Finally, it stroked Clara's hand, came close, and stood on its toes to give the hand a quick kiss before running back to the sapling and the squirrel.

A gust of wind drew Abe's attention back to the giant trees. The one nearest him said, "You have done us good service today, and we will remember it. We will be glad to see you when you next return to your usual task. Your portal waits." Indeed, it stood ready, lined on this side with leaves that fluttered in an echo of the tree's words.

Abe heard a gasp from beside him. He turned to see Clara, wide-eyed with wonder, staring up into the branches overhead. He whispered, "Can you – did you understand?" She said nothing, but her enthralled gaze answered for her.

The trees had no more to say, it seemed. Clara appeared to come to the same conclusion, looking at him with a rueful expression that combined awe and wistfulness. She looked back at the canopy above them and said, "I will remember that moment all my life."

Abe softly kissed her cheek, bowed to the trees, and said, "You have been most gracious. Until I return with more flowers, I bid you farewell." He put his arm through Clara's, and they stepped through the portal.

Somehow, after this eventful day, it was barely evening, a subdued sunset fading into dusk. The portal faced the back entrance to the office, but they turned away without a word and walked home arm in arm, leaving the car where it stood. Birds twittered softly as they passed.

Abe unlocked the front door and positioned himself between Clara and the temporary nursery, once again a prosaic spare room with an unused crib. Perhaps he made too much of looking away from it, or what he did made no difference: Clara let go of him, walked into the room, and stood over the crib, holding the side and looking at the shadows on the wall. He joined her, staring at patterns with no meaning he could find. Clara leaned her head on his shoulder and said, "It's so empty."

He could think of no reply that would hold any comfort. They stood there until Clara patted his arm and left the room. Dully, Abe started taking the crib apart. He would take it back to the rental place tomorrow.

* * * * *

The house had had no child in it for years, but the few days in which the changeling had been present made it feel forlorn. And without the distraction of the fae child, they had only the one focus, the one project: trying to rescue their daughter from the kingdom of ice. Clara and Abe spent as much time as possible at the office, busying themselves with increasingly wide-ranging folklore research, though so far finding nothing that suggested any new course of action. All that focus on trying to help Adira – and yet, Clara realized, Abe had hardly mentioned her. Had he even said her name?

He would be defensive if she pointed out the fact. Or he might simply break down, which would be painful for both of them, as well as unproductive. She would start with a less direct approach.

She had to wait until they got home from the office late one night, both awkward with fatigue. It took Abe three tries to get the key in the lock and open the front door. Stumbling in, he looked toward the liquor cabinet in the living room and leaned forward as if pulled toward it before catching himself, glancing at Clara, and going to sit down in the nearest chair.

Neither of them needed to fix dinner – they had ordered in a pizza at the office, an hour past their usual dinnertime, and left the leftovers in the office fridge. Abe leaned his head back in his chair and closed his eyes. Without waiting to see what, if anything, he would do next, she walked swiftly and silently into their bedroom, opened their closet, and rummaged in the back of it until she found the photo albums. They made a heavy armful, but she straightened up and returned to the living room. Her more unwieldy footsteps drew his attention as she half sat, half fell into the armchair across from his and opened the album at the top of the stack. She heard his long, indrawn breath, but she did not look up, turning the pages slowly. A few pages in, she said softly, "I've always loved this photo especially. Do you remember my telling you about it, the first time Adira made it to the top of the more advanced rock wall?" She turned the album toward Abe, her finger on the photo, and finally looked up at him.

He was looking away, jaw clenched, hands gripping the arms of the chair, knuckles white.

Clara slid the pile of albums onto the floor, stepped over them, and crossed over to Abe, crouching by the side of his chair, laying a hand right next to his but not quite touching. He was still turned away, but she could see he was biting his lip. She got up and sat on the arm of the chair, near the back, and put her arm around his shoulders, kissing the top of his head. He slumped forward and broke into convulsive sobs.

She waited for the storm to pass and asked softly, "Do you feel better or worse?" He only shuddered and shook his head.

Clara went back to the stack of albums and picked up the one she had already opened, taking it back to Abe's chair. She perched on the arm of the chair again and, with some difficulty, opened the book and balanced it on her knee. "I'm going to keep looking at the photos. Whatever pictures have forced their way into your mind, I promise these will be kinder ones."

Without lifting his head, Abe muttered, "They won't drive away the others. The ones from my nightmares."

Clara turned a page. "The better pictures can dilute the impact of the others. And reinforcing the good memories may give you the strength you'll need."

Slowly, Abe lifted his head and turned to look at the album. Clara let him look his fill at the open pages and then turned to the next. This time, he put his hand on the pages to stop her, and then pointed to the picture filling the page on the right. "This one."

Clara stroked his hand and considered the photo. It showed Adira at about age eight at the top of a hiking trail somewhere in the Andes, long hair tangled and blowing in the wind, arms thrown back and chin high in a triumphant posture. Abe looked at the page with an intense, avid expression, as if longing to pull her forward in time. Finally he said, hushed, "She was so strong, even then."

"Yes, my love. I remember we only had to help her a little, on the steepest parts."

Tears filled Abe's eyes again as he said in a husky voice, "I'm afraid she'll need more help this time. More than we can give."

They didn't lie to each other, ever, but there was no need to confess how much she shared his fears. "Tomorrow we'll get back to work, so we'll be ready to help her when the moment comes. Will having a drink help you to sleep?"

Abe buried his face in her shoulder and said, muffled, "It might. Having you near will probably help more."

Clara stroked his hair and said, "I could actually use a drink myself. I'll get myself some sherry. Might you prefer hot milk?"

He actually chuckled. "If you'll add a little rum to it."

She kissed his cheek, lifted his head off her shoulder, and went to get the drinks.

* * * * *

Abe tried to help Clara search their archives and every other source she could find, without either of them knowing what exactly they were looking for, but his mind kept wandering – to his past mistakes, to his fury at the viscount, to Tom, to the unknown ordeals Adira might be enduring. Clara was gentle with him at first, asking his advice, ignoring the array of craft beers and hard liquor he brought home and the speed with which he drank his way through it. But finally, after a week of this, she suggested with thinly disguised impatience, "Might it do you good to give your law practice some attention? You might be able to focus on folklore better after a little time away from it."

The only case in which he had remained active was that of the Dellors' stolen child. The fae of the Autumn Court had offered few hints of why they had stolen a human baby in the first place. They would show interest in his offer of the foster child, and then ask for the third and fourth time just how old it was, as if the age were crucial – but implying one moment that they sought a younger baby, and the next an older toddler. Still, Abe's experience told him they would eventually settle on what he offered, which would fulfill his mission of getting the human infant back home. As for other work, he had failed to return two emails and one phone call from potential new clients. His heart failed him at the thought of trying to handle matters that could only have become more difficult in the interim, if helping those would-be clients remained possible at all.

But the morning after Clara's ultimatum, the doorbell somehow emitted a bugle call, and a glowing envelope appeared on the mat inside. The Feast Realm was expanding yet again, and wished a large shipment of various human dainties: honey, cream, fine white bread, candies, and large quantities of champagne.

Abe assembled the various delicacies, as well as hand-drawn carts in which to convey them in case the fae did not arrange for a less mundane method of transport. Sniffing the odors of fresh bread and chocolate, he asked himself whether a mortal could, though in a Fair Folk realm, safely eat mortal food. He would not advise any mortal to risk it.

He opened the portal at the appointed time, and endured with good humor the fae amusement at the hand carts. The food lifted off the carts and flew through the portal, followed by the fae. They beckoned to him when he would have remained behind. "Do come through, won't you? There will be music and singing, as well as the feast."

It should be safe to attend for a little while. Even if the feasting could only frustrate him, the merriment might cheer him.

The feast was held in a meadow stretching to the horizon. An array of tables filled the same vista, some ornately carved as if hauled out of a Baroque dining room while others could only be described as picnic tables, complete with red and white checked tablecloths. Not all the Fair Folk consumed meat, but some of the tables bore immense roasts, from slabs of beef to giant turkeys to what appeared to be swans posed as if preening.

The fae filed from one table to the next, or sat at tables or on the lush green grass, or stood with plates in their hands. A few were in human form and enormously fat, as if to advertise the realm's primary attraction. Others resembled humans in other ways, though most fae found a completely human appearance too dull, and all those he saw sported some variation from the mortal norm – large pointed ears, or hair like a dandelion gone to seed (indeed, in one instance, shedding seeds), or scaled skin and gills, or feathers in bright colors or more neutral shades. Some eschewed human shape altogether, taking on the appearance of various animals – though all tall enough to reach the tables – or, in at least two cases, mobile plants, one bearing delicate pastel blossoms and the other obviously carnivorous.

As he pivoted to take in the scene, Abe noticed one fae with generally human glamour and, in some manner hard to determine, the appearance of youth. Was it the narrow shoulders, or the large magenta eyes? Or the fact that the glamour occasionally wavered, as if the fae was unused to controlling it? Before Abe could draw any firmer conclusions, the being slipped through the crowd and was lost to view.

Abe wandered here and there, smelling and fae-watching, until he began to tire and went looking for the portal to return home. He had spied it some tables away when he saw, much closer, the increasingly familiar Greek-god glamour of the ocean realm rulers. He approached them, bowed deeply, and asked, "Are you enjoying the feast?"

The queen smiled at him and said, "We have been sampling a great many of the offerings, and enjoyed at least the variety and sometimes the foods themselves. And you – no, I assume it would be imprudent for you to do the same?"

"Alas, yes."

The king gave his queen a fond, indulgent look and then grew more serious, saying to Abe, "If we had not encountered each other here, I intended to pay you a visit in the near future."

What had been the status of the oceanographer's request, the last time he paid attention to it? "I beg your forgiveness, but I have been distracted of late. Have your negotiations with Ms. McGann concluded, and her explorations begun? If not, do you have need of my participation in what negotiations remain?"

"The negotiations have concluded," said the king, "and Ms. McGann will be bringing her submersible vessel to us in a few days' time. I wished, rather, to pass on to you some news of your daughter."

Abe stood as still as if petrified. The queen reached out to pat his shoulder and said in soothing tones, "Nothing dire has befallen her – or your erstwhile client. The boy has been released from the ice sooner than originally decreed, due in part to Valentina's intervention. That has freed her to embark on a task set her by the rulers of the ice realm. That task has allowed her to leave the ice realm, though temporarily."

Abe looked around to make sure the portal had not moved or vanished, then said with a haste he hoped the fae would pardon, "I greatly appreciate this good news. I must go. My wife – I must tell her. If you should happen to learn more, such information would be most welcome."

The royal fae nodded, and Abe turned and ran for the portal, fae turning to stare at him as he ran.

By the time he reached the front steps, Abe had – if just barely – slowed down, gotten his breathing under control, and realized that if Clara saw him burst in wide-eyed, she would assume he had either dreadful or wonderful news to share.

Though it was wonderful, in its way. Alone, without support, Adira had nonetheless continued to assist their young client to a material extent, and without suffering for it – or at least, not enough for the ocean fae to regard any punishment as dire. And whatever her task, surely it was better for her to be able to leave the ice realm.

Or so he would fervently hope.

CHAPTER 8

In the School Realm

ADIRA and her escort stepped through onto what looked like a country lane, with a one-room country schoolhouse in front of them – except that to the left and right of it, and spaced every few yards up and down the lane, were other such schoolhouses, dozens of them. They looked as if they had been built, or otherwise conjured, all at one time and from a single design, and then remodeled and decorated to suit myriad different tastes. The building immediately before them – and it might be no coincidence – was painted in the colors of the ocean realm, aqua and blue and gray and green, with large windows tinted translucent versions of the same colors, and its doorway had rippled edges ascending to a pointed arch, while its roof bore a weather vane in the shape of a sea serpent. The schoolhouse to the left had been renovated to resemble a log cabin, with small windows near the roof line, but unlike the trees of the ice realm, the logs were robust and covered with reddish-brown bark, and long vines with flowers of yellow and white swooped along the edges of the roof. The building to the right resembled a miniature castle, its stony blocks incongruously pink and purple. The one next to it resembled nothing so much as a school-shaped igloo, transparent windows frosted with snowflakes, the square-cut sides glistening white in the cheery sunlight all around. Next to it, as if a variation on a theme, came a building with thin planks in the gray and white colors of the ice realm's forest, with a front step carved entirely of ice and frost covering its windows, blocking any view in or out.

How long would it take her to search all these schoolhouses? And her quarry might simply flit from one to the next ahead of her, if it didn't flee the realm altogether.

Perhaps she could bluff her way into appearing part of the routine. And in the meantime – the idea that exploded in her mind might be utterly impossible, but she would try.

She stepped back, bowed to her escort, who stared at her in obvious surprise, and asked, "Would you by any chance be willing to go to the mortal realm from which I come, the one that has lawyers who deal with the fae? I promise you I will remain in this realm, even if the means to leave it should suddenly appear. In order to improve my chances of fulfilling the task your lords have set me, I need to send a message to my parents."

* * * * *

Clara had set up Adira's desk in their office as a workspace, abandoning the home office in order to maintain some separation between research and their few leisure hours. Now Abe drank his afternoon mug of tea and watched Clara work, her attention so riveted on the notebooks in front of her that he could have dropped the mug and broken it, or for that matter jumped up and started dancing a jig, without disturbing her. Or so he thought – but then the electric prickle of a fae visitor started up his spine and, apparently, hers, for she turned away from the half-buried desk and said, "Is that a client?"

He got up and hurried to the entryway with Clara on his heels, only to see a less welcome visitor. An ice fae, though not one of the crowned rulers, stood there, and despite its immobility, it struck Abe as somehow perplexed. He stepped forward, bowed, and said, "Welcome, good fae. Pardon me for being unsure whether we have met."

The fae said, in its voice that ran up and down his spine more than the warning of its arrival had done, "We were not introduced. I bring a message from your daughter. She seeks your assistance finding one of my people, who has left our realm without leave and may have assumed some unknown glamour in defiance of our customs. It could now – though this is by no means certain or even likely – be among the pupils at one of a number of Fair Folk schools."

Clara stared at the fae and then at Abe. He was preparing to say goodbye to her, with some vague assurance of his eventual safe return, when Clara said in her most determined tones, "We will both come. Will you tell us before we go what we should be looking for, or do so after we arrive?"

"The latter. It may be that the moment we reach the Schools, Valentina or I will spy the fugitive, and you may then return here without delay."

All very well, Abe thought, *but we will greet our daughter first and make sure she is unharmed before you'll be rid of us, try as you may.*

The row of schoolhouses was a dizzying, a disorienting sight – but almost immediately eclipsed by the sight of Adira emerging from the schoolhouse directly in front of them, a building painted in a soothing range of cool colors. Her face had acquired a ghastly pallor, but he suppressed any sign of the dismay he felt. The moment she saw him, a faint flush brought her color closer to the appearance of health. She obviously reined herself in and bowed to the ice fae, saying, "I deeply appreciate your bringing my parents to assist. May I take a moment to greet them?"

"A moment only," said the escort. "We have no time to waste."

Obeying both this command and every impulse of his heart, Abe rushed to Adira and clutched her in a tight embrace, murmuring in her ear, "Are you all right? Have they hurt you in any way?"

Adira squeezed back and then, too soon, disengaged, saying, "I am quite well, though altered in ways that I hope to shed when my work for my hosts is complete."

Abe glanced at Adira's impassive escort, or guard. He had no idea how acute its hearing might be, nor was there necessarily any need for secrecy, but he felt such a need. He glanced at Clara waiting a few feet behind him and whispered quickly in Adira's ear, "What can you tell me about Tom?"

Adira also looked toward Clara, held up a finger to promise a very short delay, and whispered back, "He was released from the ice just before I left. We didn't talk long, but he seemed to be in pretty good shape."

Abe went on, as fast as he could whisper. "Tom's parents want to negotiate for his release, in exchange for some service or for one of them trading places with him."

Adira frowned. "I'm not optimistic. But if I have a chance to ask, I will." Then she darted toward Clara, who ran to meet her halfway.

After their brief but intense greeting, Adira said to Clara, "It occurs to me that you're the only one of us whom the faerie we seek will not have seen. But you are also the one of us who has no previous experience with the residents of the ice realm, which would make it harder for you to tell one from another. What might work best is for Dad and me, and my escort if it is willing, to start out looking through those windows that are clear enough, while you go inside schools whose windows are obscured or too high. You may be able to pass as a teacher, or as . . . an exhibit or specimen brought here for a teacher's use."

Clara snickered at the idea, an unexpected and heartening sound. Abe grabbed her hand, squeezed it, and asked Adira, "What should we look for, and where should we start?"

"Besides any ice fae that seems out of place, look for any fae that seems uncertain of its form, unable to maintain its glamour – though the younger pupils may have the same difficulty. Look for an instant where, between forms, it returns to the appearance of an ice fae. And if the other pupils look bored or restless, look for one of them that seems to be enjoying itself, even gleeful. I have looked inside the schoolhouse in front of us. We may as well work left and right from here, dividing our efforts as already suggested."

Abe took a deep breath and tried to don an appearance of competence and confidence. A suitable glamour would have come in handy.

* * * * *

Adira had peered through the windows of several schoolhouses. The castle's colors had proved predictive, as the interior looked eerily similar to a Barbie mansion, though the children within resembled fluorescently colored lizards. The igloo building's windows had been cold to the touch, which was unexpectedly reassuring after the long days surrounded by freezing air she was unable to feel. The glass, or whatever material, of the ocean-themed schoolhouse had proved to contain ever-moving traces of sea creatures, barely visible but distracting. Nowhere had she been able to identify a fae exhibiting the telltale behaviors she had described, and she was quickly coming to doubt that she would be able to do so no matter how long she searched.

Taking a moment to stretch out her back, she saw Mom emerging from the log cabin, whose windows would be out of reach of any of them – except, if it had occurred to her to ask, her escort, who might know how to assume the glamour of some taller creature, and might even be willing to do so. The thought of the pupils inside glancing up at the window and seeing the muzzle of a giraffe brought a smile to her face, in time for Mom to see it and look at least a little more at ease.

Adira joined her and asked, "Where do you want to go next?"

Mom looked doubtfully at the building that must belong to the ice fae. "I don't like the look of that place, but it's my turn, with the time both of you have spent in the actual realm. And there's no way to see inside."

Adira shook her head, dubious. "That'd be more of what the young fae ran away from. Why would he go in there?"

Mom got her thinking face. "How long ago did he begin this jaunt?"

Which day had it been, when they first tried to get Adira to leave Tom and go on this errand? "About a week, I think."

There was a way Mom sometimes looked at her, with a wistful expression that meant she was remembering Adira as a child or a teenager. She looked that way now. She said in a soft, remembering voice, "He's young, and he's never been away from home before. Don't you think he might be homesick?" And with that, Mom walked steadily into the school of the ice fae.

* * * * *

Abe could not simply watch Clara walk out of sight, not after what had happened to Adira. Their quarry had not been so likely to see and notice Abe during his brief sojourn to the ice realm – and one mortal might look much like another to it. But to observe some semblance of caution, he stood behind the doorway, only exposed enough to look in.

All the schools Abe had seen so far served pupils from more than one realm. He had thought the school for the ice fae might be different, given their apparent distaste for variety, but perhaps all the schools were required to accustom their pupils to some degree of exposure to other kinds of Fair Folk. Indeed, until this one, all of them had included at least a sprinkling of children with at least vaguely humanoid appearance. In this classroom, all the pupils appeared to come from forested realms, with appearances that would blend into such landscapes. Their heights differed, but whether that showed their age, Abe had no way to know. Most but not all looked like the ice fae he had seen.

There was also no way he could tell whether one of these thin, stiff, bark-clad forms was the runaway.

Clara walked calmly up the aisle in the center of the room and stood to one side of the teacher. The teacher, apparently in the middle of a lesson on elementary portal transport, looked up from the shimmering portal it had manifested and turned its head and trunk toward Clara, saying in its high-pitched creaking voice, "May I help you?"

Clara bowed to the teacher and said, "I came to help *you*, if you wish. I am a true mortal. Would it be of use for your pupils to see me and ask me any questions they may have about my kind?"

Clara's easygoing air and straightforward statement must be intended to suggest, though she could not assert, that her presence derived from some central authority. Would it work? The teacher's immobility meant little, given how little superfluous motion the ice fae indulged in. After a pause that to Abe felt dreadfully long, the teacher pointed to the nearest corner and said, "If you wait there, I will finish this lesson and then turn over the class to you."

As Clara looked remarkably calm and comfortable, Abe turned his attention to the pupils. Fully half of them had ceased to pay attention to the lesson and were twisting or leaning to get a better look at their surprise visitor. Abe was not surprised when the teacher concluded its lesson in short order and beckoned Clara to the front of the class.

The teacher gave her no introduction, nor did it instruct the children to welcome her in any way. Clara waited just long enough to be sure neither would take place and then smiled at the class, turning so her smile addressed them all in turn. "Good day to all of you! How many of you have seen a mortal before?"

Silence from the class, and then one sighing, wind-like voice from the back. "I think I did, once, if it wasn't just a glamour. I'm not sure I could tell. Do all mortals look like you?"

Abe almost chuckled, but caught himself in time. Clara, meanwhile, said, "Not exactly like me. Some of us are taller or shorter, thinner or thicker. Some of us have darker skin, some lighter. Some of us have more hair on our heads, or less, or different colors, and some of our males have beards, hair on their chins, or mustaches, hair under their noses." She twitched her nose, a skill Adira had always envied her, eliciting a few noises that might be giggles. "If you end up spending time with groups of mortals, you may learn how to tell a true mortal from a glamour. For those of you whose families don't object to your using glamour, seeing lots of mortals would help you learn how to do a better job of looking like one."

One of the ice fae children asked, its voice not yet as harsh as those of its elders, "Is it true that you only live a little while and then somehow stop living? Even if no one's hurting you?"

Clara answered, more cheerfully than Abe could have done, "Yes, that's true. At least, it would seem like a little while to you. But it can seem like a very long time to us. As we get older, we get tired, and it can hurt to move. After a while, we can actually look forward to being laid to rest. And some of us believe that after we die – that's what we call it – we have another life, one that doesn't end and where we'll be very happy."

The same child asked, "You mean after you stop living, die, then you turn into fae?"

The teacher went more rigid in what might have been shock. Clara seemed briefly lost for words, and then answered, "Not as far as we know. At least, no mortal has met a fae who died as a mortal and then became fae. But none of us know for sure what really happens."

None of the young fae asked anything more, for long enough that the teacher tapped its long fingers together. Clara could probably hear that tapping, and said, "Would any of you like to come see me up close? Or even, if your teacher says it's all right, to touch me?"

One, and then another, and then more of the children slowly left their positions and shuffled into a line. Abe mentally applauded his wife's ingenuity. Close up, she would have a much better chance of assessing the demeanor of the youngsters – or at least, those bold enough to approach her. Abe turned his attention to those who remained behind. One of them, a tall youngster with a white trunk like a birch tree and yellow leaves in place of hair, had brought up its thin arms and crossed them across its chest, as if hugging itself.

And then, one almost imperceptible motion at a time, it made its way out of the row of pupils in which it had stood, at the very back of the classroom, and joined the line.

The first two pupils had already reached Clara. The first simply stared at her before moving away; the second reached out a small twig of a finger, just barely touched her shoulder, and then almost jumped backward. As

Clara waited for the next child in line, Abe moved just a little farther from behind the door, enough that the motion might get Clara's attention – and, please God, not the teacher's.

Clara's eyes flitted toward him. Abe turned and nodded toward the back of the line, twice, and then darted back into better cover. Had she understood? The next pupil in line, resembling a shapely fir tree, had reached her, and he could not tell.

Another, and another, and another – and then, the last in line.

The fae's appearance wavered, as if a glamour had been almost lost and then restored. It came slowly toward Clara. As she waited for it, her expression and posture became achingly familiar. She looked as she had looked one of the many times that Adira had gotten into mischief, or suffered some minor injury in the process: a little sad, and accepting, and ready to do whatever she could to show Adira she was loved as much as ever, or to make the pain go away.

She looked like the essence of motherhood. And the young fae stared, and shivered so its bark rattled, and then lurched toward her, into her welcoming arms.

The teacher had appeared nonplussed at this latest development, and Clara had responded by taking the young fae's hand and gently leading it to the side of the classroom. After a brief, unsuccessful attempt to recapture the pupils' attention, the teacher dismissed the class to an early recess, and they left the schoolroom, a few dragging their feet or equivalents in the hope of seeing what other unprecedented events they would otherwise miss. When only Clara, the fae at her side, and the teacher remained in the room, Abe came cautiously forward, bowed, and explained that the teacher had temporarily acquired an extra pupil who was not authorized to attend. The teacher leaned over as if to peer at the youngster and then gave its stiff version of a nod before following its actual pupils outside.

Clara didn't turn as Abe approached, and Abe stopped a few feet away. The young fae flinched at, probably, the sound of Abe's footsteps; Clara put her free hand on its arm, stroking gently, and said very quietly to Abe, "This being would like to see its home again, but it's afraid that if it returns, it will never be allowed to leave again."

"Understandable," Abe answered. "That is not unlikely."

A gleam awoke in Clara's eyes as she said, "It sounds to me as if our young friend could use the services of a professional negotiator."

The fae twitched again, clutched Clara's hand tighter, and apparently lost hold of its glamour, resuming the form of an ice fae. Looking around wildly, it said in its piercing voice, "I don't understand! Are you going to turn me over to my parent? Please don't! Can't you help me?"

Clara started to say, "This other mortal – " She stopped in mid-sentence, probably because Abe had flinched and taken a step backward. He could go back to that realm if he must – he would do it if he could rescue Adira – but for any lesser reason . . . .

Clara looked at him with compassion and said to the young fae at her side, "I had one idea, but now I have a better one. I am not trained to persuade beings like your parent, but my daughter is, and she is already . . . planning to return to your realm. She could go with you and ask your parent, and the rulers, to let you travel again someday."

Abe heard someone approaching – no, two, and one of them not a fae, unless its glamour made their footsteps very like a human's. It was Adira, and from her expression, a mixture of tension and anticipation, she had heard what her mother had said.

* * * * *

Adira bowed to the fae for whom they had searched and said softly, "I am glad to meet you. You may call me Valentina, and I would like very much to help you."

She had not yet learned what ice fae had in place of eyes, but she *felt* the being studying her. Still in that high shriek, but with a recognizable note of pleading, it asked, "Can't you leave me here, and go back and talk to them? I promise I won't leave the School Realm until you come back and tell me what happened."

The same idea had occurred to Adira, but it took only seconds for her to realize its danger – not only to her but even more, to Tom. She shook her head, though the fae might not understand the gesture, and said, "I'm sorry. Do you know what happened to a young mortal just before you left? He was put under the ice. The rulers let him out before I came looking for you, but if I don't bring you home, they may put him back there, forever, and put me there beside him." She swallowed. "I don't know whether you can imagine how terrible a fate that is for a mortal, but I can't take that risk."

The fae let go of Mom's hand and jerked away from her. Adira stepped into his path. Had her escort joined them, ready to seize the runaway? Intent on this confrontation, she might not have noticed the scratch and slither of approaching branches. What could she say to calm the fugitive? Of course – she had already said it, or almost. "They kept Tom, the mortal boy, in the ice for only seven days – seven moonrises and sunrises. I don't know whether you knew this, but for what he had done, the usual punishment is to be put in the ice forever, as I fear they would do if I return without you. It was my parent – we have two, and I mean the one closest to me, not the one beside you – my parent and I who talked to them to change their minds. It is our profession, and we do it well."

The fae quivered as if about to resume its flight. The wrong word could set it in motion again. Did she already know what this fae could offer its masters, in exchange for the promise of some small amount of future freedom? "You can't have promised never to leave without permission, or you wouldn't be here. Am I right about that?"

The fae simply stood and looked at her.

"We will have to give them something they don't already have, in exchange for letting you travel more than most young fae in your realm do. You could promise that if they give you permission to leave some agreed number of times, you will not leave without permission again."

Now she could indeed hear her escort coming up behind her. It passed her and would have seized the young fae had she not laid a hand on its arm and said, "Please wait just a moment." She turned back to the runaway, now cringing against Mom, and said in what she hoped was an authoritative voice. "I have done the best I can for you. Please come with me, and I will continue to do so."

* * * * *

Adira's guard seemed to be growing impatient. It might whisk her away at any moment. Abe wanted to run to Adira and hold her, keep her from leaving, somehow fight with the fae now reaching for both her and the runaway, but he forced himself to move slowly and deliberately. Rather than ask, he said to the adult fae, "We will say goodbye to our daughter now." Without waiting for an answer, he pulled Adira into his arms. Clara came close and held her from the other side.

He could feel Adira shaking as she kissed his cheek and pulled gently away from them both. Then he saw the glimmer of a portal, and the two fae and Adira were gone.

He stood staring at where they had stood. Clara put her arms around him. He held her tight and then pulled back just enough to look at her. She opened her mouth as if to say something, some optimistic forecast or consolation, before she broke into sobs and hid her face in her hands.

CHAPTER 9

ADIRA, her escort, and the young fae arrived in the ice realm with Adira still reeling from saying goodbye to her parents. When would she see them again? Would she even survive to do so? How would the rulers respond to anything but a mute delivery of the fugitive into their custody?

While she had been thinking, or panicking, the three crowned rulers had appeared before her. She bowed and said, "With the assistance of my family, I have found the fae you instructed me to find, and now return it to you. To avoid any similar events happening in the future, it has asked me to speak for it." She would not say *represent it,* when the young fae would probably not understand the term.

In their unsettling unison, the rulers replied, "Did you tell this fae that you would engage in one of your negotiations?"

Running through the recent exchanges to be sure, she said, managing to keep her voice steady, "I promised to try, and to do my best for it. I am not sure I would have been able to complete my task without that pledge."

The shortest of the ruling fae turned to the escort and said, "Take the young one to its parent. We will talk to this mortal and then follow."

The tallest interrupted. "As soon as you have brought the young fae to its parent, bring the young human here to us."

Adira did her best to show no reaction, but she doubted she had succeeded. She must make sure that nothing she did gave the ice fae any reason to punish her by hurting Tom.

When the escort reappeared with Tom, he was clearly expecting some disaster, his eyes showing white all around the pupils and his jaw clenched. He barely managed to say to Adira, "What's happening? What are they going to do to me now?"

Lying while present in a Fair Folk realm might be as dangerous as lying to one of the Fair Folk itself. But she could at least present an optimistic view of the situation. "Nothing, I hope. I think they had you brought here to be sure I behave myself, and I will."

Adira had little luck winning any concession from the rulers. When she offered the young fae's possible promise not to repeat its unauthorized jaunt, the rulers brushed it aside. "We can ensure this fae's obedience without rewarding it for its transgression."

She must find some way forward. Kneeling down, she said, "If you will allow this young fae to make at least one more trip to another realm, a realm which you approve and deem safe for it, I will promise to perform some other task."

The tallest ruler laughed its terrible laugh. "We need none of your promises to require more tasks from you."

She had promised to do her best for the runaway. Then there was her duty to Tom. There was little she could do for him now, but that little required her to be aware of what befell him, and available to assist him. And she was weary to her bones of being afraid, of feeling herself at the ice fae's nonexistent mercy. Of waiting, powerless, for them to decide her fate.

She rose to only one knee and looked the rulers in the face, as much as they had faces. "My lords, you know my profession. You know that if there is some path to an escape before me, I am more likely to find it than other mortals, and perhaps even most fae. But if you give the young fae what I have asked you to give it, I will promise . . . ." She gulped, knowing she was throwing away what little remained of her own freedom. "I promise I will not look for that path, but will act as your servant, on whatever tasks you set me, until you decide I have earned the right to return to my own realm."

There was a long moment of silence, with not a breath of wind to break it. Then the tallest fae did something like snapping its fingers, a sound like the breaking of a twig, in Tom's direction. "Take this mortal back to where we keep it," it said to the escort. "We will discuss with this one the task it must perform next."

Adira had a moment of hope that *discuss* meant her preferences were to be consulted, unlikely as it seemed. She soon learned that it was not so much her preferences but her experience and abilities that were at issue. What followed could only be called an interrogation, and a perilous one, given that some of what the rulers wanted to know fell within the bounds of attorney-client confidentiality.

After she had apologetically declined to answer four questions in a row, and expected at any moment to be dragged off to the lake or some other horrific fate, one of the rulers – they had, this time, been taking turns speaking, one after another in an unvarying cycle – asked, "Have you traveled to mortal realms other than your own?"

This, at least, she could answer. "We have many different countries, which have been called realms. Some are long distances apart, which we cannot cross as quickly as you. The mortals in those countries often have different ways of speaking and other different customs. I have been to many of these different countries." As a child, her parents, and then her mother, had taken her on many folklore-gathering expeditions, and when she approached and entered adulthood, she had indulged in her own travel for the sheer love of encountering the new and different. Her childhood had prepared her perfectly for what had become her career.

Even if that career had now brought her to this cruelly bleak place, from which she might never emerge.

"When you went to a new realm," asked the next fae, "did you always know how to speak to the mortals there, or did you ever have to make your way without that knowledge?"

"I didn't always know the language – the way of speaking. Sometimes I knew a similar one, and could make myself understood or understand the people there at least a little, but sometimes I had no idea at all." In Greece and in Arab countries, she had not even been able to sound out signs on streets and shops. She didn't know whether the ice fae had a written language or understood the idea of one, so she made no attempt to add that detail.

The three fae shifted to face each other, like a smaller version of the cluster of trees where she had been sleeping.

Sleep would be wonderful. How long had it been since she had slept?

One of the ice fae had been talking, she realized, and she had somehow missed what it said. She must be falling asleep on her feet. She shook her head quickly to jolt herself to attention and said, "I beg your pardon. What did you say?"

The three fae leaned closer to her, whether to study her or to intimidate her she couldn't say. Then one of them clacked its fingers, and the escort appeared. The same crowned fae pointed into the forest. That was enough permission for Adira, and she stumbled toward her shelter, the escort staying close to her side.

She awoke to snow-filtered moonlight, and to the sound of an ice fae approaching. Crawling over to peer out the opening, she was unsurprised to see her escort. It beckoned once; she crawled out and made it to her feet without much difficulty. Whatever time it was, or would be if the ice fae kept time, she had apparently slept long enough.

The three crowned fae were waiting at the edge of the forest. They began speaking, in unison this time, as soon as Adira and her escort emerged. "There is a realm whose forest is not like ours. The trees all have many leaves, and the sun is warm and bright. The fae of this realm do not, like other fae, speak in a way that mortals or even fae outside their forest can understand. Do you know of this realm?"

Adira hoped the fae were not familiar enough with human expressions and body language to have recognized her excitement. She drew on her professional experience and adopted a tone and posture of at most mild interest. "I would like to see it."

The tallest fae made an abrupt gesture, and the escort, whose presence Adira had almost forgotten, struck her a quick sharp blow in the face. In all these dangerous days, it was the first time she had been struck, and it shocked her as if she had never been struck before – which, in fact, she almost never had been.

The three of them leaned toward her and said, "You did not answer our question. We are not fools."

The blow had scratched her cheek, and a brief instant of warmth suggested it had drawn blood. Adira bowed low, knowing she was shaking and unable to prevent it. "I apologize, Lords. It will not happen again. I should have said, as I have said to certain other questions, that my professional responsibilities do not allow me to answer."

It was, she realized, as good as an admission that her work had involved such a forest realm in some manner.

"In spite of the ancient custom that fae of one realm may visit another without hindrance, none of our people has been allowed to go there. They fear that our cold will harm them in some way." Was that a sneering tone, somehow discernible in their creaking speech? "Even if we were willing to adopt some glamour for the visit, they do not trust it to protect them. You will go there You will use your skills at learning how strangers speak. Then you will serve as a messenger to that realm when we require one."

To which the only possible response was, *OH, SHIT*. If she had not already learned the language as part of her work, she could have attempted it, and most likely failed, and then returned to beg forgiveness for that failure. But to reveal any aspect of that language now would breach her obligation of confidentiality.

Was she prepared to brave the icy lake to uphold that implicit promise?

If Adira was to find any way out of this tangle, it would be far better to go alone. But – of course! The escort was, to the leaf-talkers, just another dangerous ice fae. She would be allowed to go alone, because the rulers here had no choice.

But she had forgotten about Tom. A fae with a relatively stocky build appeared dragging a clearly terrified Tom behind it. His panic receded at the sight of her, only to surge again as the three rulers approached. The tallest one pointed its long twig of a finger towards him and asked her, "Would the presence of this mortal assist you in performing your task?"

At least they had better sense than to draft the young man as a substitute guard. And he would be a more effective hostage if he remained here. Adira contemplated the fae's question, which she did not, after last time, relish the idea of evading. "I don't see how. If you wanted them to learn our – our mortal – language, it might assist them to hear Tom and me speak to each other. I don't see how his presence would help me to learn theirs."

The three crowned fae made identical dismissive gestures, and the stocky fae began to lead Tom away. He called out over his shoulder, "Good luck! Be well!" The few words of good will threatened to undermine her composure. She waved at him and then turned away until he was out of sight.

When the escort returned alone, Adira feared she had somehow misunderstood and would have to deal with his presence on her mission, but he merely conjured a portal into existence. She bowed one more time to the rulers, took a deep breath, and stepped through.

The warm breeze caressing her cheeks, the sunlight falling on her hair, were like a benediction. She threw her head back, closed her eyes, and let the relief sink in. Then, as the shadows shifted on her face, she realized the trees might be speaking to her. She opened her eyes and said apologetically, "I'm sorry – did you say something? Your realm is such a delight to my mortal senses that I failed to pay attention."

The leaves shifted in what she thought was the equivalent of a chuckle. The language came back to her as if she had only just left. "We cannot be offended at that! And we can see that you have been ill or otherwise afflicted, and may be in need of comfort."

She looked down at her hands, still ice-pale, and said quietly, "You are quite right." How much should she explain? She looked around as she thought, and only then realized that scattered over the forest floor were patches of bright blue. "Oh, the bluebells! My father must have kept working. I'm so glad!"

"Yes, he brought the bulbs, and a mixture of mortal and fae gardeners happy to plant them – though the task is not yet complete. I believe one of them is a gardener known to you, whom your firm assisted with his own garden."

It was like a memory from another life. "Oh, yes, of course! I'm sure he greatly enjoyed the opportunity." But it was time to reveal what had brought her here. "Glad as I am to see you again, I come on a fruitless errand, and must beg your indulgence. You are, I think, familiar with the ice realm. As a result of a case my father and I undertook, I am now . . . under an obligation to its rulers. They are unaware that I temporarily know your language, and have sent me to learn it and then to serve as their messenger to you."

The leaves stirred as if in agitation. "Why did you not tell them that you can understand us?"

Adira stood up straighter. "You are our clients. You allowed us to communicate with you as part of representing you, and only for that purpose. I inferred from the terms of our agreement that even if I could share that knowledge in any effective way, which I doubt I could, I owed it to you to refrain. It was my opinion that my obligations to you extended to keeping my current knowledge of your language confidential."

The breeze seemed somehow to come from many directions at once. "That is our understanding also, and we are pleased that you honor it. How do you expect the ice fae to respond if you return and report failure?"

The sun-warmed air could not banish the chill that ran through her. "I expect them to be displeased. I cannot know in advance which of several methods they will use to express that displeasure." She felt suddenly weak. "Would it be discourteous if I were to sit down? Is there a space where no bluebells have been planted, or have spread?"

"There are still many such places. Please find one and sit, and if you like, recline against one of our trunks. If the ice fae sent you to learn a language, they would presumably grant you a reasonable time in which to learn it. You may rest here, instead, and we will consider whether there is any way we can help you."

Sunlight not filtered through ice or snow, gentle breezes, the delicate smell of nearby bluebells . . . it was no wonder she fell asleep again.

When she awoke, the air, though still soft, felt cooler, and she had only to open her eyes to see that the realm around her had greatly changed while she slumbered. Instead of the daylight she had thought always filled this forest, it was dusk. And then she saw, from the ground near her to the leafy boughs above, the golden dancing flicker of lights.

"Fireflies?" she murmured. She looked upward into the trees for an answer, though it was hard to see the leaves, let alone their shadows, in this muted light. But instead, the answer somehow came from the golden lights themselves.

"When we allow evening to come, we speak through what you call fireflies. Though they are not the insects you know, but fae of a different sort who live among us."

Adira gazed around, enthralled. "Did I sleep long? Do I need to go back soon?"

"Soon, but not yet," said the dancing lights. "And we may have come up with a way to make your return go more smoothly."

One of the lights descended, staying lit longer than a firefly would – and then transformed into a fawn, its muzzle looking softer than moss, its thin legs almost seeming to sprout from the bluebells among which it stood. Adira looked toward the lights for an explanation, but the fawn spoke to her in a sweet high voice. "I am one of the fae you called fireflies, but I can also take on other forms. I have left the forest once before, and I have met your parents." Adira gasped, but the fawn simply went on. "I could go with you to the ice realm and speak to its rulers. They can speak to me, and if there is anything they wish of us other than coming among us, they may discuss it with me – or, better, with you, on our behalf."

Adira longed to question the fawn about its encounter with her parents, but she had more urgent concerns. Would what the fawn proposed be enough to save Adira from the wrath of the ice fae? It might. It was far more reason to hope than she could have expected. "I'm so very glad. Can you make the portal we'll need?"

This time it was the remaining lights that answered. "Yes, if you are ready."

Adira looked around at the bluebells, and the spaces between them. "May I ask when you expect my father, and those helping him with the flowers, to come back?"

"Not long. But longer than you could wait for him, we think."

Adira bit her lip. It was probably just as well. It would be wonderful to see him, but it would be for so short a time, and there would be another goodbye to endure, with no more promise than before of being able to go home . . . . "I'll go, then."

She put her hand gently on the fawn's warm back, and waited for the portal that would take her back to the cold.

When Adira reappeared in the shadowless dim light of the ice realm with the fawn at her side, she was startled to see the viscount apparently waiting for her. As she bowed to it, she noted that its expression was neither its habitual smirk nor anything more hostile, though neither was it friendly. The viscount seemed, if anything, somewhat at a loss as it said, "I have been trying to guess what the rulers here would do to you when you failed. I know, you see, the nature of the language they demanded you teach them. The task is impossible. It takes a certain flexibility of mind to accept that one has demanded the impossible, and I wouldn't expect them to display such flexibility."

She wasn't sure whether the fae had noticed her companion. She asked it, "What possibilities have you considered?"

It shrugged, a gesture that failed to disturb its heavily embroidered coat collar. "They may, of course, simply put you in the lake. It would be predictable and unoriginal, not to mention kinder than some other possibilities. As for the latter, they might indulge in more or less dramatic corporal chastisement – I believe you experienced the merest taste of such before you left on your errand. If they decide on that punishment, they might, if particularly irate, invite your father to witness it. On the other hand, they might simply choose something anticlimactic, such as adding to the number of labors you would have to complete – more successfully – before being allowed to depart." A snuff box, this time coated in relatively subdued silver enamel, made its appearance, but the viscount did no more than hold it.

The viscount was noticeably failing to gloat as it listed her possible fates. "If I may ask, Lord Bloomingshire, do you have any preferences, or desires, as to what the ice lords decree?"

The viscount took a pinch of snuff, hesitated, and then blew it off his fingers rather than sniffing it. "I have heeded your plea as to using the pain of others to cause you pain. Yes, you may indeed be grateful! I do not, therefore, wish them to summon Mr. 'Alexander.' Nor do the alternatives I have imagined strike me as especially entertaining. You would be particularly uninteresting as a permanent addition to the lake. I suppose I will simply have to wait and see."

Adira must not, absolutely must not, form an expectation of success, let alone allow the viscount to discern it. But wise or foolish, she could not resist asking, "If I am, after all, able to satisfy the lords in some way, will you be very disappointed?"

Before it could answer, the three crowned fae had appeared, looming before her, and asked, almost chanting, "Have you performed the task we required of you?"

Adira could have used more time to come up with a response to that inevitable question. She opened her mouth to improvise, but before she could speak, the fawn slipped in front of her and bloomed swiftly from fawn to full-grown stag. It might or might not have been coincidence that its antlers resembled the branching crowns of the ice fae. It spoke in a reverberating bass voice that Adira found incongruously attractive. "The forest has sent me to do what may satisfy you, since the task you set this mortal is impossible for any mortal or fae to perform."

Well, that made for as good a start as she would likely have devised. Not that the ice fae appeared pleased. The shortest of the rulers leaned over the stag, only to have to jerk itself loose when its crown became tangled with the stag's antlers. It quickly recovered its composure, and the three demanded, "Explain, then." The wording and tone seemed to Adira to border on discourtesy, but she was not here as arbiter of the etiquette between the rulers of a realm and an uninvited visitor.

The stag held its head high and replied, "You could not have known, and this mortal did not know, but the language of our realm may not be learned by study, and may not be spoken outside our borders. This is not only our law, but the very nature of things. When a being is unable to visit our realm, an emissary such as myself may be made available. This happens only when we, as well as an outsider, wish for discourse. This mortal's previous services to us, and those of her family, disposed us to cooperate in the manner I have described. We have, in fact, an interest in her and their well-being."

If it wouldn't have appeared rude, Adira would have turned away to hide how moved she was. The forest realm, at least as represented by the stag, had played a card about which she had heard, but had never witnessed. Regardless of the previous relationship between them, the rulers of one realm hesitated to offend the rulers of another by ignoring a declaration that a mortal was under their protection.

And "her family," not "her father" or "her partner"? The tale of which she was ignorant nagged her like an unscratched itch.

As for the obligation Adira now owed the forest fae in return, that was a matter for another time, when and if the ice fae ever released her. It was an obligation she would gladly honor. Even if they enlisted her as an emissary in her turn, even if they insisted on keeping her among them rather than letting her go home, she would far rather spend her days in a forest of sunlight and greenery, with gentle dusks and fae like fireflies, than in this stark and icy prison.

A silence had followed the stag's statement. Now the tallest crowned fae said, "We welcome you to our realm, and acknowledge your interest in this mortal's status. As you are here, we will say again that we wish the privilege accorded other fae, to visit your realm."

Before the stag could respond, possibly shattering the tentative amity of the moment, Adira bowed to it and to the ice fae, saying, "If it would not be an unwelcome intrusion, may I offer a thought that could conceivably prove useful?"

The stag gave a regal nod, while the ice fae rulers stood in rigid silence. Adira chose to take that as permission and went on. "Lacking the magic of the fae, mortals have made do, when they cannot trade for the benefits of such magic, by using other means of achieving various desired ends. The mortal realms include great extremes of heat and cold. We have therefore learned how to protect ourselves against those extremes. If you are willing, lords, Emissary, I could assist in obtaining protective garb – what we call 'insulated' garments – for the ice fae to wear. Such garments would protect the forest from any cold the ice fae might otherwise exude. This solution would also eliminate any need for the ice fae to alter their traditional forms for such a visit."

Despite their lack of visible eyes, Adira had the distinct impression that the ice fae were looking into and through her. They responded together. "If we decide to pursue this option, we will summon your parent to assist us. For you, we have another task."

Adira bit her lip, and could only hope the ice fae knew little about the signs of human disappointment. "I cannot promise he would come, while I am kept here."

The tallest ice lord made a gesture of dismissal. "It is of little current importance."

Silence again, until the stag bowed its noble head to her and said, "Until we meet again." With an identical – no deeper – bow to the ice fae, it turned toward a suddenly manifested portal and stepped through, back to its kinder climes. The faintest warm breeze marked its departure.

CHAPTER 10

HELPLESSNESS was infuriating, and then debilitating.

Clara had read every book and notebook twice, both hers and Abe's, and listened to every recording. At least, she'd read or listened to everything she'd brought with her, and everything she could find at the house. There were notes she thought should be here somewhere, but neither she nor Abe had found them. Finally, she jolted awake at 4 a.m. one morning with the realization that she had sent those notes to a transcription service in Edinburgh two months ago. Ironically, she had wanted to have them available in digital form so she could access them anywhere in the world that had Internet service. She'd been staying in a village with no copy machines, let alone scanners, so she had entrusted the originals to the friend who had suggested the place, as he was heading home for a wedding.

What had happened to that transcript? Had it vanished into some long-emptied spam filter? Or had she given them the email address she had abandoned some weeks back, after too many frustrating encounters with their so-called customer care center?

As soon as she'd dashed cold water in her face and drunk some cold coffee Abe had left overnight (when had he gone back to drinking the real thing, instead of decaf?), she found the outfit's website and sent them a message. If they adhered to their stated policy, they would have retained a copy of the transcript and would have it for months yet – if they were still in business, and hadn't had their projects in progress wiped out by fire or flood or other catastrophe.

The brief burst of energy had run out. Clara shuffled back to bed, maybe even to sleep.

She did, in fact, fall asleep until Abe's groan woke her two hours later. She rolled over, saw the tears on his cheeks, and kissed them away. He opened his eyes, looked at her blearily, and reached up to touch her face, muttering, "Thanks, hon. Sorry I disturbed you."

She patted his hand. "It's all right. I need to check my email anyway. I might have something from Scotland."

He looked confused and then intrigued, but the thought of explaining made her more tired. She got out of bed and dragged herself to her computer.

Lo and behold, the transcription service had replied, full of apologies and explanations. The employee to whom her job had been assigned had gone on maternity leave, and the contractor who was supposed to replace her had gone AWOL, and then the next employee had trouble with Clara's abbreviations and was embarrassed to say so, and hadn't they let her know, so terribly sorry! The contractor working on it presently was doing so from a somewhat remote location, but they would ask her to make a copy and bring it in, or to scan it if the village had a scanner. . . .

Clara left the email open as she went to the kitchen and replaced the cold coffee with a fresh pot. Filling her largest mug, she took a grateful sniff and sat in the breakfast nook to drink coffee and think. When she heard Abe's slippered step, she looked up at him, checked that he was fully awake, and said, "I may need to go to Scotland."

She explained while Abe puttered around getting his own coffee and some sort of packaged breakfast bar. It gave her a pang of affectionate dismay: when had he last baked? Coffee and bar in hand, he sat down across from her and asked simply, "And then what?"

She looked in his eyes, trying to read them. "And then – I come back here, and we go through those notes. Don't we?"

Since Clara came home, Abe had at various times looked depressed, despairing, soul-sick, angry, and on too-rare occasions, interested and absorbed. Now he simply looked sad.

"Almost right," he said quietly. "You go to Edinburgh and get those notes. You make another copy, and mail it to me. And you get back to work. Your own work, in Cairo or Scotland or better yet, somewhere new."

She put her half-empty coffee mug down on the table with a clunk. Abe reached out his hand and put it over hers. "Just stay somewhere with phone or Internet access close by. We can both read those notes, and if we have thoughts to share, we can still do it. But there may be some answer or clue waiting in tales you haven't heard yet. The only way you'll find it is if you go places whose tales you haven't already collected and combed through. And in the meantime, you'll be doing what you love, what gives you satisfaction." He took a shaky breath. "We could very much use satisfaction. And I would share in yours, in my fashion."

The feeling that arose in her bore some resemblance to hope. Clara squeezed his hand and asked, "Are you saying this just to make me go back?"

He shook his head. "My love, I'm saying it to make you go back and because it's true. You do what you do best, and I'll get back to my own work, and either of us might stumble on something we can use."

* * * * *

Two days later, Abe drove home from the airport, looked from the driveway at his now deserted house, and pulled back out. Minutes later he walked into the office, where the dangling doorbell did its best to cheer him. He set it swinging, listened to its faint chiming – just a bit like the changeling's laughter – and trudged to his desk.

The reminder of the changeling boosted his resolve to turn his attention to his work. He had done his duty, and more, by the changeling. Now he would concentrate on doing his best for his bereft client and the child whose place the changeling had taken.

After the longest and most difficult series of negotiations Abe could recall, Abe decided he had extracted sufficient protections for the foster child, including enforcement mechanisms to prevent some unforeseen creative interpretation of the contract provisions. The one thing he couldn't do was ensure that if he were incapacitated, someone else would follow through. But he had insisted on the most rigorous language he could devise to bind the fae of the Autumn Court to their obligations.

It was time to make the exchange, stolen child for unwanted one.

There had been only one mention of the changeling, the day before the exchange was set to take place. Just as Abe was getting ready to go, the faerie with whom Abe had been negotiating said casually, "By the way, you haven't mentioned the infant you claim we left in this child's place. We rather thought you might."

Abe did his best to echo the fae's tone. "That infant has left our world. No doubt it has returned to the realm from which it came."

The fae cocked its head and regarded Abe with the faintest air of amusement. It might know very well where the changeling had gone. At any rate, it asked nothing more.

Abe took charge of the foster child, who had if anything lost weight and become less responsive to adult attention during the interim, and endured the excuses of the overwhelmed foster mother. Back in his office, he knelt down in front of the boy, who sat huddled in their smallest armchair clutching a threadbare toy lamb, and said, "We're going somewhere magical! Have you heard about magic? Or faeries?"

The child shook his head and put one of the lamb's forelegs in his mouth, sucking it rhythmically. Abe stubbornly kept talking. "Even though it's still spring here, it's autumn there, and everywhere you look, there are trees with bright-colored leaves on them, yellow and orange and red and red-purple. Lots of the leaves don't fall from the trees, not like leaves here. And the people dance around, and make the leaves – the ones that do fall off the trees – dance with them. Have you ever danced?"

The boy looked up at him, wrinkling his forehead.

"May I pick you up? So I can show you about dancing?"

The boy looked at Abe with wide eyes, breathing so quietly Abe could hardly see his chest move. He took the lamb's leg out of his mouth and held it up. Abe nodded and said, "You can keep holding your lamb if you want to. I can hold you and the lamb both." He walked over to the radio in the corner of the room and switched it on, tuning it as quickly as possible to an easy-listening station. Then he went back and lifted the boy in his arms, grimly noting that it was all too easy. He turned and turned in the closest he knew to a waltz step, singing along with a "dum-dee-dum, dum-dee-dee-dum . . . ."

So quietly that Abe almost missed it, the boy started mimicking Abe, saying, with no particular melody, " . . . dum . . . dee . . . dum . . ."

Abe swallowed hard and kept dancing. He couldn't pretend to know what the boy's future held in the Autumn Court, but it should be less bleak than his past.

An hour later, Abe stepped through the portal with another child, a younger one, in his arms.

The fae had showed no reaction, either compassionate or indignant, to the foster child's condition, but whatever their reason for wanting a mortal child, the offered toddler apparently satisfied it. They handed over his client's baby son with a moment of hesitation he judged was intended purely to disconcert him.

He had once again rented a crib, placing it this time in the office conference room, and obtained the favorite blue blanket from the baby's mother. He set the baby in the crib as soon as he had unlocked the office and gone inside. The baby picked up the blanket and babbled in an odd, musical way, hauntingly familiar, and a stark contrast with the child Abe had traded away. Abe called the mother as soon as the baby had snuggled down into the crib and, as far as Abe could tell, fallen asleep.

"He's not the same! He's *changed*!"

She was holding the baby so tight Abe was surprised the child wasn't squalling. Had the boy changed any more than the passage of time should have changed him? It had been so long since Adira was a baby, and Abe had seen few babies since. Still, he doubted it. "Ma'am, that wouldn't fit with the usual Fair Folk preferences. Either the fae who took your son delight in babies, and would if anything have kept him from growing any older, or they prefer a child old enough to need less care, and would have enchanted him to be several years older." He looked around the house, confirming the absence of either other children or the clutter that usually came with them. "He's your first child?"

Ms. Dellor bristled. "Are you saying that because he's my first, I don't know what he's supposed to look like?"

"I'm not saying you wouldn't know your own baby in a group of babies, not at all. It's just that it can be startling how quickly and dramatically infants change in their early months. I remember, even though my daughter is grown now. I could hardly believe it." And he had better not let himself relive those memories now.

The woman's anger faded into uncertainty. "Do you have . . . can you show me any pictures from when your daughter was a baby?"

Abe clenched his teeth, and then forced himself to relax his jaw before the woman noticed. "I don't have any immediately at hand. You could look online at babies of different ages to get an idea. And I'll make a bargain with you, ma'am. You get used to having your baby home, and let the trauma of these last weeks fade a little, and watch him as he keeps growing and changing. If you're still concerned, call me, and I'll hunt up those baby pictures of my daughter. All right?"

Ms. Dellor relaxed her grip slightly, gulped, and nodded. "All right. And thank you, Mr. Alexander. I didn't mean to – to ignore what you've done for us."

Abe wished he had been wearing a hat, just so he could tip it. Instead, he forced a smile. "You're most welcome. Now, if you don't have any more questions, I'll be on my way."

He should have gone back to the office. Instead, he drove home, locked the door, and made himself a white Russian, carrying it into the cluttered room he and Clara called a library and Adira called his burrow. Clara had put the photo albums there when she left, on top of his large, shabby desk. He set his drink down next to the stack.

It would hurt, without Clara there to turn sharing the memories into a sign of determination and hope; and the hurt would make it hard to stop with one drink. But he couldn't help himself. He opened the album to the beginning.

CHAPTER 11

ADIRA's captors might have a third task for her – they had said so, and they could not have lied outright – but the days appeared to pass, without even the horrible occupation of her former lakeside vigil, and nothing happened, no summons or demands or threats. Had they even decided what task to give her, or had they fallen back on a vague, general notion that they would come up with one sooner or later?

It was a poor time for Adira to remember one of the innumerable folk tales she had heard from her parents. Some legendary prankster had agreed to provide a much-desired benefit – was it gold, or some service? – to a man in exchange for giving him three whacks with a belt. The man endured two whacks, comforting himself with anticipation of the reward, only to find that the prankster intended to postpone the third whack indefinitely.

With eternity before them, would the ice lords wait months or years? Would she grow old here, or linger unchanged, while her parents grew old or even died without her seeing them again, without them seeing her, neither knowing the other's fate?

Adira tried to distract herself by wandering as much as she dared, partly to find whatever variety the ice realm offered and partly in the hope of spying Tom. She worried about his welfare, and different as they were, he would have provided some company. But while she found what might have been the cave in which he had first been held, she saw no trace of him. Nor could she tell whether any of the ice fae she saw might be the young fae she had compelled to return, saving herself and condemning him to an unknown fate.

Adira had not even the normal mundane events to vary her days. No errands, no meetings, no chores, no work. Not even meals. Not that whatever enchantments lay on her allowed her to feel hunger. At times, she missed even that.

And then things changed.

The first sign was the dream. She had not dreamed in all this time – and had not even realized the fact, as if the ice fae had wiped away even the concept of dreaming. But she awoke that morning from a dream of . . . breakfast. An enormous breakfast, far more than she could have actually eaten: oatmeal with a pat of butter and a pitcher of cream, a brimming bowl of soft scrambled eggs, a plate of crisp bacon and sausage hot from the pan, and strawberries and melon and more cream to pour on them. And a tall glass of orange juice, and a mug of hot chocolate, and an urn of coffee.

She had had time only to sip the hot chocolate and to look for another mug into which to pour the coffee before she awoke to the bare ground, and the surrounding pale trees, and the dim light . . . and hunger.

At first, she thought it was a lingering remnant of the dream. But the sensation stayed with her and grew more intense as she stooped to leave the shelter, stretched her cramped muscles, and took as deep breaths as she could in the somehow unsatisfying air.

It could not have simply happened. The ice fae had arranged it. And that explained how the fae, who didn't dream, could somehow plant a dream in her. They hadn't – they had just made her hungry, and given that strong a stimulus, her sleeping mind has overcome whatever had kept her from dreaming before.

But was this hunger meant simply to torment her, or did it have some other purpose?

Three nights of tantalizing dreams, from which she awoke each morning to a hunger that only increased. On the third morning, as Adira was alternating between recalling the luscious details of her dream the night before and trying desperately to forget it, the three crowned ice fae appeared with a fourth, shorter and slighter. She could not recognize it by its appearance, but the air it somehow projected of disappointment or even hostility, tempered by cautious hope, identified it as most likely the fae she had followed and retrieved.

The rulers formed an arc halfway surrounding the young fae, facing Adira, and said together, "This young one has completed its penance, and we have decided to allow it some measure of the freedom it sought."

She waited, but the rulers made no mention of the pact she had proposed when she and the runaway returned. Had their silence at that time constituted an acceptance? She would have to assume as much.

"We will not, of course, allow this fae to wander about unsupervised wherever it will. Nor do we wish to consign any of our number to be its escort. As your next task, you will perform that function. It has promised not to move between realms without your permission."

Any lawyer, let alone a lawyer dealing with the fae, knew that an offer or deal that seemed too good to be true must not be taken at face value. But this was neither an offer nor a deal. It was a pronouncement, and she had no power to refuse, whatever dangers might underly it. She would have to comply, and extract any shred of pleasure she might find while watching for lurking hazards.

"How will we travel, and where will we go?"

The three fae extended one hand each and pointed at her. She could feel no effect, but they pulled back their hands and announced, "You may now create a portal to any fae realm this fae wishes to visit. You will be able to control the portal to prevent your charge from sneaking through it. If you at any point lose sight of this fae or cannot lay hands on it, you will both find yourselves back here at once, and will face suitable punishment for disobedience. Go now."

The idea of herself as an escort for a possibly troublesome youth reminded her suddenly of Tom, whom she had not been able to find, and for whom she had promised to convey a message. Adira bowed and said, "Before I go, my lords, there is another matter. The family of the other mortal wishes to know whether you will accept their services for his release earlier than you would otherwise grant it, or would allow one of them to take his place here."

The rulers responded in a syncopated chorus. "We will not tolerate any further discussions of that mortal. And you will not speak of him to other mortals, or you will be the worse for it."

She was pushing her nonexistent luck, but she asked, "May I see him before the young fae and I leave?"

The three snapped out as one, "Denied."

Even here, with her captors, she dared not be less than polite. There was nothing she could let herself say that would not condemn her and possibly Tom. She kept silent.

Adira might find it convenient to call the young fae by name. Did the same constraints about revealing names apply to Fair Folk? She had never found out, or even thought about it. She led the fae away from its rulers until they should be out of earshot, and then asked, "What would you like me to call you?"

The fae turned to look back over its shoulder and then said softly, "I would like a new name for while we travel together. Can you give me one?"

She found the request oddly touching. It made her want to please the youngster if she could. What did she know of its likes and dislikes? Something important, come to think of it. "How would you like me to call you Explorer? That means that you go new places and even find places that others of your people have never seen."

The ice fae straightened up and shivered so that its bark and twigs rustled. "I would like that very much!"

"Then Explorer you will be. We'll start with places I know, but where you've never been, if that's all right. Later, we may find places new to me as well."

"Yes, yes! Let's start!"

Where should they go first? The destination that had so thrilled her, not long ago, might delight Explorer as well, and she knew that realm's rulers to be well disposed toward her. Would their benign attitude survive an unheralded appearance, and with an unfamiliar fae accompanying her? Well, she would trust her diplomatic abilities to rise to the occasion.

She took the young fae's hand, pictured her destination, and led her charge through the portal that appeared.

They found themselves on a grassy plain, with the sound of distant waves and the wind off the ocean her clues as to which way to walk. The ice fae looked around eagerly, leaned precariously backward, and pointed up. "Oh, look! What are those?"

Puffy white clouds dotted the sky, sailing serenely on the wind. "Those are called clouds. They're made of tiny drops of water. Some people like to find shapes in them." She pointed at one of the larger ones. "For example, to me, that cloud looks like a castle. Does any of them remind you of something you've seen?"

The fae – Explorer – made a whistling noise like wind through barren trees. "I haven't seen very much." Then, in a brighter tone: "Maybe after you take me more places, I'll see pictures in clouds the way you do."

They walked a few steps on before the fae said abruptly, as if blurting out a secret, "I think I like mortals. You've been . . . kind to me, if I know what that means." Adira's throat felt tight as she wondered what to say, but the fae went on, "And that other mortal told me stories – about its brother and sister and some other girl."

Adira stopped in her tracks and swung around to face the fae. "Where did you meet that mortal? At home, or while you were, um, traveling?"

"At home. I was wandering around, looking for anything I'd never seen before, and I saw a clear space in the snow, and a digging stick lying along one side, and a sapling ready to be planted. Next to it, the mortal was leaning against a tree making a noise like this." The thin wailing sound could have been Explorer's attempt to mimic crying. "So I stopped and asked what it was doing, and it didn't answer me, but somehow we started talking anyway."

Adira began walking again, more slowly, and the fae fell in step beside her. It must be talking about Tom. He must have been terribly lonely – lonely enough to talk to the only being nearby who was willing to talk to him.

Explorer went on reminiscing. "I only got to talk to it that one time. One of the adults found us and told me to go away. I tried to find the mortal again when – after you brought me home. A while after, when you'd gone off on your next task. But I couldn't." It started to say more, and then fell silent.

Adira stopped again, pulling the fae to a halt and then letting go. "You couldn't find the mortal? Did anyone tell you what happened to him?"

The fae turned away, toward the sound of the sea, and then back again. "I'm sorry, Valentina. I'm not supposed to say."

Adira bit her lip so hard she felt it start to bleed. The fae leaned toward her and asked, "Are you all right? Are you . . . are you angry with me?"

Adira took a deep breath and blew it out as slowly as she could. By then, she was able to speak. "No, Explorer. Not with you."

They soon reached what looked like the same cliff on which she and Dad had arrived on her earlier visits. From here she could better smell the full-bodied salty air, and hear in full force the rumble and hiss of the waves reaching the shore and receding again, the cries of pipers and gulls. She felt the twitch and scrape of twigs in her hand and realized it was the ice fae. She let it hold her hand and watched it looking around. If it had had visible eyes, she was sure they would have been wide open.

It pointed at the waves curling and crashing and said in a hushed voice, "I may have been here before, but inside that – that moving substance. I felt much lighter, except not exactly lighter – the substance moved me around, but I could also make my own movements. What is it?"

"That's water." She felt its incredulity and added, "Not the same kind of water as in your lake. What you smell – that is, can you smell?"

"Yes. What am I smelling?"

She smiled at it. "That's salt. Mortals, and maybe some fae, use salt to make their food taste better." Immediately she wished she had not mentioned food; her hunger, from which she had been distracted for the last few minutes, came roaring back to her awareness, but she ignored it as best she could. "This water is full of salt. And there are also living things in it, like the one your glamour copied when you came here – I don't know if they're all fae, or something else, but there are fish living in the water, and birds – flying creatures that make some of the sounds you hear – that eat the fish. At least, back in my world, birds eat fish."

She would have liked to sit down, but that might make it too hard to keep up with Explorer if it decided to suddenly move away. Instead she willed her legs to remain steady and awaited more questions, sure they would come.

"What fae live here? Besides the things in the water that may not be fae at all?"

As if in answer, the two enormous waves appeared almost at the horizon, and then rushed toward the cliff as if determined to overwhelm it. But they slowed near the shore, as before, and Adira said, "I believe you are about to meet two of them, the rulers of this realm. You should address them as Their Majesties."

Before either Adira or her charge could speak, however, the taller wave spoke to her. "Welcome back, Valentina. We are glad to see you again, especially in somewhat better health than previously."

Startled, Adira looked down at her arm. Instead of the sickly pallor, it had the blessedly ordinary appearance she had known all her life, with variations according to the season and whether she had spent time in hotter countries. The restoration of her hunger must be somehow responsible, or at least connected.

But the ocean ruler was awaiting an answer. "What you see is, in fact, a mixed blessing, but I am nonetheless relieved. Your Majesties, may I make known to you Explorer, a young fae from the ice realm where I have been . . . staying."

The other wave spoke in its higher voice, saying, "Welcome, Explorer. Our realm must seem strange to you, but we hope you will enjoy your visit."

"Oh, yes!" said the ice fae. "It is so different, and wonderful! I could never have imagined it."

Adira expected more in the way of conversation, though she was hardly entitled to do so, but the waves receded as swiftly as they had arrived. Crestfallen, she almost jumped when the two full-grown harp seals appeared on the grass a little farther from the cliff edge. The ice fae actually did jump backward, tripping on its root-like feet and barely avoiding a tumble.

Lest the ice fae show less than the necessary respect, Adira hastened to explain, "These beings are Their Majesties, even though they now assume such a different glamour." As if to make that assertion even more unlikely, the seals came closer and ran their black noses over Explorer's trunk. The touch must have tickled, little as Adira had ever imagined one of the ice fae being ticklish, for the young fae wriggled and laughed, its laugh somehow less unsettling than that of its elders.

The harp seals were almost the same size, but the taller and bulkier spoke with a voice that recalled the bass rumble of the King. It asked the ice fae, "What other realms have you seen, beyond your own?"

Explorer held up its twig-fingers and counted on them, surprising Adira into another smile. "The School Realm, just before I . . . had to go home. And a terrible dry place – it frightened me, and I left there right away. And a place as cold as home, but with great glowing lights in the sky, and no trees." (Had the fae somehow seen the Northern Lights? Adira had never seen them, and felt a brief throb of envy.) "And a wonderful place full of food! All we eat at home is snow. I had no idea food could be like that!" It asked Adira eagerly, "Could I go back there? With you, of course. There was so much I didn't have time to try!"

Adira could refuse. Or could she? She paced back and forth as she tried to remember the ice rulers' exact words. She and the young fae could go to any realm it wished to visit – but they had not said that if it wished to visit one, Adira could refuse. Abe had long since drummed into her that any ambiguity could be a trap of the most dangerous kind.

From the earliest days of her childhood, when she was hearing stories from folklore instead of from Dad's practice, she had known that any mortal who tasted food in Fair Folk territory could never return to the mortal realm. Could she endure being surrounded by food? She stopped in her tracks, struck by unwelcome insight. That was quite likely the ice rulers' plan in making her hungry! – to lure her into trapping herself, so that her own actions would make a mockery of any permission they might give her to go home.

Well, she would neither succumb to that temptation nor take the risk involved in avoiding it. She turned to Explorer, watching her in apparent confusion, and said, "Yes, we can go to the Feast Realm, whenever you wish."

The young fae clasped its hands, the twigs intermingling. "Let's go right away!" It bowed to the harp seals. "Might I come back sometime? I would like to see more here – after the food."

The harp seals, in the blink of an eye, transformed into the godlike forms Adira had seen before. The goddess nodded graciously as the image of Poseidon said, "You may indeed."

Adira had failed to anticipate the aromas that filled this realm, each more enticing than the last. She inhaled deeply and groaned. Explorer pivoted toward her and asked, "Is that a sound of pain?"

"Not exactly. It's hard to explain. Where would you like to go first?"

The fae pointed to one of the closest tables. "Maybe there. What is that color? I saw a little of it on the outside of one of the schoolhouses. I never see it at home."

It was yellow – a platter piled high with scrambled eggs, almost like her dream three days ago. Adira could have groaned again. She looked away and tried not to smell the eggs as Explorer helped itself. At least it finished its portion quickly. There was such a wide variety of food that she was able, without feeling that she was cheating the youngster, to draw its attention to those tables whose offerings she did not find as tempting.

She soon noticed that the other fae in attendance were not only cheerful, but sociable. Many of them, presumably meaning to be helpful, offered to move so she could take her turn filling a plate, or pointed out their own favorite dishes. Some simply commented on how particularly fine the weather was for this eternal picnic, or asked her if this was her first visit to a Fair Folk realm, or struck up a conversation with the ice fae at her side. She paid close and nervous attention to these exchanges, not sure what the ice fae might say that could land either it or herself in difficulties, but unhappily certain that such could occur.

At a table displaying the glistening roast of an oversized pig, an even more oversized fae, with the general appearance of an eight-foot-tall clean-shaven Santa Claus, beamed at her and said, "You're a mortal, aren't you? Then you, or one of you, is responsible for this delightful scene!"

"I beg your pardon?"

The white eyebrows shot up, in diverging directions. "Why, this splendid feast came from a mortal's dream! My, that fellow must have been hungry. When he woke up, he told a friend who knew some Fair Folk, and luckily one of them was interested enough to buy it. Of course, the dream didn't include every food you see around you, but the buyer had no trouble filling in some more details. And even though – " The fae stopped short, smiled awkwardly, and then went on as if nothing had happened. "Now *every*body comes here to enjoy themselves!"

Adira said something innocuous and stepped away, still keeping the ice fae within easy reach. Her thoughts whirled in confusion. She had known that humans sometimes sold dreams to fae – Dad had even mentioned it not long ago, something about a graveyard and deer? – but she had always imagined a sort of mini-realm, something that could accommodate only a very few visitors at a time. This endless vista of tables, crowded with what could be thousands of Fair Folk – it had begun as images, as desires, in the sleeping thoughts of a single human being?

Meanwhile, the ice fae had gobbled its slice of pork and was moving on to a table of distinctly human desserts: dark chocolate cake with creamy chocolate icing, banana splits, sherbet in cool pastels, cinnamon rolls, tiramisu. Adira gritted her teeth and followed. She could not hold out much longer. To what other realm could she tempt the fae to go before she succumbed?

What was it the young fae had first noticed, when it spied the table full of breakfast foods? The color – that was it. The fae had marveled at the bright yellow of scrambled eggs. Its home had whites and grays and dark greens, the palest of blues now and then in the skies, faint bluish shadows in the ice. Whichever desert place it had visited, it had been so uncomfortable that it might not have noticed any vivid colors there. What realms had Adira seen that might offer a visual feast instead of this literal one?

A memory surfaced from the first days of Dad's practice. She had been lazing about in the back yard, ignoring her book to stare upward at the sunset, and he had offered to show her something she might enjoy even more. . . . And there was one other feature that might hold some appeal.

She tapped the young fae on the shoulder. "Excuse me. We've been here for quite a while. I noticed that you admired the color yellow at the first table. How would you like to go somewhere with many colors just as vivid, stretched all across the sky, and reflected below?"

She was far from sure that she could find the place again, but she concentrated as hard as she could on those years-old memories, called up her hard-won ability to travel in Fair Folk realms, and pushed through.

And there they were, standing, or hovering, on the surface of a sheet of water stretching in every direction. Everywhere they looked, across the water and above, stretched sheets and streamers and clouds of color, oranges and yellows and magentas and purples and reds, because this was a realm of unending sunsets, gradually shifting from one to the next, all different, all splendid. The reflections in the water added blue tones to the palette, deepening them without completely stealing the warmth from the colors.

Adira sat herself down on the surface of the water. That was something else Dad had delighted in showing her, how she could not only stand on the water but sit or even lie on it, the better to gaze up at the sky. The ice fae, less flexible – did they ever lie down, to rest or for any other reason? – stayed on its feet, but it turned around and around like the central pillar of a carousel.

There was nothing the ice fae wanted to say, it appeared, and nothing Adira had any need to. The silence between them let Adira hear the faint ambient ringing, varying from one sweet high tone to the next, just at the very border between silence and sound. It had no melody, but it could almost have been a lullaby.

Adira climbed to her feet again and asked her companion, "How long would you like to stay here?"

Its voice came back to her hushed, almost soft. "A long time. I love it so."

Adira let out a long breath of relief. "So do I. If you promise to stay next to me, I'll rest for a while."

"I promise."

Adira lowered herself back down as she said, "Please let me know if you're ready to leave before I get up again." Indulging in a luxurious yawn, she sat down, lay down on her side, curled up in fetal position, and let herself drift off to sleep.

Adira woke from her nap to find the ice fae standing beside her, fidgeting. She climbed quickly, if clumsily, to her feet and said, "I hope I haven't kept you waiting long."

The fae said shyly, "Oh, not long – but I was hoping we could go back to the ocean now. The rulers were so kind, and I did say I'd go back there after the feast. That was almost a promise, wasn't it?"

As Adira remembered it, it had been considerably less, and involved no particular schedule or sequence of events, but there were few fae realms she would rather be in. "By all means, let's return to the ocean. It's good to have friends, let alone powerful friends, and I believe you've begun to make such friends there."

They arrived within sight of the cliff, but a little farther away from the shore. Adira saw what looked like a combination of a work site and camping ground. A clothesline of sorts had been erected beside the one-person tent, and from it hung a pair of rubber flippers.

Adira's heart started pounding. For the first time in uncounted days, she remembered the oceanographer whom she and Dad had escorted to this realm. If Ms. McGann was here, was it possible Adira might find Dad here as well?

CHAPTER 12

Meanwhile . . .

VISITING Scotland had always made Clara feel closer to Faerie. She used to relish that feeling, despite Scotland's particularly nasty set of supernatural beings. Now she had to resist the frequent urge to look over her shoulder. She had planned to make this a brief, efficient detour, but when she arrived on a Friday afternoon, the transcription business had closed early for some combination of inventory and training. That might be Clara's doing, if her inquiry had made it more difficult to ignore longstanding office difficulties.

Making the best of the delay, she bought a train ticket to Dundee, supposedly the oldest city in Scotland, where she had never been. With a little poking about, she should be able to find some wise woman or other elder with tales to share.

The old lady, a Mrs. Muir, had a few bristles of beard, an equally bristly accent, and what used to be known as a dowager's hump. She offered Clara black tea with milk and some tablet, the particularly sugary and buttery Scots version of fudge. Clara gratefully accepted both, asked for and received permission to take notes, and settled back in her comfortable chair.

It became less comfortable as the woman launched into one story after another about the evil fae creatures collectively called Wicked Wichts. She had less interest, it seemed, in the Guid Folk. No, she would rather impress her visitor with the Cailleach, the giant hag who strode over mountains on her cruel errands, toward whom Mrs. Muir seemed to feel an almost familial pride, as of an older and more imposing sister. Then came an array of faeries who curdled milk, sickened cattle, and stole babies, that last a reminder of the changeling and Ms. Dellor's stolen (if recently restored) little son.

"And then," said Mrs. Muir with relish as she refreshed Clara's tea, "there's the Each Uisge. They're like the Kelpies, but they live in deep lochs rather than rivers or streams, and their powers are greater, oh, much greater."

Clara closed her eyes for a moment as Abe's description of the frozen lake in the Ice Realm surfaced from memory. She forced herself to open them and reach for her cup. A sip calmed her enough to say, "Yes, I think I've heard of them, though I hear about the Kelpies more often."

"Here's something you won't have heard before, I'm thinking. There's a type of Each Uisge that keeps to the north, in lochs with ice over them. If a mortal so much as sees them, the mortal freezes to a statue, and only a faerie from the Seelie Court can bring them back. And then there's the Cailleach Bheur, the Blue Witch – you've maybe heard of her. Skin of ice blue and her hair like snow. She does much the same. Your travels won't be taking you too far north, I trust?"

Clara bit her lip and struggled for self-control. Mrs. Muir made a soft clucking sound and reached over to cover Clara's hand. "Must you go there, then?"

"It's not that." Clara could hear her voice shaking and went on anyway. "My daughter . . . she's run afoul of some fae almost that bad. And I don't know how to help her."

"*Losh*! I could ask how she came to such a pass, but I won't. Well, you've got your own troubles and no mistake. Is that why you're here asking questions?"

Clara shook her head and smiled weakly. "No, I've always been doing that. It's long been my trade, and it was my joy, but it's my trade still. So I thank you for your welcome and your tales."

The woman got up and pulled a cloth napkin from a drawer. "Take you some of the tablet with you, then. And if you find other people to answer your questions, you can give them a piece and tell them Granny Muir made it."

The man Clara interviewed next, an old man whose long wispy beard and matching physique suggested a wizard, accepted his portion of Mrs. Muir's fudgy treat with childlike delight. He could hardly be engaged in substantive conversation until he had eaten every crumb. When he finally folded the napkin and gave Clara his attention, he added few details to Mrs. Muir's account. The Each Uisge had a particular interest in human women, it seemed, while fae from the Seelie Court did indeed sometimes intervene to assist their victims. The former might shed some light on the past, but none on their current options. The latter might suggest some faint cause for optimism, though Abe had given her the impression that the rulers of one realm rarely interfered in any active sense with the schemes of another.

Clara's host rose to refill the teapot, surprising her by returning with a plate of fruitcake. "Dundee Cake, this is, and a favorite of English royalty, which makes it less popular with some good Scots, but I favor it. By the by, did you know that King James III had a royal dream interpreter? There was a man who took dreams seriously. Could be his people believed the Fair Folk creep into dreams and make mischief."

Clara swallowed her bite of fruitcake and asked, "Is it common, to believe that?"

"Och aye, common enough. Care for more tea?"

* * * * *

Abe talked to Clara the day after she finally retrieved her notes from the transcription service. She gave him a report of her latest research, her tone unnaturally impassive as she described types of fae who resembled those holding Adira captive. As he was wondering whether and how to attempt comforting her, she moved on to Scottish fancies concerning dreams, and added, "It made me remember what you said once about the Fair Folk buying dreams. Do they somehow use them against the mortals who sell them?"

That was a daunting thought, but he had no reason to believe it. "I don't think so. It's a good point, though. If I ever sell the Fair Folk a dream, I'll make sure to protect myself. And now you've reminded me that I had one I thought of trying to sell."

"Best of luck with that, if you do try. If the ice fae were interested, you'd finally have at least a bit of leverage over them."

That was as close as they came to the quest that so consumed the thoughts of both. She told him she was headed to Thailand next, and he wished her a safe and easy journey. As he hung up, he contemplated his dream with the deer and the graveyard and the gentle, wondering ghosts. Could that dream possibly appeal to the ice fae? His loathing for them made it hard to imagine them appreciating anything so serene and soothing, but it was possible. And he might be able to find other more suitable dreams, belonging to other people if not to him.

Maybe some Fair Folk more friendly to him and to Adira would be willing to share their thoughts on the matter. Even if they themselves had an interest in his dream, they would necessarily tell him the truth about the ice fae's likely attitude – if they knew it, and if they were willing to talk about it at all.

It would be most appropriate to make his inquiries while he was there for an already authorized purpose. He called his floral supplier and was relieved to hear that she had more bluebells in stock, ready for planting. Then he went down his list of willing volunteers.

By the next afternoon, he was ready.

Even without his additional motive for coming here, the soft warmth and ever-shifting golden light of the place would have been a balm to his wounded spirit. And it was gratifying to see how the bluebells had already spread beneath the trees, even as the gardeners planted new bulbs wherever the flowers remained sparse.

In fact, fulfilling the bluebell contract shouldn't require another visit. He would need to broach his business before he left. Even if it would not be presumptuous of him to come again without that justification, it was unlikely he would retain his ability to speak to the trees after he left today. He walked over to one of the tallest, broadest trees, one whose size would in an earthly forest have betokened great age. He bowed deeply and said, "I hope you have been satisfied."

The tree's leaves rippled in reply. "Quite satisfied. You have done as we asked, and with as little disruption of our peace as could be expected."

"I'm gratified to hear it. My visits to your realm have been among the most delightful of all my career. Before I leave for what may be the last time, there is something I wanted to ask you, in an area where my expertise is incomplete. May I do so? I should add that my question may stray into delicate territory, and I will fully understand if you choose not to answer."

The leaves rustled and clapped softly together in what came to Abe as a sort of chuckle. "I am intrigued. Say on, and whether we answer you or no, I pledge not to be offended."

"You may be aware that my partner – my daughter – has been required to stay in the ice realm, or to leave there only as its rulers command. My wife and I have tried to think of any inducement we could offer them to release her. We now wonder whether it is possible, and if so, how likely or unlikely, that they might take a dream of mine in exchange."

The tree's leaves grew still, and then moved again. "An interesting notion. What is the nature of this dream?"

"The dream I have in mind has solemn overtones, but it is gentle in mood, and many mortals would find it lovely and soothing."

A wave of swaying and rustling swept through the treetops. When it died down, the tree under which he stood addressed him again. "It is difficult to be sure, of course, but most of us are inclined to doubt that a dream of this character would suit the ice fae's sensibilities. Do you have anything harsher and more dramatic in mood?"

Abe had not, prior to Adira's imprisonment, been prone to nightmares, at least not as an adult. As for his recent dreams . . . whether they showed Adira herself subjected to some evil fate, or more general scenes of pain and disaster, he felt ill at the thought of the ice fae watching such a dream, gloating over the suffering it showed – perhaps even forcing Adira to inhabit it. No, he did not trust them with any of his more dire dreams, and the more they wanted it, the less willing he would be to put it in their hands. "I have nothing suitable to offer, my lords, at least not at this time."

Abe's shoulders sagged. He hated to leave, and most likely for the last time, on such a fruitless, unproductive note. But there was, after all, something else he could do before bidding this realm farewell. He straightened up and asked, "Would you by any chance be interested in obtaining this dream yourself? I believe it would be more to your taste."

The wordless language of the leaves somehow suggested sympathy. "Our curiosity, at least, has been engaged. You may say more."

Abe did his best to describe the dream. Fortunately, the tree was familiar with the concepts of grassy open spaces, of animals, and of human mortality, but conveying to an immortal fae the purposes of a graveyard, let alone its atmosphere under the right conditions, proved difficult, and explaining the idea and appearance of ghosts even more so. The leaf shadows suggested incredulity as the tree asked, "So humans die, but they are sometimes thought to leave a visible spirit behind, but in fact do not? And this dream places these nonexistent surviving mortal remnants among the markers declaring that they have in fact died? And these 'ghosts' are touching living animals, and the animals sense as much and welcome it?"

Abe smiled politely. "You have, in fact, understood me better than I could have hoped. It will, however, be easier to see the attraction of this dream if I may show it to you." From what he had heard, it would be possible if and only if the fae made it so.

The leaves rustled in the equivalent of a considering humming sound. "It will be easier to arrange if you do this during twilight. I will discuss with the others when that twilight should occur, as we do not require a regular cycle of day and night. In the meantime, you may remain after we send your helpers home."

Abe gladly agreed. Clara would not be waiting for him, and he had nothing else at home to compare with this rare chance. He found a sunlit spot between trees, asked and received permission, and sat down to wait.

Abe didn't know when he had seen anything more beautiful than the soft blue-purple dusk, filled with dancing, flickering firefly lights. He was sorry to interrupt his immersion in it; but it would be a pleasure to see the dream again, and to assure himself that it was as serene and, at least for him, as moving as he remembered.

It was that, and more. After the emotionally fraught time he had been spending in immortal realms, dealing with the fae's inhuman points of view and their frequent absence of comprehensible emotions, the homely beauty of the deer in the melancholic peace of the graveyard and the poignant gratitude of the ghosts brought tears to his eyes. When it was over, he was glad of another moment of twilight before the forest fae banished it and restored the sunshine.

He returned to the large tree and asked, "Did the dream please you more than you expected?"

In slowly moving shadows, as if the tree was considering each word, it replied, "It did. Your description, able as it was, did not capture the dream fully."

"In that case, my lord, shall we discuss terms on which you could acquire and make use of it?"

The leaves still shifted, the shadows still moved, but they conveyed nothing except hesitation. Finally, they became speech again as the tree said, "We will have to discuss this further. There are more considerations than you know. It will help that you have dealt with us fairly and done us great service, but this is always a difficult decision."

Why would it necessarily be difficult? What didn't he know?

The tree went on, something implacable in its tone. "If we decide to discuss obtaining this dream, we will let you know, and give you back the gift of understanding us. Until then, when you leave today, you leave that behind – except for any message we find it necessary to send you. I hope you have appreciated and enjoyed it."

Abe bowed again, his heart heavy. "I have done both. I will always cherish the memory of it, even if I am not allowed to speak with you again."

Maybe he would even dream of it.

Days passed, and no message came . . . until one did. He had just finished a second cup of coffee, and as he had failed to do any baking in weeks, there was nothing to eat in the office but packaged snacks, stale crackers, and cheese he suspected had grown mold. He opened the front door to go get some lunch and stopped in his tracks to find leaves falling, falling where there was no tree to be shedding them. And faintly, like an echo or some song carried on a breeze from distant hills, he sensed the words, *We wish you well, but we will not be purchasing your dream.*

The last leaf fell, and there was nothing but the whir and click of a bicycle passing by and the distant bark of a dog. Abe scooped up the leaves, went inside, and tucked them away in his deepest desk drawer, where they would rest undisturbed.

Now that Abe had begun trying to sell the dream, he was loath to abandon the project, make-work though it might be. After a quick and barely tasted lunch, he returned to the office, wrote Clara a quick email describing his unexpected difficulties, and rummaged through his files and his memory for another likely purchaser. This time, he might be better off focusing not on the landscape of the realm but on the character of its inhabitants. The forest fae, with the slow deliberate habits appropriate to their chosen form, considered dream transactions a weighty concern. What fae were more careless in their manner, more devil-may-care, more eager for novelty?

What came to mind, at first, was the viscount. In all the time Abe had been working with it, the sardonic, dandyish fae had never mentioned its home realm, and Abe had never asked. It seemed to flit easily from one realm to the next, peering through its quizzing glass with equal casual curiosity at each. Was this attitude, which Abe had somehow assumed to be a personal attribute, actually a characteristic of an entire people?

It was certainly worth finding out. The idea, however, posed one problem. In all the years of his practice, any meeting between them had always been at the viscount's initiative or pursuant to some prior arrangement. He had no way to summon Lord Bloomingshire, nor to visit whatever realm it called its own.

It was always possible that the viscount somehow kept watch on Abe's and Adira's premises. Feeling a fool, Abe stepped out on the front step and said, not quite loudly enough to surprise any passersby, "Lord Bloomingshire, would you do me the very great favor of appearing?"

He waited for almost five minutes before giving up and trudging inside.

Abe slept poorly that night.

In the morning, stumbling into his office, he double-checked his files and saw that Ms. McGann, the oceanographer, was due to make her fourth and last descent in her submersible the next day. He could meet her there and inquire whether she sought an extension of her explorations and, if so, whether the rulers were willing to negotiate it. And while he was there, he could see if the rulers could help him contact the viscount. They, if any fae, were favorably disposed to both Adira and himself. What they thought of the viscount might be another story, but he could hope any unfavorable impression would not prevent them from assisting.

Abe stepped through the portal at the appointed time and found himself on the beach. He edged back from the oncoming surf, stepping around a large towel and the ingredients for building a fire. Peering out to sea, he saw some sort of floating buoy. Ms. McGann must have already entered her submersible and . . . submerged.

The rulers, in their glamours as Greek divinity, appeared on both sides of him, making him feel somewhat like an adolescent under supervision. He bowed to right and left. "Your Majesty, Your Majesty. I hope all is going well?"

"Quite well," said the queen. "Such a quaint and entertaining mortal! We rather hope she will decide to conduct further explorations, though from her comments, she has gathered enough data to spend a good deal of time studying it."

"I'm delighted to hear it." Did their gratitude extend far enough to embrace the help he sought? Only one way to find out. "In addition to seeking such news, I come with – I have a request, which I hope you will not regard as inappropriate presumption on my part. If you would rather not entertain it, I will say no more."

"Of course we will entertain it!" said the queen with reassuring warmth. "We would like to help you if we can."

"Indeed," rumbled the king. "Say on."

The buoy was moving more now. The waves disturbing it seemed to have no connection to the general movement of the waters, and probably came from movements of the submersible instead. Was it ascending? Should he wait to speak of his own concerns? But the king had told him to continue. "When my client has completed her work, if she does so today, I'm hoping you can either grant me passage to a realm where I have never been, or persuade a fae from that realm to meet me somewhere we can both reach."

The king stroked his long, green-tinged beard and asked, "Is there a particular fae with whom you would most like to meet, or will any fae from the realm of which you speak suit your purpose?"

Abe had been thinking only of the viscount, but was their prior relationship truly an advantage? He thought as quickly as he could, and reluctantly concluded that it was, if not exactly an advantage, at least an inescapable fact. He could hardly begin dealing with the viscount's realm for the first time and not include that fae in those dealings, not without angering a fae who had already proved dangerous. And that anger might well fall on Adira as well as himself. Abe suppressed a sigh and said, "I am already well acquainted with, and should at least initially speak to, the fae who goes by the title of Lord Bloomingshire."

The queen let out a laugh like birdsong. "Ah, yes, the viscount! Another original character – though, you may find, not quite so singular as you imagine. We can certainly contact it on your behalf. But I see your client's vessel is emerging from the depths, and will soon come ashore. Let us prepare to meet her." And with that, the king, embodiment of Poseidon, ruler of an ocean realm stretching to the horizon and beyond, picked up the towel, apparently prepared to offer it to Ms. McGann or even to wrap her in it when she appeared.

The submersible returned to the beach and its hatch opened, the oceanographer emerging with an ear-to-ear grin. As she shook herself like a wet terrier, the king stepped gravely forward, towel spread wide. She bowed, took it, and said cheerfully, "That'll save time on getting the wet suit dry – and then it'll be a dry suit, won't it? Hello again, Mr. Alexander. How kind of you to witness the last day of this incomparable adventure!"

"I gather it's been everything you hoped?"

Briskly drying the suit, she replied, "Well, I could hope to spend even more time, but it's been incredibly productive. If I didn't have so much to do with the data, I'd bend your ear for a week just describing what I've seen and sampled and measured. But if you'd care for it, I'll send you a copy of my report."

Smiling at her, Abe said, "I'd like that very much. But you might want to delay finishing it, given that Their Majesties have informed me that they would permit you to conduct more research, if you're so inclined."

Ms. McGann spun around to face the fae. "My lords! If I weren't disinclined to get sand on my suit, I'd collapse from sheer delight! I'll have to get a handle on what I've already found and figure out where the gaps are, and I'm just about certain there will be gaps enough to justify more work. And if not, I'll find some anyway!"

The queen's and king's laughter made for a marvelous harmony. The king stopped first, saying, "Your conversation has been an unexpected gift. We have rarely, if ever, had such a window into mortal customs pertaining to oceans. I hope that with more time available, you may be able to tell us more."

"Absolutely! But now, if Your Majesties will excuse me, I've got work to do." Ms. McGann inspected herself and, apparently deciding she was dry enough for the moment, strode to what proved to be a path from the shore up the cliff. The king turned back to Abe and said, with an enigmatic smile, "We will meet you at the top." And the two fae vanished.

When Abe and his client reached the top of the cliff, he was panting and she was spry and energetic as a cricket. He stood catching his breath while she bustled off to what appeared to be her campsite and into her tent, probably to take off her suit and don something more comfortable.

And then, a voice from behind him: "Dad?"

He spun around, fatigue forgotten. There stood Adira, with the crooked smile that meant she had too many feelings to encompass in one expression. As if struck dumb, he opened his arms, and she hurtled into them.

He held her tight against him as if holding her could solve everything, could save her from all dangers, could let him bring her home. And then he loosened his hold and stepped back just enough to look her over. He couldn't tell, even so, whether she looked better or worse than the last time he had seen her. She no longer had the deathly pallor that had so dismayed him, but there were lines of strain in her face, as if she were enduring some stress or pain and had been enduring it for too long.

What had they done to her? And what was she doing here – with, he now saw, the young ice fae close at hand?

That fae clearly recognized Abe, stepping backward as if intimidated. Abe smiled in what he hoped was a reassuring manner, if the fae had learned anything of human expressions. Should he bow? It could do no harm. He did, and the fae, with an air of confusion, bowed back before saying in its thin high voice, "I apologize for my behavior before. I should not have left home without permission."

It was hardly Abe's place to absolve the young fae of its hierarchical sins, but he nodded and said, "Of course. I'm glad to see that you've been allowed to travel to other realms in spite of that incident."

"Yes, with your daughter as escort. I am not giving her any trouble." It turned to Adira. "Am I?"

"No, indeed you are not. You have behaved just as you ought," Adira answered with what Abe heard as sincerity, though weariness and sadness lay underneath it. "Dad, did you come to make sure everything had gone well with our oceanographer client? I'd forgotten she might be here. Explorer loves this realm and wanted to spend some more time in it."

"Yes, that's why I came . . . ." He hesitated and then, chest tight, asked the young fae, "Would you excuse me for a moment, to talk to my daughter more privately? Do the terms of her and your obligations allow it?"

It shifted from one twiggy foot to the other as if uncertain. "We need to stay near each other. But I can try not to hear." It demonstrated its meaning by putting its hands on both sides of its head where its ears must be, though none were visible.

Abe looked doubtfully at Adira. "Will it be all right, do you think?"

Adira bit her lip and nodded, moving a couple of yards away. Abe put his arm around Adira again and whispered in her ear, "I had another errand, a work matter with which I've had difficulty. I want to see whether the viscount could assist me, loath as I am to deal with him. I'm guessing you'd rather not be at hand if he appears."

He felt her shudder against him as she shook her head and whispered back, "You're right about that. I'll find something for us to do, away from this spot."

He gave her another hug, murmured, "Stay safe, sweetheart," and let go. Adira took two deep breaths, located the ice fae, and said to it cheerfully, "Let's go down to the shoreline, if Their Majesties don't mind. There's nothing like seeing the waves rush toward you from up close."

The regal pair nodded their permission, and Adira led her charge down the path Abe had just ascended. When they were well out of sight, Abe said heavily to the ocean fae, "Whenever it pleases you, Your Majesties, I'm ready to proceed."

The ocean rulers had gone off together to contact the viscount in whatever manner they had decided to do so. Abe stood watching the breakers roll in and retreat, waiting for the rulers to return, breathing in time with the waves as an impromptu form of meditation.

"My *dear* Alexander! What an unexpected pleasure."

The voice came from behind him. Abe turned around and bowed low. "Lord Bloomingshire. I had hoped you would be available to meet me."

The viscount had arrayed itself in a particularly colorful outfit, a sky-blue topcoat with long tails, open to reveal broad violet and pink stripes. Its neck cloth was so stiff and high that it should have restricted the movements of the viscount's head, though it somehow failed to do so. Abe suspected the fae had chosen one of its most outrageous glamours for the pleasure of watching Abe try not to respond to the fact. Raising its quizzing glass and peering through it at Abe, it drawled,

"I understand you may wish to speak to others of my people, or to visit our realm. I may be failing to recall, but would this not be the first time you expressed any such interest?"

Choosing his words with extreme care, Abe replied, "I would not have contemplated such an intrusion merely to satisfy my curiosity. Indeed, if you are willing for us to conduct our business without such a journey, I am of course content for us to do so. But I am sufficiently ignorant of the customs of your realm that I thought it possible my visiting there might prove helpful."

The viscount smirked, a relief after its more hostile expressions in the recent past. "How pleasant to hear that my past efforts have met with your satisfaction! Do explain what it is you wish for me or my fellows to do for you."

The king and queen had returned in the viscount's wake and stood benignly by. Only then did Abe realize that he had sought their intervention without telling them his purpose, let alone offering them the first opportunity to buy the dream themselves. Whether sensing Abe's discomfort or conforming to some faerie etiquette, the king said, "We will leave you to your discussion. Mr. Alexander, should your business with the viscount take you elsewhere, we look forward to our next meeting."

Abe bowed low and hoped the posture concealed his flush of embarrassment. The god and goddess vanished, and the huge waves appeared and then rapidly receded toward the horizon. Abe returned his attention to the viscount, who was watching him as if fully aware of his discomfiture and enjoying it.

"My business today involves a dream . . . ." Abe was relieved to see the viscount's indolent air give way to avid interest as he described the details. When he finished, the viscount clasped its gloved hands dramatically together and said, "But how marvelous! Markers for mortals who have died? Lingering images of them, as if they could survive their mortality? And mortal animals as well! We simply *must* see it." It raised its quizzing glass again, suggesting Abe had betrayed surprise. "My dear sir, can you possibly have thought that among all the residents of my country, only I am interested in mortals and their habits? You must, you simply must, accompany me there and see for yourself. Though I admit I pride myself on my acute understanding of your world's Regency period clothing and accouterments."

There was nothing truthful Abe could say in response, and any other comment was out of the question. He bowed his head in ambiguous acknowledgment of the viscount's boast, and awaited transport to a realm apparently filled with ardent students of mortals like himself.

The viscount brought him to what looked like a marketplace, its stalls filled with all kinds of human bric-a-brac – spools of thread, wooden and steel and silver spoons, picture frames, bicycle tires, dog collars, embroidered waistcoats such as the viscount wore – perhaps his outfits were not all glamour, after all? – crude and elaborate rocking horses, wooden pencils, wristwatches from a variety of eras, thick leather-bound tomes, atlases, cheap and expensive editions of paperbacks, electrical wires, cowboy hats, shoes, jewelry, children's pajamas, bottles of medicine. Abe imagined that the viscount and others of his ilk would find the medicine deliciously ironic, and pictured them pretending to drink it and asking each other gleefully if it had rendered them immortal, as humans no doubt hoped would be its effect.

The shoppers turned to stare at them as they passed through, the viscount radiating smugness at the reaction. Abe gave little bows in all directions. At last they reached the far end of the market, which gave onto a boulevard as broad as the Champs Elysees. At its end stood a palace combining architectural features from a bewildering range of countries and periods, from spires to onion domes to expanses of glass to modest red brick. A wrought-iron gate, painted white, blocked their way, flanked by two impassive guards considerably shorter than Abe and dressed like those at Buckingham Palace. The viscount airily announced, "A visitor for the emperor and empress!" The guards silently opened the gates and turned to gaze once more at the empty road ahead of them.

The palace doors opened of, apparently, their own accord, revealing an entry hall filled with enough furniture to render it a maze. The viscount steered Abe to an overstuffed armchair upholstered in pink brocade and instructed him to sit. "I'll report your most intriguing offer to their Imperial Majesties. Unless I miss my guess, they'll summon you forthwith."

The viscount would never, in any realm Abe had visited or imagined, be called laconic. Abe was therefore not surprised to be kept waiting for perhaps fifteen minutes, though it would have been rude of him to look at his watch. He passed the time by imagining all the items in his house that might sell well in the market – only to stop, appalled, when the photo albums came to mind.

The viscount finally returned, now clad in a less flamboyant outfit of black coat, black breeches, and snowy white waistcoat, with a dangling silver quizzing glass. Interesting – perhaps the fae had changed before actually attending its audience with the rulers, in conformance with some royal dictate. Abe glanced down at his own clothing, to which he had given no thought beyond finding something not conspicuously in need of washing. It was at least neutral in color, gray slacks and a white button-down shirt with professorial tweed blazer.

Should he have somehow procured a tie, possibly at the market? Too late now. The viscount was beckoning, with an impatience suggesting it had done so once already. "Come, my good man! You are called into the imperial presence. Pray do not waste the opportunity."

The room in which the emperor and empress held their audiences was vast, with high ceilings and many multi-branched chandeliers spaced so closely together that the tall flames of their candles almost overlapped. Their Imperial Majesties, both dressed in ornately embroidered versions of the viscount's attire, sat side by side in plushly upholstered thrones rising high above the polished parquet floor. They proved to be the smallest fae Abe had encountered in this realm, less than four feet tall and petite in build, with an alert air that reminded him of chickadees. The viscount ushered him in, performing an obeisance that involved spreading its coattails and combining elements of a bow and curtsy, before taking a position to the empress's right. Abe bowed as low as he was able and held the bow until the empress said, in an incongruously deep voice, "Rise, sir – or should I say, 'At ease?'" It beamed in pleasure at, he presumed, its own knowledge of human customs. In case it knew more about military training than he thought likely, he assumed the appropriate posture, though bending at the knees a trifle more than a young and physically fit member of the army would do.

The emperor leaned forward eagerly and said, "Our courtier has given Us your description of the dream you offer, but of course no words can truly convey its nature and quality. Show Us!"

It felt painfully incongruous to conjure up that dream of wistful peace and gentle twilight in the blazing brightness of the audience hall, but Abe put aside his inconvenient scruples and obeyed. This time, Abe paid attention to his audience rather than to the dream with which he sought to entice them. The emperor leaned even farther forward, almost to the point of toppling off its throne; the empress clasped its hands and then produced a white silver-embroidered handkerchief as if to dab away the tears it was incapable of shedding. Abe looked last at the viscount, and for the first time saw no trace of condescension, amusement, or hostility. It looked, instead, like a young boy confronting his first elephant, or perhaps a first view of the Milky Way in a wilderness night sky.

As the dream ended with a final aged-looking ghost stroking a fawn, Abe waited for one of the fae to break the silence. He was about to give in to impatience and ask for their reactions when the empress sighed dramatically and said, "How unutterably lovely. Lord Bloomingshire tells Us that such scenes may not actually take place?"

Abe, finding unexpected sorrow rise up in him, swallowed and said, "I believe not, Your Imperial Majesty.

Though there have been many mortals, in many places and times, who have claimed to see ghosts, most often in places the living person had frequented."

The emperor scooted back in its throne, barely, and declared with great satisfaction, "Then if We purchase this dream, Our realization of it would not only feature customs uniquely important to mortals, but sights Our fellow Fair Folk could not simply travel to mortal realms to see. Excellent." But then it grew more sober in mien and turned to the empress and the viscount. "Of course, it is essential to take proper precautions. Lord Bloomingshire, you know this mortal well. Do you believe he will include all the necessary provisions in any agreement he prepares?"

The viscount bowed, with less flourish than usual, and replied, "My role has been more a matter of introducing him to various Fair Folk than taking part in the ensuing negotiations. However, I have often spoken to the fae who have been involved, sometimes long enough afterward for difficulties to have presented themselves, and none of them has expressed any serious dissatisfaction."

While Abe absorbed the fact that the viscount had, in essence, been collecting reviews of his and Adira's performance, and would doubtless have spread any problematic ones far and wide, the emperor nodded and said, "This time We wish you to represent us in all pertinent discussions, as Our responsibilities require Our continual attention." Its gaze flicked over to Abe, as if to catch him revealing any reluctance. Abe, long accustomed to guarding his expression, hoped he presented only a sedate willingness for the viscount's assistance.

"Very good," said the emperor. "Lord Bloomingshire, you may conduct these negotiations at your convenience. Keep Us informed."

Abe would not have called the viscount a being notable for its straightforward approach, but when they sat down in a book-lined, somewhat stuffy chamber to begin their negotiations, he found the being even more cryptic and elusive than he had expected. When he was able to get past the initial layer of obfuscation, he found that the first obstacle had to do with which mortals would be allowed to visit the embodied dream. He thought at first that he must be misunderstanding. "Can you be saying that Adira and other mortals, even strangers, would be allowed to go there, but that I would be excluded?"

The viscount gave him an encouraging smile, like a teacher whose slow-witted student has finally managed to master the alphabet. "Why, yes, Mr. Alexander, that is exactly what I was hoping to convey!"

Abe took that in, reminding himself that there was nothing particularly important about this proposed transaction. He had, after all, undertaken it primarily to occupy his mind in the hope that some inspiration for helping Adira would strike him while he focused on other things. But he found himself stubbornly unwilling to comply with such a condition. It had been, after all, his dream, the fruit of his own desires and sorrows, even his unconscious and unexamined hopes. If he agreed never to visit after its realization was supposedly complete, how could he know what changes the fae might make to it?

He rolled his neck around to work out the stiffness and said, in an apologetic tone that little reflected his feelings, "I'm afraid, Lord Bloomingshire, that I cannot agree to such a condition. I could, however, countenance a set number of visits after the realm is complete, visits limited in time. Will that satisfy their Imperial Majesties, and avoid disappointing them with a failure to come to an agreement?"

The viscount took an unnervingly long time to answer him, and Abe could not help remembering the anger and malice the fae had revealed when springing the trap in which Adira remained caught. But then it shook its head and said in a tone of reluctant admiration, "Of course I did not expect to have every point decided as I could wish, not with the mortal who has negotiated with fae of every description and prevailed! . . . I believe my masters would be able to accept three visits – you know, I am sure, our fondness for that number – spread over one of your weeks, subject to supervision at our discretion and lasting no more than a third of an hour. What say you, sir?"

Abe gave a small seated bow and said, "I am glad to find you prepared to show flexibility in this matter. But my lord, I must inform you that if the visits are to be limited to three, they must be spread over a considerably longer span of time. . . ."

By the time they had agreed on five visits, the first two visits two days apart and the last three at intervals of one, two, and finally three weeks, lasting twenty minutes apiece, Abe could no longer ignore his hunger and fatigue. He stood up, drawing a quizzical expression from the viscount, and said, "Please pardon me, my lord. I am not able to continue without food and rest. Shall we resume tomorrow morning, as my realm marks the time?"

The viscount rose as well, its manner all that was solicitous. "But of course, dear sir! I apologize for detaining you so long. A recess will be most opportune, as I can relate the details of our discussions to the emperor and empress and receive any additional instructions those details may prompt. Let us meet again in three days' time."

Suddenly Abe remembered the precautions he had intended to take, based on what Clara had told him of Scottish lore. "I apologize, my lord, but I have just recalled a provision that we must include. If there is any way that your ownership or possession of this dream could be used to exercise any power over me, power of any kind, then our contract must state that neither your rulers nor anyone else in this realm will exercise that power."

The viscount raised one manicured eyebrow. "But of course, my dear sir." Its expression was unaccountably amused.

It did not appear that Abe was expected to bid their Imperial Majesties farewell, and he was just as glad. He might have stumbled in some way, and that could have repercussions beyond the business of this particular bargain. He would go home, and ponder whether the unexpectedly complicated matter of selling a dream to the fae – even fae so obsessed with mortal ways – could shed any light at all on his more pressing problem.

CHAPTER 13

CLARA returned to the hostel after a warm rainy day filled with long conversations and longer walks. As soon as she arrived, she hung up her raincoat to dry and sought out the small office available to the guests on a first-come-first-serve basis. She found it occupied: a girl with a wild and gorgeous tangle of turquoise hair was scrolling through some website in a leisurely manner. Clara privately admired the girl's hair while inquiring politely how long she expected to be using the office. The girl looked at Clara, the screen, and Clara again, finally replying, "In a while?"

It was just as well, Clara reminded herself. She did need a shower. "I'll be back in a bit, then," she said firmly, and went to grab her robe and towel.

She resisted the urge to take her shower in record time. The girl might not be done yet. On the other hand, someone else might duck in ahead of Clara when the girl left . . . Clara rinsed off hurriedly and gave her hair only the most cursory squeeze to dry it before hanging up the towel and hustling to her locker. She extracted her laptop and the large envelope bulging with papers, doublechecking to make sure none had somehow migrated to the locker's depths.

The office was empty this time. Clara went in, closed the door, and emptied the envelope out on the splintered wooden desk, smiling in welcome at the notes that spilled out. Those notes, restored, gave her back years of work, or at least the assurance that she need no longer trust her memory for what those years had taught her.

She opened her laptop and made a new document: *Highlights from Old Notes*. She would leaf through the pages quickly before starting at the beginning and choosing what to record.

On the third page, a blurry set of fingerprints made her stop and catch her breath.

She remembered helping Adira make those fingerprints. It had been Clara's turn to stay with Adira while Abe did interviews. The last two days had been hot enough to discourage even Adira from playing outside, and their hut had little room to move around in. Modeling clay, coloring books, and colorful beaded dolls had held the child's attention through that morning, but by afternoon she was bored with those options. "Umama, I want to do what *you're* doing!"

Their supplies of paper were running low, but Clara could spare a sheet or two. "Would you like to write up your research, the way I'm doing?"

"Umama! You know I can't write!"

Indeed – and it showed an interesting self-awareness that Adira knew and acknowledged as much. "Hmmm. All right, then – would you like to put something in *my* notes?" A drawing would inevitably take up a good deal of room . . . . "I know! You can put your fingerprints here, in the margin, and then we'll always remember that you were here today, wanting to help. All right?"

Adira pursed her lips. "What's a finger-print?"

"I'll show you." Clara fetched some blue paint almost the same color as the ink she was using and painted the index and middle fingers on Adira's right hand. Adira giggled, and Clara guessed that full-scale fingerpainting lay in their future as she guided Adira in pressing those fingers on the paper, holding the little hand steady so the paint wouldn't smear . . . .

A drop of water fell just beside the small blotch of paint, and Clara hastily fished out a tissue to blot the tear before it spread and caused damage. She clenched her teeth to make sure no more tears would come, then relaxed her jaw, stroked the fingerprints, and turned the page.

* * * * *

The ice rulers had not given Adira a deadline by which she must return Explorer to their control, and the two travelers shared a similar dread of that prospect. She showed Explorer realms she had visited and enjoyed, so long as nothing in their nature seemed problematic. Explorer had overheard a few cryptic hints of unfamiliar realms, but so far those fragments had not been enough for Adira to find what they described.

They returned several times to the familiar ocean realm, which Explorer adored – until it began to find the waves' restless motion and turbulent energy exhausting, and Adira would seek the slower changes of the sunset realm. Or they would travel to forest realms, once Adira had asked the ocean rulers and been assured that not all such realms forbade ice fae to enter. Explorer had never witnessed or conceived of spring, and the Spring Court had gardens in which visitors could see the season progress at whatever pace they chose. Both Adira and Explorer delighted in the stately shifts of the leaves from yellow-green to purer green, crocuses peeking out of new grass, and the appearance one by one of the taller daffodils. Nor did daffodils wilt as quickly as they came, only doing so when blossoming fruit trees demanded attention. As they approached what looked like a crabapple tree and saw deep pink blossoms appear before their eyes, Explorer clapped its twiggy hands together with a clacking sound and exclaimed, "Oh, this is so much better than home!"

Adira stiffened and stopped short. Explorer must have spent enough time with her to understand at least that much of her body language. It uttered a shrill whine and said, "Something is wrong! Are you hurt?"

Adira took deep breaths until the surge of anger and exasperation and grief subsided. The scent of blossoms made it more difficult, but she finally mastered herself and replied, "I am as well as I can be. And this is indeed a more pleasant place, for me, than your own realm. As for my home, it is similar in some ways and different in others, but at this moment, I would rather be there than any other realm I have seen or could imagine."

Explorer whined again, more softly, and then hushed. Adira closed her eyes and said, "Let's move on."

They visited the realm where all the trees and moss and ferns had colors from palest pink to deepest magenta, the trees occasionally dropping their leaves on rocks and streams for variety. There was even a realm somewhat like the firefly-lit dusk of the realm the ice fae were forbidden to visit, with the lights glimmering from beneath fallen gray-purple leaves and the twilight matching the leaves in a darker hue.

That forest reminded Adira of her father's description of his dream. Back at the Ocean Realm, while Explorer played tag with the breakers, she mentioned the fact to the rulers as they swooped and dived near her in their gull glamours. She added idly, "I wonder if Dad ever tried to sell that dream. He talked about trying to."

The gulls flew closer together, hovering in mid-air, and then descended to assume their Greek-god forms. The king held both hands in front of him and raised them up; three sculpted seats arose from the sand, two side by side and one facing them. The rulers took their seats and motioned for Adira to do the same. Mystified and a little nervous, she complied, glad her seat faced the water's edge where Explorer had taken to collecting seashells.

The rulers looked at each other and back at Adira with unreadable expressions. The Amphitrite figure spoke first, saying, "Has your father made such attempts before?"

"I don't know. We've never done it together, but I don't know if he sold a dream or tried to sell one before I joined him. Is there some reason he shouldn't?"

The Poseidon figure shook its imposing head. "It is not forbidden, but it is fraught with difficulties. You know, do you not, that with all the enchantments at our command, we cannot dream, nor reproduce a dream unassisted in order to add it to our realms?"

Adira glanced over at Explorer, now arranging the shells it had gathered into some sort of picture, before saying, "I did know that. Does it . . . annoy many fae, or offend them, for mortals to remind them of that fact?"

The goddess smiled. "Indeed it may, though only the most vain would see the offer in that light. No, the complexities lie elsewhere. And if you or your father intend to market mortal dreams, you should learn about those complexities."

Just then, Explorer came up to where they sat, dragging its feet in the sand. "Valentina, could we go somewhere else for a while? Someplace quiet?"

The god and goddess stood, and the goddess took the young fae's hand, paying no apparent mind to the cold of it. "There's another forest realm, one where the trees are tall and have white trunks, and the leaves are all yellow and gold. It might appeal to you."

The ice fae perked up immediately. "Yellow! I love yellow. Please, Valentina, let's go there!" It let go of the ocean fae's hand and reached for hers. She took it, pausing only to say, "I hope we can continue our discussion when we next return."

"Of course," said the king. "And if we see your father before that time, we will discuss the subject with him."

Adira's curiosity, starved for lack of nourishment these past weeks, as well as her concern for her father made it hard to wait. But her duty lay elsewhere, and she followed it.

Adira and Explorer spent hours in the realm of the yellow leaves, with its unending meandering rows of white-trunked trees. She wondered idly whether the trees were based on birches, the whitest, straightest trees she knew, though these reached a far greater height than any birch ever achieved. She had little else to think about as they wandered the long narrow paths, or at least little else pleasant. She still had her hunger, which would stab at her suddenly just when she thought she had grown accustomed to it, and her future, of which interludes such as this one were the best she could have any confidence in anticipating.

Explorer, when it finally became bored with that realm, was not yet interested in returning to the ocean. She had a sense, based on she knew not what, that it might be growing homesick again, but she dreaded returning to the ice realm. Once they spotted her there, the rulers might decide she and the young fae should not be allowed to go wandering again. What other realms had Abe told her of, during the years she waited eagerly to be old enough to see for herself? Was there one more familiar to Explorer than this one, but yet offering some novelty and excitement?

Yes ... yes ... that might do. She donned an encouraging smile, though she still couldn't say what her charge would make of it. "How would you like to go somewhere with ice, but nothing like your lake? Ice reaching far up the side of a mountain, in blues and greens, with a blue-green lake below and clouds above, clouds that look like a whole other realm themselves?"

The young fae bounced in excitement. Where had it picked that up? In the School Realm, perhaps? Maybe they could go there again. For now, she took the fae's reaction as consent and whisked them away.

Adira's travels through faerie realms, and especially her present circumstances, had somewhat dulled her capacity for wonder. But the awe-inspiring sight of the glacier, cascading in centuries-long slow motion down the jagged black mountain, its base plunging into the milky blue-green waters of the lake, its heights far beyond her sight, almost stopped her breath – and that was before she saw the reflection in the lake, far clearer than an actual glacial lake could have shown it, and with mysterious swirls of dark cloud circling the reflected peaks. On the upper slopes of the glacier, figures so small she could see nothing of their nature speckled the ice, clustered together or moving even farther upward.

Explorer drank in the glorious vista and then reached toward the glacier, as if hoping to touch the icy surface. Finding that its finger reached across no appreciable distance, it made a petulant noise, rather like wind forcing its way through some small fissure, and asked, "Can we get closer?"

"I wonder. Let me try something." She had never used a portal to move from one part of a realm to another, but her former escort had done so. She visualized a spot just to one side of where the glacier touched land, stepped with Explorer through the portal . . . and they were there. The ice fae let out a shrill ear-piercing sound and sprinted toward the ice sheet.

Which was how she, and perhaps Explorer, learned that it could somehow climb ice.

Watching the fae scramble upward, she suddenly realized that it was far out of her reach, unless she attempted another short transport onto a surface where she had no way to anchor herself. She brushed aside her unease as best she could. As far as she knew, the fae could not create its own portal, and even if it climbed out of sight, it would eventually return when it was ready for new amusements. In the meantime, she could try to guess what was so complicated about selling dreams to Fair Folk. Did the dream reconstructions fade away too soon, the way real dreams did? Or did they include stray threads of nonsense that an actual dream might include, though the dreamer forgot them upon waking? Could the fae prune away such fragments?

Tired of speculating and tired in general, Adira sat down cautiously on the narrow shelf of rock between the mountain and the lake. She had never been able to meditate as such, but perhaps she could gaze up at the heights, or into the depths of the lake, and lose herself for a time.

She must have succeeded to some extent, because she had no sense of how long it took until movement caught her eye, not on the upper reaches but lower and moving down. With impressive speed, the ice fae descended until, with a whining sound of effort, it leaped free of the glacier and landed close beside her, saying, "That was wonderful! Now I'm ready for the ocean again. Will you take me there?"

Adira stood up and brushed herself off to dislodge any pebbles or fragments of ice. "Certainly. I'll be glad to see it again." Or, more precisely, to see its rulers, and to continue their conversation.

When they first stepped into the ocean realm, Adira could find no sign of their hosts, neither as waves nor seals nor pipers nor gulls nor any other possible form. There were only the everyday-sized waves rolling into shore and ebbing away, and the salty breeze, and the short grasses of the cliff. Explorer scampered happily down the path to the shore, leaving Adira to follow as fast as felt anything like safe.

Explorer paused briefly to admire a good-sized spiral shell, swirled in subdued blues and deep browns. Adira looked at it in her turn and was startled to see scaly feelers sticking out of it and wriggling at her. She crouched hastily to slip to her knees beside it. At worst, she would be kneeling to one of the creatures that inhabited the realm, with who knew what qualities of mind. But when another shell sprouted similar limbs and dragged itself up next to the first, she was fairly sure she had guessed aright.

From the first shell came an echoing voice that sounded as if it had bounced around inside the shell before emerging. "Did we surprise you this time?"

Adira laughed and replied, "Indeed you did, Your Majesty! How delightful to be reminded how much I still have to discover, in your realm and elsewhere."

From the second shell came a similar but lower voice. "But you can't be comfortable, kneeling like that . . . You may want to step back a few paces." Adira scrambled to her feet and complied, and was not, this time, surprised to see the hermit crabs vanish and the two enormous waves rush toward her and stop just outside the breakers. The ice fae jumped backward before moving down the beach to resume its game of tag with the surf. Adira bowed and waited.

The rulers changed form yet again, this time assuming their harp seal shape and wriggling in the direction opposite to where the ice fae had gone. "It occurs to us," said the larger of the two, "that what we wish to tell you might be better kept between us, which will be easier if we are no longer looming so large."

Adira swallowed and said, "Certainly, Your Majesties, though I must keep Explorer within view. I will be glad of anything you can tell me about the sale and purchase of dreams, and why my father should expect the process to be challenging."

The seals moved a ways up on the beach, beyond the reach of the waves. "Sit, if you will," said the smaller one, "and we will explain." She did so, leaning back on her arms and glad to be able to stretch out her legs. Then, wondering if the pose was too casual, she shifted into sitting tailor fashion and sat up as straight as she could. Once she stopped fidgeting and was still, the larger seal asked, "What do you know about the kind of transactions we speak of?"

"Very little," Adira admitted. "I know that it's possible, which it wouldn't be between mortals. And that the fae who buy a dream turn it into something, like a realm but smaller, a sort of preserve that they and other fae – and mortals, I think, if they're allowed – can visit and see."

"All that is true, as far as it goes," said the seal in its hoarse bark. "And you may assume that only favored mortals, or those who have rendered service to the fae in question, would be allowed to visit. But there is another factor, one that has to do with the connection between the dreamer and the dream."

Adira held her breath, then let it out as the seal appeared to hesitate. It was the smaller seal that spoke next. "If we go on, if we give you the knowledge you lack, it may affect whether fae – even we – will be willing to purchase dreams from you in the future."

The immediate future, in particular her father's, mattered more. She said as much, and added, "I've never seriously considered it, and now that I do, I don't think I'd want to sell any of my dreams. Mortals require varying levels of privacy to feel comfortable, and I prefer quite a lot. I'd rather describe a dream to a few friends, at most, than to set it loose, as it were, for who knows who to – " She almost said *to gawk at*. "To walk through or look at for the rest of my life and beyond."

"Very well, then," said the seal. "This connection we speak of could be better described as a power. A power the dreamer holds over the dream, or rather over the separate realm built from the dream, so long as the dreamer is present within it."

Adira could feel her heart racing as she asked, "Can you tell me more about this power, what the dreamer could do?"

Another pause. She more than half expected the fae to refuse to tell her anything else. The answer, when it came, surprised her more. "There have not been many transactions in dreams since the fae realized this power existed. For that reason, we cannot be certain we know its full extent. We do know the dreamer can alter the dream, in the absence of a promise not to do so. There are tales of dreamers creating something entirely new, not based in the dream at all, in the realm given over to the dream, but these tales are never told by a fae who has seen it happen, and no fae has admitted to having been involved."

The other seal spoke next, in as close to a whisper as a harp seal could produce. "It is also said that the dreamer, always a mortal of course, may leave the dream realm to return home whenever it will, even if it has no fae escort and has not been dismissed. We cannot say whether any mortal has ever used such a power to travel from that realm to another fae realm. It seems likely that even if the mortal could do this, it could go nowhere else from the second realm, but even that is more than we are sure of."

Could Adira sell a dream to the ice fae, and then use this power to leave their realm behind forever? Aside from all the uncertainties, it might be seen as breaking her word, a fatal breach of the rules binding any human dealing with the Fair Folk. Besides, would so unbending and dour a people have any interest? She could at least ask: "Have you ever heard tell of the ice fae purchasing a dream?"

The seals both shook their whiskered heads.

The ocean rulers had apparently not told Dad any of this, unless it had happened since her last visit. Would he have had any chance to learn it? In case he hadn't, was there any way for her to reach him?

Adira got to her feet in order to give the fae a proper bow. "I am enriched by the knowledge you have shared."

The seals tossed their heads in what might have been some return gesture. In an instant, it was the ocean gods standing before her, and then nothing, until the giant waves appeared again, crashed down in a maelstrom of froth, receded, and were gone.

Once her nerves settled, Adira went back to hunting for seashells, alert this time for any more fae manifestations. She had found a clam shell lined with the iridescent sheen of mother-of-pearl and a delicate crescent shell before the ice fae approached her and said, "I'm ready to go somewhere else now. Do you have any ideas of a place I'd like to see?"

"Let me think for a minute." Adira looked out over the waves, trying to remember. It was imperative, now, to try to find Dad. In what realms had they had unfinished business, before all these disruptive events had befallen them? There was that case of the changeling for whom a client wanted to substitute another child . . . but she had no idea how that case had progressed in her absence. Nor was the Autumn Court a safe, or reliably hospitable, destination. She could not take the ice fae there.

If her father had completed the negotiations and delivered the foster child to the fae, that child would know nothing of his – its? – no, his new world. Might the Fair Folk wish to provide the child with an appropriate education? Did the School Realm include anything like a kindergarten or nursery? And if it did, might Dad go there, if he could, to see how the child was weathering the transition? The odds were slim, but she had nothing to lose by trying.

She looked back at the ice fae and said, trying for a persuasive tone, "You had to leave the School Realm before you had seen that much of it, or learned everything you could. Would you like to go back there and see more of what it had to offer, or meet more of the other young fae?"

Explorer looked down at its branching equivalent of toes and dug them into the sand. "The ice fae teacher might wonder what I'm doing there."

"We don't have to go into that building. And if we do encounter that teacher, I can whisk you right away again, or we can stay and I can explain that I'm escorting you, whichever you prefer."

The fae looked up at her, its minimal expression somehow conveying a trust that brought a lump to her throat. "Let's go, then. I know you'll take care of me."

Adira and Explorer landed in the School Realm just where she had hoped not to land, almost directly in front of the school for ice fae. Aligned in intention, the two of them hurried away almost stride for stride, Adira steering them toward a stretch of buildings arranged by color, each one next to its neighbor on the color wheel. They approached a building painted bright yellow, Explorer hurrying toward it and stretching out its arms as if basking in sunshine. After standing there for a few minutes, it pointed to the door and said, "I want to go inside! Will you come and ask them if I may?"

"Of course." She opened the door, waved the fae in, and followed immediately after. Inside, the room was lined with what looked like sunflowers. The majority of the pupils bore a glamour like giant honeybees, and did not sit but flitted about in circles. As Adira entered, the teacher, who had been making a gentle buzzing sound, shifted abruptly to an angry whine more like a hornet whose nest had been attacked.

Adira made haste to bow almost to the ground, and said even as she straightened up, "Your pardon, gentle fae, for our intrusion. I come at the request of this young fae to ask if it may visit your school, as it longs to do. I will withdraw immediately if you wish."

The whine grew less piercing and became speech. "Of course this young fae may attend the class for a short time, so long as you remove yourself. Do so at once."

The ice fae glanced back at her with an air of apology. She smiled to reassure it and backed out the door.

Now what? She could not search the entire School Realm for her father, or even wander out of sight of the building from which the ice fae would at some point emerge. The best she could do was investigate the nearest schoolhouses and hope that one of them – perhaps the green one, its color like spring leaves – might prove to be devoted to young children.

The green schoolhouse, as she might have predicted, contained children from tree and garden realms. Heading to the other side of the yellow building and trying the orange one proved more fruitful, its students all appearing to be the equivalent of toddlers and preschool children. But of course, she didn't find Dad there. The chance had been vanishingly small. She could wait until Explorer grew bored, but it would make little difference. She looked toward the sunflower school again and saw movement at the door. The being that emerged was nothing like a bee, but it didn't look like Explorer – the colors, brownish and drab, were wrong, the silhouette wider, and the stride longer and looser.

By the time Adira reached the schoolhouse, the figure she had seen had vanished and Explorer was walking out the door. It greeted her with excitement. "The students were learning all about how to fly and drink honey. I wish I could do that! Maybe if I practiced that glamour, I could do it another time. Just as I was thinking I should go, another fae looked in. The teacher didn't like it much more than it liked you – "

Explorer stopped and looked down in obvious embarrassment. Adira laughed and said, "Please don't fret. I know very well that it didn't care for a human in its classroom. What was this other fae like?"

"It was as tall as I am, but I couldn't tell much more than that, because it was wearing something that stood out all around it – not stiff, because I saw whatever it was ripple and change shape, but still taking up a lot of space. When the teacher told the fae to leave, it stopped and talked to me on its way out, saying that I was welcome to visit its realm, that I'd find it much more lively and interesting than where I must have come from. Can we go there?"

Adira wrinkled her forehead. "That doesn't give us very much to go on. It didn't say what its realm was called, or anything else about how to find it?"

"I guess not," Explorer admitted reluctantly. "But we can try, surely?"

Adira patted its hand. "Yes, we can certainly try."

CHAPTER 14

ABE HAD three days to wait before the next negotiating session with the viscount. He spent the first of them seeing to his practice, starting by visiting the garden enhanced by Fair Folk enchantments. The gardener, quite at ease with him since the bluebell missions to the Forest Realm, was delighted to show him around, repeatedly offering him one or another fruit or vegetable – not only the original tomatoes, but pumpkins, beans, sweet peas, strawberries, and grapes all benefiting from the spell. Abe explained again, for perhaps the fourth time, that any human even sampling such would be taking unknown and possibly grave risks. Only the samples intended for judging at the county fair had been guaranteed free of such effects. Imagining how many other visitors might have received similar offers, he cajoled the gardener into giving him a list of those visitors, and vowed to check up on them.

Abe then contacted the senior aide for the politician being guarded by fae security. He should have inquired earlier, but he would probably have heard, at high volume, if there had been any trouble which the security failed to avert – or caused. Fortunately the report amounted to "so far, so good," protesters and any would-be assassins having either failed to materialize or taken the measure of the man's escort and kept their distance. When Abe had ended that call and made another to the oceanographer, ecstatic about her data but too busy analyzing it to chat long, it was time for two tasks he both longed for and dreaded. He procrastinated by leaving the office for home, but all too soon he was settled in front of his home computer.

First, he wrote an email to Clara.

My most beloved wife,
How is Thailand? I'm glad you've finally made it there, after all the times we discussed it and even planned itineraries that were somehow derailed by events. Have you been delving into the darker tales? I know you'll tell me at once if you find anything I'd want to know.

After sharing the few details of his cases that fell outside the bounds of confidentiality and might amuse her, he edged closer to what mattered.

I'm doing as well as either of us can reasonably expect. I miss you terribly, but I'm glad you took my advice to get back to your own work. It'll do you good even if it has no immediate payoff for us. There's no knowing what will turn out to be a clue, in my work as well as yours. I certainly have plenty to learn about the customs and concerns of the Fair Folk, and have been learning some small part of it in recent days as I've been trying to sell that dream of mine. It turns out the viscount comes from a realm full of people similarly obsessed with humans, and its rulers are eager to buy.

Let's talk soon. Hearing your voice is no substitute for your presence, but it's a precious privilege, one I appreciate the more when you're far away. Be well, sweetheart, and if you're so inclined, pray for our daughter and for your baffled but determined
Abe

Next, he wrote a letter to Adira, one he had no way to send her. He could have made it an email instead, but he was unreasonably terrified of accidentally hitting "Send," as if the lack of a response would take on some special significance. He could write a letter and then save it, keeping it close as if it would somehow bring Adira closer.

He had to be careful not to turn it into a journal, confiding or confessing things she would rather not hear.

Dearest Adira,
In the midst of all my fears for you, I know that you are a brave, brilliant, resilient, and resourceful woman, and that you will withstand the difficulties you face at least as well as I would if our positions were reversed. I nevertheless wish with all my soul that they were. Parents don't stop wanting to protect and aid their children, no matter how many years have passed since those children outgrew any special need for it.
I'm confident that when you are finally free to come home and to take up our work again, you will bring to that endeavor knowledge gained by your experience, and which neither of us would have been likely to gain any other way.

And that was as much hope and confidence as he could muster, or even pretend to find in his heart. He turned away from the keyboard and stumbled to the kitchen for a drink. Ale, maybe, or port. Or even gin, and he hated gin.

Abe had thought the viscount might keep him waiting for more than the three days mentioned, but it appeared so early on the appropriate morning that Abe had barely arrived at the office and had not even started the coffee. It had abandoned its more sober garb and now presented a dazzling, even disorienting, array of colors and embroidery to Abe's sleep-fuddled gaze.

Deciding, or rationalizing, that it would improve his negotiating position if he asserted himself, Abe welcomed the fae and told it he would accompany it as soon as the coffee finished percolating and he had drunk a cup. The viscount responded with aplomb, professing an interest in the process and taking apparently appreciative sniffs of both the coffee grounds and the finished product. It declined Abe's offer to taste, however, and as soon as Abe drained his mug and rinsed it in the office sink, the fae manifested a portal composed of windblown silver streamers and invited Abe to step through. Abe did so, with a moment of nervousness that he might end up somewhere altogether unexpected, but he found himself back in the same room, although the books lining it appeared to have changed in appearance and arrangement.

The viscount seemed even more reluctant, this time, to come to the point. After going over the matters they had already settled, and attempting to win concessions Abe had already declined, it finally folded its long thin fingers and said, "Let us refine, then, what you will be permitted to do during the visits we have already arranged."

Abe would have thought the agenda for those visits fairly obvious, but apparently there was more to it. "What needs to be agreed upon?"

The viscount leaned back in its ornately carved chair as if relaxed, but Abe was almost sure the fae was anything but. It unclasped its hands and ticked off items on its fingers. "First. On your initial visit, the only one for which their Imperial Majesties see any need, you will ensure that the dream is manifested just as you showed it to them, with nothing taken away or added."

Abe replied cautiously, "I cannot make binding promises as to a process that has been under your control, namely making it possible for me to display my dream, nor as to how precisely my memory of the dream – either as I dreamed it, or as their Imperial Majesties viewed it – matches what you will create. But I will scrutinize it carefully, and will tell you about any and all discrepancies I find."

The viscount gave a grunt rather out of keeping with its excessively refined clothing and manner. "That will have to be acceptable. Second. As soon as you confirm that the materialized dream is as complete and accurate as you are able to make it, you will await my escort for your return to your own realm, without . . . any kind of wandering about or disruptive behavior."

Abe suppressed a fleeting wish to see more of the realm, and then decided there was no point in suppression. "I will admit I am curious to see what must be many marvels as fascinating as the market through which we passed. But if your rulers would rather I earn such a privilege in some separate fashion, I will of course accept that decision."

"My dear sir, that is hardly a complete response, is it? Pray continue." The viscount leaned suddenly forward as if unable to continue disguising the intensity of its interest. Abe sensed that somewhere in what the viscount had said or was about to say was a clue, one he must not miss.

Until he puzzled out what it was, he must promise as little as possible. But he had already learned that at least one inhabitant of this realm could be dangerous when offended. He would have to tread even more attentively than usual. After reviewing what he was about to say as carefully as the situation allowed, he answered, "I agree, then, that I will not intrude uninvited into parts of your realm that I have not, by then, been allowed to see."

The viscount peered at him, while Abe tried to appear only as alert and engrossed as he would for any other contract negotiation. He had the sense that the fae would have liked to press him on some point, but thought it imprudent to do so. After a pause whose length he was in no condition to measure, the viscount touched its next finger and said, "Third. This same condition applies to the later visits we are allowing."

Abe nodded his head as if considering the matter, little as he knew about what required considering. "Very well. The promise I have already made shall apply to the later visits as well."

"Fourth. Except for the visits herein agreed, you will make no attempt to use your portal to return here without express permission, which nothing in these discussions may be understood to include."

For far from the first time, Abe was struck by how much the fae's natural caution and cunning resembled the habits ingrained by legal training. "Agreed."

"Fifth and last." The viscount, rather than moving on to its thumb, had sprouted an additional forefinger. "After we have accepted the fixed and final form of your dream, you will neither alter the dream nor add to it in any way, on your first visit or subsequent visits."

"Agreed." Abe waited for the fae to add any more conditions, its declaration to the contrary notwithstanding. But the viscount arose, with an air of relief that appeared genuine, fluffing its coattails to ensure they lay smooth and bowing to Abe for one of the few times he could remember. "My masters will be pleased with your cooperation. Shall we begin?"

Abe desperately wanted more time to think, to track down that faint impression of some subtext. What could he truthfully say to give himself the time he needed? "My lord, I have cases I should review and perhaps attend to, as well as correspondence unfinished. I would prefer to begin tomorrow, if you and their Imperial Majesties would be so kind."

The viscount shrugged. "Remain here, then, while I consult them." It vanished, leaving Abe to fret. He must avoid the appearance of being uneasy – there was no way to know if he was being observed. To appear as casual as possible, and to pass the time, he got up and approached the nearest of the bookshelves, looking over the gold lettering on the leather-bound spines. He was immediately intrigued. Was there really a book titled *Glimpses in the Gloom: Mortal Tales From Before First Contact*? If it was a true book and not mere set decoration, he and Clara might both find unique revelations inside. Could he take the book off the shelf and look at its contents, or would that be too presumptuous?

He put off decision by looking at the volume beside it, but the words on the spine refused to come into focus, blurring and jumping around as he looked at them. He was rubbing his eyes when the sound of a tapping foot behind him made him start and turn around. It was the viscount, twirling its rainbow-sequined quizzing glass. "Dear Mr. Alexander, would you rather stay and amuse yourself with the collection? And here I just informed their Imperial Majesties that you wished to delay your task, and obtained their gracious permission for you to do so."

"My apologies, Lord Bloomingshire. The treasures of your library distracted me from my purpose, and your return reminds me of it."

Now that he thought of it, the viscount's choice of meeting room might not have been a random one. If one was to prepare a snare for a former folklorist, what could be more ideal? But if there had been any plan to trap him rather than simply to toy with him, the viscount had apparently changed its mind, and he had better not test his luck.

The fae called forth a portal of violet mist and led him through. Abe stepped onto the lawn behind his office with mixed feelings of relief and regret, bid the viscount farewell, watched it vanish through the portal, and almost ran to the door. He needed to sit in familiar surroundings and set himself to figuring out whether there was in fact some crucial information, some knowledge not meant for mortals, almost within his grasp.

Abe spent the next morning writing down everything he could remember about the previous day's negotiations. It would have been better to take detailed notes at the time, but his intuition had told him the frequent interruptions and delays involved would have made the viscount more contrary and intractable. When he finally finished and no revelations had emerged, the energy he derived from an urgent professional task ebbed quickly away, with all the emotions he had temporarily put aside now waiting to swamp him.

He had known for years that when a problem seemed impossible to solve, the best thing was to put it aside and busy himself with other things while his subconscious mind worked on it. This wise advice became almost impossible to follow when solving the problem was absolutely essential. How could he turn aside from the trail, however faint or even illusory, that might lead to a way to bring Adira home? But the glare of his attention was drowning out any trace of that trail. He buried his face in his hands, pressed on his temples until meaningless patterns of light appeared behind his closed eyelids, and fell back in his chair with a groan. Then he hauled himself out of the chair and fetched his list of active cases.

He started by calling the people to whom the gardener had offered samples of his enchanted produce. Their responses, when he spoke to them rather than leaving messages, were not always reassuring, but his responsibility to them was limited, and he had discharged it. Next on the list came Ms. Dellor, the mother who had traded an orphan child for her stolen baby. He had more empathy, these days, for her initial desperation and determination.

If he could, might he not trade some languishing prisoner for his own trapped daughter?

Ms. Dellor accepted his call almost immediately. To his considerable relief, she was in better shape than he had ever seen her: relaxed, well groomed, her cheeks rounded and pink rather than hollow and pale. "Good morning!" she almost sang. "It's good to see you again. I never properly thanked you for all you've done for us."

Abe managed something like a smile, though not the one her words and his own apparent success deserved. "I – we only did our job, and are very gratified to have been able to complete it. How is your little boy doing?"

"See for yourself!" She got up, walked over to a playpen, and returned with a wriggling, healthy baby in her arms. "Isn't he wonderful? *Aren't you wonderful, you sweet boy, you darling thing?*" She bounced the baby in her arms, eliciting a delighted giggle. "You know, I don't think he remembers a thing about it!" She stopped bouncing the baby and held him tighter. "Except when he first wakes up, in the morning or from a nap, he looks around as if something's missing. But I'm probably imagining it, don't you think?"

"Very likely," he said in a low, soothing tone, while privately doubting it.

* * * * *

Clara had made it about two-thirds of the way through her recovered notes. It had started out as a task, but soon become an escape and a pleasure. Not only were the various tales engrossing in themselves, well worth remembering, but many of them called to mind the times and places when she had collected them – cottages and huts and stately centuries-old residences, warm stale air and icy breezes, strong thick coffee and deep red wine.

She stopped reading to stretch, and to contemplate the waning of the day. She would take a walk soon, and then she should really plan her schedule for the next few days. But first, she'd read just one more page.

Halfway down the page, she stopped, looked hard at the words, and read them again. Then she grabbed her laptop to email Abe.

* * * * *

Abe read his notes over for the third time, still unable to pin down what had been behind the viscount's intensity. Was there some knowledge or history concerning transactions in dreams of which Abe was ignorant? How could he learn it?

So framed, the answer to the question leapt to mind. He must visit the Library Realm.

Most realms to which he was allowed to travel were doing business with the firm's clients, or, more rarely, were clients themselves. The Library Realm, however, welcomed anyone that its rulers' magic identified as a book lover. Once a client mentioned the realm's existence, Abe was able to use his portal to reach it, submit himself for inspection, and enter a bibliophile's heaven.

A visitor arrived not on stone steps flanked by sculptures of lions or gryphons or some other imposing creature, but on a meandering cobblestone path leading to a modest storefront resembling a bookshop. The interior was no closer to his initial expectations, which had been along the lines of the Old Library of Dublin's Trinity College, with multiple stories of shelves stretching to the distance on every side and up to a cavernous vaulted ceiling. No, the scale was closer to cozy, if still ultimately uncanny. Whichever way one turned, or however far one walked, one saw a reading room with one-person desks and an array of comfortable-looking armchairs, the latter equipped with tables on each side big enough for an armful of books. Surrounding these small oases, there were indeed shelves of books, arrayed like the spokes of a wheel or the rays of a stylized sun, with large easily read labels on each shelf describing its contents.

Most of the rooms Abe had seen had windows: Earthlike ones looking out on anything from sunlit green fields to a steady fall of large and intricate snowflakes; others showing various fae realms Abe had seen or heard of or even more fantastic sights, eye-watering spirals of pulsating colors, upside-down worlds. Every room had the hushed and peaceful quiet a library should have, and was redolent with the incomparable perfume of leather and old paper even where the books he found looked as if they had been published yesterday. Searches could be conducted according to the technology with which the visitor was most comfortable, the more old-fashioned visitor finding a row of wooden chests containing card catalogs, and those more attuned to the digital having a choice of desktop or laptop computers. And somehow, he could read every one, just as he could understand the speech of realms into which he had been properly invited.

Of course, this library, or these libraries, did not merely contain books penned by mortals. Many, quite possibly most, of the offerings were written by Fair Folk: histories of one or another realm, poetry, and scholarly books like the one that had intrigued him in the viscount's realm. There were, however, no novels from fae authors, or none he had found. That particular form of creativity was either disfavored or beyond Fair Folk capacity.

Abe entered just behind a small group of Fair Folk children, who vanished immediately into some section particularly suitable for their education and enjoyment. He longed for a glimpse of it, but even if he could have been admitted, he had too urgent an errand for such an indulgence. In the years during which the Fair Folk had been purchasing or contemplating the purchase of mortal dreams, surely one or more of them had written down the precautions the purchaser should take, and any powers either the purchaser or the dreamer might otherwise be able to exercise.

He was old enough to have used card catalogs in his youth, then welcomed digital alternatives, and ultimately enjoyed the pleasures of nostalgia when seeing card catalogs again. He accordingly started there, finding the drawers of "D" entries and flipping through to find "dreams." His pulse picked up as he found two books listed. One covered numerous possible transactions with mortals, while the other dealt solely with dreams: what they were, mortals as the exclusive source, what a purchaser should know ahead of time.

Now to find the books. Here, too, the libraries offered options. He could simply walk from shelf to shelf, checking the signage to see their contents; or he could pick up one of the pencils conveniently available in a basket atop the catalog, point it in any direction, and proceed with something like the game of "hot or cold," according to the color and brightness of the pencil tip; or he could look for a librarian to assist him. Seeing no librarian close at hand, he picked up a pencil and followed its guidance.

It took only a few minutes to find the first book, in a shelf devoted to the quirks and habits and varieties of humanity. Collecting it, he kept searching and, with somewhat more difficulty, found the other volume, shoved far back on its shelf and notably thinner than the books surrounding it. He looked to each side of it, in case the catalog had somehow failed to list other books on the same subject, but found none. Satisfied nonetheless, he returned to the reading room with his prizes.

He started with the book devoted to dreams, finding the initial mention of this mortal phenomenon charming in its somewhat bemused attempt to explain them. It dealt meticulously with the few rumors of Fair Folk dreams and the ways they had been debunked, shown to originate in accounts of mortal dreams distorted through multiple retellings. It discussed the possibility that a dream would involve mortals or even Fair Folk telling lies, and the philosophical implications of that possibility. And finally, at the end of a left-hand page, it began to set forth what a purchaser of a mortal dream had better know beforehand.

Any well-traveled or well-informed fae knows the history of the Feast Realm, nor is it the only realm with

But the text on the facing page concerned the process of manifesting a purchased dream, and some historical examples of the compensation paid. He checked to compare the page numbers, only to find that there were none.

Abe brought the book up close to his eyes and examined the binding. He could see no sign that one or more pages had been torn out – but such crude methods were no doubt unnecessary in a fae realm. That left several questions: who had excised the pages, whether they had been preserved, and whether they could be restored. It was time to find a librarian.

The librarians Abe had seen on earlier visits varied widely in the details of their appearance, but they had all been around Abe's height, stooped slightly, and wore old-fashioned spectacles with no glass in them. The one he found this time resembled an owl with brown and white feathers. Abe explained his problem and opened the book for the librarian's perusal. The owl studied the book, its equivalent of eyebrows drawing lower and closer together. Then it closed the book with a bang and clacked its beak. "This book has, as you see, been altered. It must be replaced."

Frustrated, Abe picked up the other book, checked its index, and found the listing for dreams, only around three pages long. To his glum lack of surprise, those pages too had disappeared. The librarian clacked its beak twice more and reached out to take the book.

Abe asked, "How long will it take to replace the books?"

The owl ruffled its feathers. "We rarely need to replace a book. When some anomaly like this occurs, we must first investigate how and why. Then, either we commission a replacement, which typically takes longer than we would wish, or the book is removed from our collections."

Abe gritted his teeth and then desisted to ask, "Without this investigation, does your experience suggest any possible causes?"

The owl spread its wings a little and relaxed them again, in what might have been a shrug. "The information in the removed pages may have been disputed, or proved to be based on rumor or on unreliable mortal sources. Or a fae of importance may have considered the text to be insulting or otherwise impolite. When you next visit us, you may inquire whether any conclusion has been reached."

Abe had no time to wait for investigations or replacements. He would have to do without. In the meantime, he would have liked to find something else to read, some book in which he could lose himself and forget the still unsolved puzzle. But his mind insisted on running in circles, and after a few frustrating minutes, he gave up and trudged toward the door.

Abe stepped through the library portal, lined with open books whose pages seemed to wave goodbye to him, and arrived on the path to his office door. He stared at it, turned around, and walked toward the street instead. He would go home. Maybe he could still lose himself in a favorite novel, and set his subconscious free to search the library of his mind.

One of his favorite comfort reads, reread many times over many years, pulled him in to the point that when he next looked around, the afternoon had faded into evening. Realizing he was hungry in spite of an uneasy stomach, he assembled a supper out of store-bought prepared foods and brought the book to the table to keep reading while he ate. He was washing up before he realized that he had not checked his email since early morning.

News summaries, updates from professional organizations, pleas from politicians . . . and an email from Clara, with URGENT in the subject line.

Dearest Abe,

I hope this hits your inbox before you see the viscount again. Race on, noble steed! . . . Whoops, I've been reading too many stories of desperate late-night rides.

Should I not attempt any levity? It's such strange territory we're trying to survive and navigate.

I hope my subject line hasn't raised your hopes more than my news justifies. But I wanted to tell you, or remind you, about a certain legend, and I was afraid I'd forget or garble something if we did it by phone – not to mention that it's late here, and I almost fell asleep over my keyboard.

I was looking through those old notes I retrieved, hoping for some tale about trapped mortals and how they got free. I didn't find any, but I did come upon an Abenaki creation myth I first heard many years ago. You heard it too, though you probably haven't thought about it for quite a while. I certainly hadn't.

It's one of the stories involving turtles, with the Great Spirit creating the world by slapping mud on a turtle's back, but that's not what I wanted to highlight. After it finished coating the turtle with mud, the Great Spirit waited and pondered what sort of creatures should live on this new land. He fell asleep and dreamed of all the animals and people of the Earth – and when he woke up, there they all were!

You told me the other day that the fae seemed surprisingly cautious about dreams, and I wondered whether it could have something to do with the power dreamers have. After all, if a dream could populate a whole world, dreamers must seem formidable to beings who lack that capacity.
This may be a meaningless coincidence, but I thought I'd let you decide what to make of it.
I'm kissing the screen.
All my love,
Clara

Abe kissed his own screen, hoping he might have lucked into kissing a spot matching the one Clara had chosen. Then he wished the thought had not occurred to him. He would need all his luck for the task ahead of him.

Did the Abenaki legend suggest anything useful? He could ponder the question as well or better walking as sitting still. He headed out to the street.

It was a lovely evening on the cusp between spring and summer, the leaves full-grown but retaining something of the freshness of spring green, and the last of the fruit blossoms giving way to the beginnings of the fruit they had heralded. The sheer animal relief of moving instead of sitting, and of breathing fresh air, wiped away his cares – for a minute or two at most, before the near paradise surrounding him made him picture, against his will, the very different conditions Adira might be enduring. He gritted his teeth and increased his pace, seeking and soon enough achieving the burn of neglected muscles forced into sustained activity. He turned around only when his sore legs filled his awareness and drove imagined images away.

He had, he saw, returned to his office. Limping across the lawn, Abe felt the familiar prickle up and down his spine and limped faster so as not to keep his visitor waiting. He opened the door to find a merman and mermaid, the shining scales of their lower bodies curled on the floor in almost perfect circles, their upper bodies splendidly nude. He had never seen this glamour before, but as he thought about how to phrase an inquiry, the merman saved him the trouble, saying, "Greetings, Mr. Alexander. You may be surprised to see us again so soon, but we have discovered a need for us to speak."

Abe put aside his surprise, and did his best to keep both his curiosity and his concern from taking precedence over courtesy. "Welcome, my lords. Please make yourselves comfortable, unless you would rather I follow you elsewhere."

The merman king looked around with interest. "Is there some portion of these premises customarily used for private meetings? If so, indicate its direction, and we will relocate there."

And so it was that in a very short time, two merpeople sat with coiled tails, quite at their ease, in the leather armchairs of the office conference room.

"Mr. Alexander," said the queen, "let us first report to you that we have seen your daughter Valentina recently, and that she appeared well and had been given a not unpleasant duty to perform, acting as escort to a young ice fae."

Abe closed his eyes and let his head fall back against his chair. For that moment, he could think of nothing except the relief that filled him. The visiting royalty waited in patient silence until he opened his eyes and began to apologize. The king held up its hand to silence him. "We are in no way offended by your very natural reaction. But we did not come here only to give you this news, though we were glad to do so. During her visit to our realm, Valentina mentioned that you were thinking of selling a dream to the Fair Folk. We explained to her why this is a more serious and delicate matter than mortals may assume, and have now come to tell you the same."

Abe bid farewell to his visitors with every courtesy at his command, in lieu of the thanks that Fair Folk etiquette forbade him to utter. He kept to himself the futile wish that he had possessed this background knowledge a few days sooner. But he could, if he liked, review the now-concluded negotiations and quite possibly find explanations for the points on which the viscount had been most insistent. Even if he could no longer resist, or seek more concessions in exchange, there might still be some purpose in better understanding the transaction.

More important, he could use every bit of his professional acumen to search out those areas in which, the viscount's best efforts notwithstanding, Abe might still be able to use the powers he now knew he possessed. And given that the boundaries of those powers remained unknown, he would explore them to their very limits.

CHAPTER 15

T HE NIGHT after the ocean rulers' revelations, Abe's dreams brought no terrifying images, no desolation. Instead, they were filled with visitations from Adira, at every age from eager toddler to blossoming adolescent to triumphant adult. Waking briefly between dreams, he imagined Adira clasping his hands between hers and insisting, "Don't take any risks for me! I can handle myself!" And in his mind he replied: "I'm your father. Taking risks for you is part of what I'm here for. It's who and what I am."

On the morning when the dream was to take shape, Abe wasn't sure whether he should simply use his portal to return to the viscount's realm or wait for the viscount to fetch him as it had the last time. He decided to wait a few minutes and passed the time asking himself what, after all, he hoped to accomplish. He was finding it hard to keep straight the events of these last days, even with the notes he had made, but he had definitely agreed to ensure the dream was realized just as he remembered it. So how could he add anything to it, even if he could imagine any addition that would somehow help his daughter?

But there might be some maneuvering room in the precise terms, if he could recall them. Or . . . as the viscount reappeared, Abe said to him, "Given my mortal failings, neither my memory nor my written notes are necessarily as accurate as our business requires. It would greatly assist me in fulfilling our agreement if you could provide me with a written recital of its precise terms. I would keep this writing constantly at hand during my time in your realm."

The fae gave him a contemptuous version of its habitual smirk and replied, "We will of course be happy to supply you with such an *aide-memoire*." It produced a portal composed of a dazzling array of interwoven ribbons and feathers. Human and fae stepped through into mist, stretching as far as Abe could see in every direction.

"This," said the viscount, "is where your dream will take shape. All you must do is to display it, as you did before, and you will have the privilege of seeing it transformed into reality."

Abe hesitated, but before he could speak, the viscount flourished its hand, the lace of the sleeve beneath its topcoat fluttering as it did so. A scroll appeared in mid-air, partly unrolled. "And here, my good sir, is the writing you require."

Abe held up his hand just long enough to make sure it wasn't trembling, and then reached out and took the paper. "I will display the dream and then review the list while the transformation takes place."

He cleared his mind, reached back into his memory, and performed the wordless operation that brought forth the dream. He glanced at it as it shimmered into shape, then cast his eyes hurriedly down the writing on the scroll. Rather than a formal recital of terms such as he would have composed, it was a word for word reproduction of his negotiation with the viscount, from first to last. He scanned quickly down to just below his caveats about his memory of the dream.

What had he promised to do and not to do after the dream had taken shape? He read the terms dealing with those points, and read them again. Then, before his study could become suspicious, he looked up to see what was happening around him . . . and drew in a long, quiet breath, enthralled.

At first, it seemed that the mist he had found on his arrival blended seamlessly into the drifting fog of the graveyard. But looking closer, he saw that the edge of the mist was thickening even as he watched and becoming a wall, the wall he had barely noticed surrounding the graveyard, now a complete and sturdy-looking structure built of roughly joined stones with little mortar remaining between them. The tombstones were there, some partly obscured by the fog and others showing clear. The deer were appearing one by one, looking about and then stooping their delicate heads to graze on the grass. And there, arriving from behind the tombstones and from the wall itself, came the ghosts, their eyes wide with wonder.

He had not consciously remembered the ghosts' faces, but seeing them now, there was a rightness to them. They must have been part of the fabric of the dream, called forth by the enchantment that allowed him to display it. . . . Except – what was *that*?

A ghost emerging from beneath a tombstone, its forehead lined and its hair with the texture of gray hair despite its lack of color, nevertheless bore Adira's face.

He could not possibly have dreamed her there. Even if she showed the signs of a longer life than she had lived so far, the sight would have jolted him awake. Whether through some bizarre mischance or Fair Folk mischief, the dream had been altered.

Abe took a moment to calm himself before he spoke, his voice seeming out of place in the almost sacred silence of the dreamscape. "Lord Bloomingshire, it is my duty to point out an error. This ghost here – " In spite of himself, his finger shook as he pointed. "You may well recognize its face. And I assure you, my dream did not include it."

To its credit, the viscount did not assume an air of innocence. Instead, it beamed and said, "Indeed, sir! I will correct the error immediately." It faced the ghost and blew out toward it. The ghost rippled and reformed, and this time it was the shade of a young girl, with no resemblance to Adira as a child.

If Abe had harbored any qualms of conscience at seeking, and even skirting, the boundaries of the agreement binding him, they were swept away as surely as the fae's breath had swept away the semblance of his daughter. He read through the scroll again, more slowly, and rolled it up, already making his plan.

What he hoped to do, what he would try to do, could not be done in this first visit. It would have to wait for his second. For now, he waited with the calm of resolution, watching as the ghosts approached the deer, as the last translucent hand stroked the last furry neck. Only then did he realize that his dream, like all dreams, had had an end. Would this scene melt away at any moment? Surely the fae who traveled here to see it would want more time to appreciate it.

He cleared his throat and said to the fae, "A dilemma has occurred to me. I do not know the exact duration of my dream, nor whether the time of a dreaming human corresponds to the time of this realm or any other. What you have created here is all I remember, and I can and must so certify. But what, if anything, comes after?"

The viscount smiled smugly. "An excellent point, my good man. I will make sure their Imperial Majesties consider the matter. I think it likely that they will allow the dream to continue, with appropriate random variations, so as to offer a more satisfying experience, more likely to attract visitors who have not previously considered our realm worth their attention." A hint of anger glinted in its eyes at the disrespect it attributed to the fae whose attitude it described.

Abe nodded gravely and said, "I rejoice in having raised an idea of possible merit." He could truly say so: if the fae themselves altered the dream, it could only improve his chances for success, or for escaping retribution if he did succeed. But he would not, must not, absolutely would not smile at the thought.

Instead he bowed and said, "If you agree that our work is done, I will return in two days' time. Are you ready to provide a portal?"

The viscount adjusted its neck cloth and brushed nonexistent dust off its coat. "Certainly, certainly. And now I must report the satisfactory completion of this task to my masters. Good day, good day!" The portal it waved into existence was the simplest oval, this time, and Abe was more than ready to step through.

* * * * *

The young ice fae was as eager as Adira had ever seen it, and she saw no reason not to indulge it. The difficulty came in discovering how to do so. She consulted it on how to frame their first attempt. "Should we ask to go to the realm of the fae with flowing shape? Or – what color was it?"

"I don't know. The thing it wore was like our sky at home, or a little darker."

"Hmmm. Gray, we might call that." What else could she ask? "Did what it was wearing cover its whole body?"

"Almost. Its hands almost showed a few times, but it always pulled them back in. Its head showed, though."

That was odd. What sort of fae would hide its own appearance? Of course, it wasn't among its own people. Maybe fae from whatever realm it came from had a strong sense of privacy. Or maybe something about their appearance repelled or frightened most fae, though with the variety of glamours she had seen and heard of, it was hard to imagine.

Back to the motion inside the garment, or shell, or whatever it was. Perhaps the form within was simply delicate. The thought gave rise to an image. "Have you ever seen a butterfly? There aren't any in your realm, but I can't remember whether you might have come across one somewhere else, or even in the sunflower classroom. They're about the size of a very small bird, and they have wings, but not like birds . . . . Hold on a minute." The road on which they stood had a thin layer of dirt, and she used her finger to draw the outline of a butterfly in it. "They're shaped like this, and their wings flutter, like this." She did her best to imitate the movement with her fingers. "Is that anything like what the fae's clothing looked like?"

Explorer shuffled its feet, making random patterns in the dirt beneath. "I don't know. But it sounds pretty. Can we go look for a realm of butterflies?"

Maybe there was one. And maybe it had hills on which one could sit or lie, looking up at a sky full of fluttering wisps of color. "I'd like that. Let's give it a try."

There was indeed a butterfly realm, and she found it on her first attempt, stepping onto just such a hill as she had imagined and longed for. Explorer came right behind her, and butterflies came to greet them, butterflies as small as her thumbnail and as large as her two hands spread wide, and every size in between. There were more with pastel colors than starker ones, though she did see a few that looked like black swallowtails, the kind with blue dots lining their lower wings. The smallest were white or pale yellow or sky blue, while many of the larger ones bore patterns both more and less intricate: some with eye-shapes reminiscent of peacocks, some with wings in shades of purple divided like stained-glass windows, or of green edged with rust-red. They fluttered over her head, or lit on her outstretched arm, or flitted back and forth between Adira and Explorer, who did not need wide-opened eyes or beaming smile to show its delight and wonder.

The movement of the butterfly wings reminded her of the forest realm, where she had briefly possessed the ability to read the movements of leaves and shadows. Did these hovering and darting butterflies also have their own speech, and if she could stay here, if the rulers of this place met and approved of her, would she learn to speak it? But for now, it was enough to watch them and know herself welcome.

Adira looked around at the hill and asked the fae, "Shall we rest here for a while?" It hesitated, and she wondered how easily it would be able to lay itself down on the slope. "I could help you get comfortable."

Explorer came closer and said, "Oh, would you? I would like to look at the butterflies without turning back and forth so much."

Adira, silently giving thanks for her possession of a more movable neck, took the ice fae's hands, grasping them carefully to avoid breaking any twigs. "All right. Bend at the waist a little, so the middle of you reaches the ground first, and I'll lower you down. Yes, that's it." The fae was a little heavier than she had thought, and she gritted her teeth, determined not to drop it. "There you go . . . almost there . . . There!" She stepped back as the fae relaxed against the grass and gazed upward. Satisfied, she sat and then lay down herself.

It was lovely, even idyllic, and she kept herself awake so as not to miss any of the display. The light changed as she watched, ebbing toward dusk, and new butterflies came with it, or perhaps moths, their muted colors blending with the shadows.

In spite of her intentions, she felt her eyes drifting closed. But then she felt a touch on her cheek, too soft to be Explorer's fingers. She pushed herself to a sitting position and saw Explorer still lying beside her, watching the butterflies and crooning softly with a sound that lacked the usual grating or hair-raising tones. The touch on her cheek had been a breeze that had arisen and now shifted. It brought to her the scent of what might have been cider.

She had almost taught herself to ignore her hunger, to shove it into the background of her mind. But now her mouth watered, and her muscles tensed. Suppressing a curse, she sat up, startling a blue and brown butterfly that had been resting on her knee, and looked for the source of the odor. At the base of the hill, she saw a path, made by she knew not what fae or other creature, leading to a grove of trees.

It was from the trees that the breeze blew. It would have been easier to ignore the scent if it had been constant. But the breeze played with her, tantalizing her, dying away and then growing stronger. Clearly her idyll was over. She stretched, yawned, and tapped Explorer on the shoulder, saying, "I'm very glad we found this place, but it isn't where we intended to go. Should we keep looking?"

* * * * *

Abe barely slept the night before his return visit to his dream realm, dropping off and waking again and again. He awoke for the final time just as dawn touched the sky, and scrambled out of bed. He had waited as long as he had bound himself to wait, and now he would go and find out just what if any powers he had.

Fortifying himself with the quickest breakfast he could grab, he donned a jacket with large pockets and half walked, half ran to the office, where he got the coffee going while he read through the scroll two more times. Pouring the coffee while it was still dripping, he gulped it down and stuffed the scroll into one of the jacket pockets, shrugging the coat on as he ran to the portal, and stepped out into the fog and the graveyard.

He had hoped to find himself alone. Instead, he came upon none other than the emperor and empress, arm in arm, all oohs and ahs and appreciation. Had the dream been something he consciously crafted, he would have been gratified. When they beamed at him and congratulated him, he avoided the etiquette breach of thanking them and merely said, "It does indeed capture every nuance of my dream, as best I could recall it. It is Lord Bloomingshire, or the magic of your realm, that merits your congratulations."

Now how could he get them to leave? Whatever he attempted, it would need privacy. But not only might they stay far beyond his allotted twenty minutes, but other fae might arrive at any time, and who could say how long those fae would linger?

He pulled the scroll out and unrolled it as casually as he could, reading quickly through it and stowing it again. Then he cast his mind back to what the ocean rulers had told him. There had been a great many unknowns in what they disclosed. He would have to test the boundaries of what they had been sure of, or he would have no hope of rescuing his daughter. And what he had in mind to do first, if it worked, would not, he was almost sure, violate any term of the agreement. Though if these royal fae ever learned of it, they might not care about such technicalities.

Ambling away from their Imperial Majesties, pausing to stroke an inquisitive fawn, he mentally formed the silent command, *Leave, Emperor and Empress, as if of your own accord. Leave now.*

He began to recite it again, only to be interrupted by the deep voice of the empress saying, "We will leave you to contemplate your success, with which We are well pleased."

He turned toward her while thinking, *And let no one else come while I am here.*

Immediately she went on, "And that you may enjoy your limited time here without spending any of it on pleasantries or answering questions, we will ensure that no one else intrudes until your departure."

Concealing his emotions, he had long ago ascertained, did not constitute deceit in the Fair Folks' eyes. Bowing low, hiding his exultation, he said, "You are most gracious, Your Imperial Majesty." He almost slipped and thanked her for her consideration, barely catching himself as the two of them waved in acknowledgment and disappeared.

But the empress's words reminded him that he had only twenty minutes in all, and he had already spent some of them. He must move quickly to his next and more important experiment.

Everything depended on his reading of the negotiated terms, his opinion that they did not forbid him to make changes within this miniature realm per se, or at least were ambiguous on that point. But to hedge in every way he could, he strode to the stone wall surrounding the graveyard and leaned over it, looking beyond. As he'd hoped, the mist did not abruptly end where the wall did, but extended about two feet further.

Abe hoisted himself onto the wall, dangling his feet on the far side. He could argue, if put to it – if given the chance – that he remained within the dream realm over which he had power, but was not, at that moment, inside the dream itself. If he could summon Adira to him and control the summons so that she landed next to him, or at worst within arm's reach in the mist, he could say truthfully that he had not added her to the dream.

Abe held his breath, closed his eyes, and said out loud, in case his voice had added power, "Adira, come to me. Come to me now!"

* * * * *

Adira had tried instructing her portal to reveal a realm where the inhabitants wore loose clothing, or one where they hid their bodies, or even one where their bodies were balloons. All three times, nothing happened.

The ice fae grew more dejected with each failed attempt. After the third, it said, "You've been so good to me, all this time, and you're trying so hard. And I've never done anything for you. I wish there was something I could do to make you happy, the way seeing all these new places makes me."

Adira started to say that she would rather play tourist with Explorer than wander the cold forests of its home or stare at the wooden walls of her shelter-prison. Then she remembered. "There is something you could do for me. But it's something you've been ordered not to do, and I won't ask you to break the rules."

The ice fae's trunk sagged a little, as if bent by too strong a wind. "You want to know what they did with the mortal."

"I do. I feel responsible for him. I negotiated with your rulers about his fate. If they've – if they've killed him, I'll feel not only grieved, but betrayed, even though they never promised in so many words to keep him alive."

The fae gasped, a sound like a tree creaking in a wind that might topple it. "Oh, no! They didn't do anything like that! They . . . they sent it away. Back where it came from. So it wouldn't talk to me any more, or to anyone else. They said it could cause more trouble than keeping it was worth."

Adira staggered, and might have fallen if the fae hadn't leaned into her and braced itself. She pulled herself upright and said, "I am very glad you told me."

The rulers must have considered Tom a bad influence. Explorer and Tom had first spoken before Explorer went adventuring. Perhaps this also shed some light on why Adira had been given the task of escorting it. The rulers might consider Explorer contaminated by that contact with Tom, and prefer that no other ice fae be exposed to it.

And they had kept the fact from her. Or would she have known, if she'd only asked? Probably not – they could not lie to her, but they could refuse to answer her questions.

Had they returned Tom home, or stranded him in some distant country? If she ever escaped, she would make it her business to find out.

But now, to her present task. Adira looked at the ice fae and shrugged. "Do you have any other ideas about how to find the realm the fae at the school came from?"

Explorer scuffed its feet and answered, "If I were the one the portal obeyed, I could tell it to go where the people were like the fae I saw. But that would need my memory, wouldn't it? And you don't share it."

Adira pursed her lips, thinking. "It wouldn't hurt to try something a little different. Take my hands. Now, think hard about the fae you saw, about how it looked and sounded and everything you can remember."

The fae did so. Adira focused on their joined hands, on the connection between them, and commanded the portal, "Go to the realm that is home to the fae Explorer is remembering."

The portal appeared, its shape oddly unstable. The ice fae let out a high shriek of excitement. Leaning toward the portal, it said, "I see yellow, and some other colors almost like yellow! The fae I saw didn't look like that, but maybe that's what was under that suit it wore. And the colors are moving, just like the clothing did, and more. Oh, how pretty!"

Adira stared in shock at what the portal showed them. How could Explorer not realize? But then, how could it? In its realm of ice, where to light a torch condemned one to an eternity under the lake and only a foolish mortal lured to his doom would ever dare, how would this young fae have ever seen flames?

The suit of loose and undulating cloth must have been fireproof, shifting shape with the hot air within, protecting those around and incidentally hiding the nature of the beings who even now danced and frolicked and came closer to their side of the portal, only their heads constant in shape. The ice fae, excited and eager, made as if to push past her and step through the portal to greet them. Any moment, its arm or leg could enter the waiting realm and catch fire. And she had nothing with her and no enchantment that could save it once it was ablaze.

With one mighty shove, Adira sent Explorer reeling backward. Then she stepped through and sealed the portal behind her.

The flame beings did not immediately advance on her, instead studying her, their flames jumping higher as they looked at her. Were they marveling at her solidity, or feeling a cold wind from her very presence? If so, it did not make them retreat. Instead, one of the smaller beings edged closer to her. It might be a young fae, coming to welcome her. It couldn't know. She spared a thought from her mounting terror to feel for the confusion, and then dismay and sadness, it would feel to see her charred body drop to the ground and move no more.

And then –

* * * * *

Abe felt a wave of energy surround him, leave, and return, almost sending him toppling off the wall. In the next moment, Adira was there beside him, standing precariously on the wall, paler than ever before, her fists clenched and her eyes frantic. He grabbed her legs as high up as he could reach, steadying her, and said hoarsely, "It's all right. Whatever it is, you're all right. Can you sit? Yes, there, sit right there. You're safe." He wiped away the tears streaming from his eyes, the better to drink in the sight of her. "You're safe."

Adira looked wildly around. "I don't understand – wait. This is your dream, isn't it? Maybe I do understand. Is this what the ocean fae told me? You had the power to bring me here?" She looked around, but not at the graveyard or its deer and ghosts. "Where's Explorer? It was with me, and then I closed the portal behind me to save it – but it can't go anywhere without the portal. Can you bring it here too? I can't just leave it . . . ."

Abe looked at his watch. "We don't have much time. Do you really – "

"Yes, yes! It's safe, at least for now, but I can't just leave it there, without a word, without explaining what I did and why I had to. Please!"

"You'll have to catch it, the way I did you. Ready?"

Adira gave a jerky nod, and Abe sent out the power again. And there stood the ice fae, warbling in ear-splitting distress. Its narrow, rigid body did not yet need steadying. They were almost out of time, and Abe wasted none of it. One last glance at the beauty of the dream, then one more surge of power. Barely comprehending that it might be the last thing he ever did in Faerie, Abe sent all three of them to the world that he and Adira, at least, called home.

CHAPTER 16

T HE ICE fae had never been inside a building except in the School Realm, and had never seen anything like the office. The novelty of the opportunity distracted it long enough for Abe to get all three of them inside.

Finally, Abe could envelop Adira in his fiercest hug. She hugged him back just as hard, and when he could finally bring himself to let go, she said, "I'd better explain things to Explorer. In the meantime, is there anything here to eat? And do you know how long it's been since I had coffee?"

Abe laughed, almost carefree, though they still had cares enough if he let himself think about them. "I'll raid the snack cupboard and get coffee started. You talk to your young friend."

Adira led the fae to their conference room, where she sat and it stood. By the time Abe met them there with an armful of snacks and a mug – Adira's favorite – of coffee, she had almost finished telling him what fire was, and what fire would have done to it if she hadn't forced it back. The fae was whimpering, and Abe could easily have done the same. She had stepped into a realm of fire, alone, to protect the fae she had been forced to escort?

He could not really be surprised. It was like her. He could only be appalled, and terrified in retrospect.

The young fae had gone quiet. When Adira was done, it reached out to grip her hand. If the bare twigs of its hand hurt her, she gave no sign of it. In something like a hushed tone, it said to her, "You saved me."

She looked at it with what Abe could only call affection. "Yes. Of course."

"And then your parent saved you."

Tears glimmered in her eyes, and she blinked them away. "Yes, he did."

"And then you had him bring me to you – why?"

More tears, and Adira bit her lip as she wiped them away with her free hand. When she could speak, she said, "I couldn't just leave you there, knowing you didn't know why and had no way to get home. You could have been in worse places, but you wouldn't have wanted to stay in the butterfly realm forever, with no one to talk to."

Despite the fae's lack of visible eyes, Abe felt it staring at him. "You didn't stay there, in the place where you brought me."

Abe cleared his throat and said, "We had to leave. I'd agreed not to stay there any longer, and Ad – Valentina needed me to bring her home." He paused to catch his breath after his narrow escape from revealing her true name. "And she hadn't had time to tell you what had happened – what had almost happened." He chuckled weakly. "So here we are, we three."

The fae looked at Abe and back at Adira, saying to her, "You could send me home, couldn't you? Back to my own place. But – would you have to take me there?"

Adira shrugged. "I could try to send you on your own. And if I couldn't, my father might be able to. We won't know until we try."

There was something Abe desperately wanted to know, but neither Adira nor the ice fae could tell him. The fae was the one to ask. "Valentina. Will my people let you stay here, when they didn't say you could?"

Adira closed her eyes as if gathering her strength before opening them and saying, "Explorer, I don't know. The third task they set me was to escort you wherever you wished to go. Let me think . . . . They said they would not allow you to 'wander about unsupervised,' and that you'd promised not to go anywhere without my permission. It's not entirely clear whether an 'escort' has to accompany you when you go home. Even if that's not the case, they haven't released me. They said I was to 'remain,' and then . . . ." Her voice faltered. "I said that if they let you travel to at least one more realm, I would not try to escape, and would perform whatever tasks they set me until they decided I had earned the right to go home. I didn't try to escape – my father rescued me without my knowing it was happening. And the rulers haven't set me any other tasks, though . . . I may not have finished this one. But if they've decided I'm entitled to go home, they haven't told me so."

The silence that followed her words reverberated in Abe's head until he thought he would go mad. If he had had more time, was there something else he could have done, some safer place to send her? He could go back – he had more visits coming, if he chose to make them – but the emperor and empress might well feel he had abused his privileges, violated the spirit of the agreement if not the letter. Even if they did not, or he could persuade them otherwise, he could think of no way to use the dream realm's power that would place Adira more thoroughly out of reach.

Abe had almost forgotten Explorer standing there until it suddenly spoke. "I can tell them I don't want to travel. I will tell them. Then you will have finished the task they set you."

Adira looked up and said slowly, "But you still want to see more places. I know you do."

"I have already seen many, thanks to you. And because of what I didn't know, the last one could have destroyed me. I do not have to rush, as you would, to fit everything I want to see into a mortal lifetime. I can wait, and learn more, and know how to be more careful, before I travel again. And maybe, if I show myself obedient, my masters will be willing to send *me* on their errands, instead of you."

Adira sat up straighter as if from an infusion of hope. She looked at Explorer with the gratitude faerie etiquette forbade her to express and said, "It's kind of you, and generous, to say all this. But that still leaves the biggest obstacle. I promised to perform tasks for them until the rulers decided I deserved to leave. It's up to them, not you and not me, whether they have more tasks for me to perform."

And then the familiar tingle and chill ran up and down Abe's spine. A fae had arrived. He knew, before he looked, which fae it would be.

* * * * *

Adira longed to run to the file room and hide behind the cabinets. There was enough room. But the viscount was tall, and could probably lean over the top and find her, trapped like a mouse facing a cat ready to play with her before devouring her.

Instead, she stood up and walked, neither fast nor slow, to the entryway, where the viscount stood in a silver topcoat, white waistcoat, and white breeches, polishing its gleaming white boots with a spotless white glove.

It snapped the glove into nothingness as she approached, saying, "Well, well, if it isn't the truant mortal run to Papa! Whatever shall we do?"

"She didn't run to me. I snatched her away." Dad had run up behind her and now grabbed her arm and thrust her behind him. "She didn't know it was happening and had nothing to do with it."

"Indeed," the viscount purred. "And will you now convey her back to where she belongs?"

The fae was obviously needling Dad to get a reaction, and was all too likely to get one. Adira stepped back in front of Dad. "There is some question, my lord, as to whether I ever properly belonged in the ice realm – I presume that is the meaning of your reference – in the first place."

The viscount lifted its elegant eyebrows. "And I presume you are referring to the circumstances under which you first found yourself in the ice realm. I admit that I played a hand in that episode, under the impetus of a grievance that has, I may say, run its course. But your subsequent bargain was not with me."

A memory came to mind from one of Dad's coaching sessions as she had studied for her Negotiations class. *Whatever the person across the table just said, look behind it for any concessions they may have made or implied.* The viscount had just, more or less, declared that it was no longer her enemy. What difference might that make? The ice fae were not dependent on this one fae to act on their behalf . . . but isolationist as they were, how many alternatives did they have, particularly for a mission that would amount to kidnapping? And were they prepared to extend their dispute with this one mortal into a potentially wider conflict?

Might they, rather, have some interest in a way to save face?

For that matter, why was the viscount here? As the ice rulers' agent, or for some other purpose?

"Lord Bloomingshire," Adira said with all her hard-won skill at politesse, "I apologize for keeping you standing at the door. Won't you come in, and take a seat in our conference room or anywhere else you prefer? And would you like some refreshment? We have relatively few offerings, but I could easily go down the street and procure a greater selection."

Dad still stood close by, but she seemed to have rendered him speechless. The viscount produced its quizzing glass, this time an incongruously contemporary-looking contraption, and peered through it. "How very kind of you."

Adira had to laugh. "Overdue courtesy, you may well think, and I fully acknowledge it. We have hot chocolate here, or tea, and I believe we even have a bottle of wine, though I'm not altogether sure about a bottle-opener."

She led the way into the conference room and waved toward the chairs. The viscount seated itself, looked up, and pursed its lips. "I have often heard you and your esteemed father mention coffee, and once refused an offer to sample it. I believe I'll take a cup today."

In the midst of all this cordial discussion, the ice fae erupted into the room with all the drama of an adolescent that had worked up its courage. "My lord! You mustn't, I mean they mustn't, make her go back! I'll go with you, and I can explain it all to them, and if they're angry . . . ." Its stream of words faltered, and it fell back on repeating, "I'll go."

The older fae tucked away its quizzing glass and stared sternly at the younger. "Indeed you will. That is not in question."

Adira put her hand gently on the ice fae's shoulder. "Explorer," she said, "Would you like to tell our esteemed guest about your and my most recent adventure? I'll go and get the cup of coffee it requested."

When Adira returned, Explorer was still talking. It must have started with its return to the School Realm and its encounter with the intriguing and mysterious fae it met there. Abe was sitting very straight, tense as an over-tightened string as he waited for the details of what it had already been hard for him to hear. Adira placed the mug of coffee where the viscount could reach it and took a seat next to where the ice fae stood, stammering and waving its hands back and forth.

"I didn't know. I should have known – we all learn about it and that it's dangerous, but I'd never really imagined it. When I saw the yellow and the other colors dancing behind the portal, I just wanted to get closer – I was so rude, Valentina, I'm so sorry, I pushed past you so you didn't have time to explain – "

The viscount held up a long white hand. "Excuse me, my dear Explorer, but I believe in your earnest effort to convey the emotional tenor of the occasion, you have omitted the actual substance."

As several times before, Adira thought that the youngster would have blushed if it could. She reached over and patted its hand. "That's all right. Just take your time. Tell Lord Bloomingshire what you saw through the portal."

"Fire, my lord. I saw fire. Fire people, with flames for bodies. I don't think they wanted to hurt us – Valentina, do you think so?"

She had wondered, in that moment and several times since. "I don't know. They didn't hurt me – "

"Didn't they?" Dad growled, and seized her hand, bringing it up toward her face. "Isn't that a burn?"

Adira stared down at the red, angry streak beneath her thumb. "I didn't even feel it. Not then, and not after." She grimaced. "Not until now."

"I'll go get some ice." Dad shoved back his chair and walked quickly to the kitchenette, while Adira tried to remember what she had been saying. "I guess one of them touched me, but I don't know if they meant to, or knew what would happen. I don't know why the fae Explorer met encouraged it to come. Maybe someone will find out, some day." She looked at her hand again, resisting the urge to rub it. "I'd rather it not be me."

Explorer looked solemnly at her. "I don't want you to go back there, and I never could. But I'd like to look at them again, sometime. The flames were so pretty. . . ."

Dad came back with an ice pack, the kind with a strap one could fasten to keep it in place, and gently put it on her before he sat down again. The viscount stroked its clean-shaven chin. "I regret that I am still missing a piece of this puzzle. You, Explorer, wanted to pass through the portal and even, most regrettably, pushed your escort out of the way to go through sooner. Yet she was the one who was burned. How did matters sort out in this manner?"

The young fae hung its head and put its arms around itself as if for comfort. Adira took up the tale. It was quickly told, but she was sorry Dad and Explorer had to hear it.

When she finished, Dad sat hunched over the table with his head in his arms, while Explorer regarded him with a tangible air of misery. Adira got up, stood behind Dad, and massaged his shoulders, murmuring, "It's all right. I was barely singed, and now I'm here."

Dad lifted his head and looked up at her, eyes red. "For how long?"

The ice fae straightened to its stiffest and tallest. "Remember, sir, I'm going to tell them I'm done traveling – just like I said before, uh, Lord Bloomingshire arrived. And besides, you saved my life! That has to count for something!"

Dad sat up and nodded slowly. "Yes, it must. In fact . . . the ice realm's rulers are bound, like any other fae, to speak only truth. Even if they refuse to speak at all, I believe they are unable to deceive themselves, at least where the truth is sufficiently clear. Lord Bloomingshire, do you agree?"

The viscount took out a silver snuff box and took a pinch. "Indeed I do, though what truth is in fact sufficiently clear may be a matter for philosophers." It sniffed up the snuff, sneezed delicately, and tucked the box away again before saying with a shark-like smile, "Or for lawyers."

"I submit, then," Dad said, looking the viscount in the eye, "that by her demonstrated willingness to sacrifice her life for the fae the ice rulers entrusted to her – a willingness that would have led to that tragedy, had my intervention not occurred in the nick of time – my daughter has demonstrated, beyond reasonable dispute, that she deserves to be released from any further obligations to the ice realm, just as her death would have released her."

Adira bent down, kissed Dad on the top of his head, and quietly took her seat again, saying to the viscount, "I may not be objective on the point, but I think my father makes a compelling argument. Are you willing to share your thoughts on the matter?"

The viscount had assumed what Adira would call a poker face, though she wondered what 19th century term the fae would have used. Slowly, it pushed back its chair and rose to its feet, towering over the ice fae and the two seated mortals. "I will, as you suggest, share my thoughts – with the rulers of the ice realm." It stood looking at Adira, then Dad, then Adira again, before breaking into a smug smile as if it had won its hand. "And I believe you will be pleased with the results."

Dad breathed in sharply and reached for Adira's hand. She took his and caressed it, saying to the viscount, "I am gratified and relieved to hear it. Is it your opinion that when you endorse my father's argument, as I gather you intend to do, they will be receptive to it?"

Back to the poker face. "There is, of course, the issue of testimony. You are the only witness to what occurred after you closed the portal behind you."

The fae waited for Dad to jolt backward in shock, as if from a blow, and for whatever reaction escaped Adira herself, before donning its habitual smirk. "But fortunately, something akin to the arithmetical commutative property applies. You have described to me what happened, and since you know better than to do so falsely, I can relay what you said to those fae to whom you owe – or, I will assert, owed – the obligation."

Explorer had lurched toward the viscount, and now stumbled to a halt. Obviously bewildered by the exchange, it said shakily, "I did see through the portal. I didn't know what flames look like, but the rulers must. Don't they?" At the viscount's condescending nod, the ice fae went on, "Well, then, I'll tell them what I saw, and they'll recognize it. And I saw Valentina go through the portal."

The viscount moved toward Explorer, who took a step back and then stepped slowly forward again.

Dad spoke carefully, as if feeling his way. "My greatest concern and my overriding goal, ever since Adira was detained, has been her freedom and her safety. I am greatly relieved that we may be on the cusp of seeing that goal realized. There remains, however, the question of my own status."

In all the flurry of activity, and then in her self-centered fear for herself, Adira had forgotten that Dad had risked offending the rulers of a Fair Folk realm in order to rescue her. She could hardly breathe as Dad asked the viscount, "How do your emperor and empress view the manner in which I brought my daughter home? Do they consider me in breach of contract?"

"How conscientious of you to ask." The viscount's condescension was such that Adira could almost imagine it chucking Dad under the chin. "In fact, when their Imperial Majesties pondered the matter – and rest assured, they did so – they decided that you had rather cleverly construed the terms of the agreement, and tiptoed, as it were, to the very boundary but not beyond. After all, your lovely dream remains unaltered and unspoiled."

Dad's shoulders slumped in relief, though he muttered something under his breath – something about *what else I did.* She couldn't tell whether the viscount heard, and if so, what it might make of those words. It said nothing else to Dad or herself as it stood and tossed its coattails behind it with an elegant flourish. Beckoning to the ice fae, it said, "It is high time we were on our way. Say your farewells, if you wish."

Adira and Dad both stood. Explorer turned and bowed to Dad and Adira, but then hesitated and said to her, "Would it be appropriate, and would it hurt you, if I . . . I think the word is 'hugged'?"

Adira went to the ice fae and put her arms around it, not pulling back when the rough edges of the bark texture scraped her arms. The fae tentatively hugged her back, at first barely touching her and then pressing a little harder. After enough time passed that Adira began wondering how to extricate herself, the fae let go, stepping back with a noise like wind in branches.

The viscount reached out gingerly, took Explorer's hand, and winced dramatically at the touch of the twigs. Adira and Dad stood close together and bowed to the viscount, who made its quizzing glass appear and twirled it cheerily in response. "I'll stop by and tell you what happens – when I find the time. Until then, *au revoir!*" With that, the viscount waved up a portal of glittering, shifting crystals and stepped through, pulling the ice fae after it. The coffee she had served it remained untouched.

And now, for the first time in such a very long time, Adira and her father were alone, and on familiar ground. They stood for maybe half a minute, simply looking at each other, as Adira basked in the rattle of the office air conditioner and the occasional creak as the old building settled on its foundation. Dad broke the silence first. "We've got to call your mother. Right away!"

Adira smiled, beamed, laughed. "Right away! And then, let's go out and get the biggest bowl of soup in town. I'm overdue."

Adira gave herself the rest of that day to indulge in the fundamental, reassuring pleasures of food, relaxation, Dad's company, and finally sleep. The next morning, after grabbing a quick breakfast, she double-checked her memory of the directions to Tom's family home and headed there. She should have called or texted, but every time she tried to find the words, her mind went blank. In person, if she found someone home, she could play it by ear, responding to whatever met her, whether it be welcome or reproach, anger or gratitude or wariness or solicitude.

The walk through the woods reminded her of the forest realm, though the leaves, a darker green by this time of year, moved with no message behind them. She sighed for the realm left behind and then focused on what she might find ahead of her. Soon she came to the small patch of cleared land surrounding Tom's home. A little girl who reminded Adira of herself as a child – alert, energetic, with long dark hair mightily tangled from who knew what activities – answered the door and studied her with knowing eyes. "You're the other lawyer, aren't you? The one who got stuck the same place as Tom? Except they didn't put you under the ice, did they?" The girl's mood shifted to wide-eyed unease, and she hugged herself tightly. "That sounded *awful*."

Adira, still on the doorstep, shifted her weight from foot to foot and then made herself stand still. "No, they didn't do that to me. I saw Tom there, and it did look awful. I'm so sorry I couldn't keep the fae from doing it."

The girl stared. "But Tom says you're the one, you and your father, who made them let him out, instead of keeping him there forever and ever!"

Adira stood a little straighter. "It was our job." And they had done it. If not for them, Tom might still be in the frozen lake, staring up at the ice with a soundless scream.

Though if the viscount had not been angry with her, Tom might never have been lured into the ice realm in the first place. Did she owe it to this child, to Tom's parents and his girlfriend, to share those misgivings? She could not be sure . . . and it would do them no good that she could see.

A man's hand appeared on the little girl's shoulder. "Who's come to visit, kitten?"

Adira introduced herself and explained her presence, incompletely, by saying, "Events proceeded so quickly, and then took such an unexpected direction, that we never had the chance to meet. I know you've talked to my father, but if you have any questions for me, I'd be happy to answer them if I can. And I was also hoping to see Tom."

The man gently moved the child out of the way and ushered Adira inside. "Please come meet my wife, and Tom's brother! I'm afraid Tom isn't here just now." He chuckled. "He's been spending more time with his girl than with us since he got home."

A woman bustled out of the kitchen carrying a plate of cinnamon rolls, setting them on a low table. She brushed off her skirt and said, "Would you like some coffee with these? I just made them this morning, and they're still warm."

Indeed, Adira could smell them from where she stood. "They look marvelous, and I'd love some coffee. Could you use any help?"

"No, no, you just set yourself down. I won't be a minute." And she hurried out again. Tom's father sat down in an armchair near the table and beckoned Adira toward another.

As soon as she was seated, he leaned forward and extended his hand. She held out her own, and he gripped it tight, saying, "We haven't had a chance to thank either of you for getting Tom sent home. As a parent, I'm sure your father has some idea how relieved and grateful we are."

It felt like deceit to relax in this family's home and eat cinnamon rolls in the face of how little they knew. They had no idea that Adira's careless behavior toward the viscount had led to Tom's captivity. And while she and Dad had been able to reduce the rigor of his sentence, they'd had nothing to do with the timing of his return home. She relieved her feelings somewhat by saying, "We had very little to do with when he came back to you. So even though our feelings can't come close to yours, we're very relieved as well."

The little girl reached for a cinnamon roll, but apparently changed her mind and chewed on her lip instead. "And none of us has to go there to take Tom's place? Don't I even have to sew clothes for the faeries?"

Adira smiled and shook her head.

The child looked let down, but persevered. "I could make some anyway. As a present. Would they like that?"

Adira hated to frustrate the girl's good intentions, but felt obliged to explain, "Even if they would have liked you to give them clothes, they can't accept gifts. It's against their rules, and so would it be for you to offer them."

It was the little girl's turn to shake her head. "I love getting presents! The Fair Folk must be really strange."

Adira sat back against her chair, while her hostess brought the coffee and a plate, putting a cinnamon roll on the plate for good measure. Adira surrendered to temptation, picked up the roll, took a big bite, and said to the child, "You're absolutely right. The Fair Folk are strange indeed."

This largely pleasant meeting, with neither negotiation nor danger in it, should not have tired Adira, let alone exhausted her, but she was apparently still recovering from her experiences. By the time she got near the office, her tentative resolve to catch up on her and Dad's cases had ebbed, and she made her way home instead. There she discovered that Dad had restocked her kitchen, and she made herself a large hot lunch of scrambled eggs with everything she could think of thrown in. As soon as she was done, she gave the dishes a quick rinse, stumbled into her bedroom, threw the curtains open wide to the afternoon sunshine, pulled a quilt out of her closet, and went back to bed, the quilt wrapped close around her.

She awoke at dusk to her father's knock, and then his anxious voice calling her. She made some groggy noise; he opened the door enough to peek in, his forehead furrowed with worry until he got a look at her cozily untidy arrangement. He started to close the door again, but Adira sat up in bed and held out her arms. Hesitantly he came in, taking small steps and then bigger ones until he reached her and almost lunged to give her a hug.

She got up to go to his house for dinner and then went home and back to bed again.

And the next day, Mom was home.

Mom fretted less, or less visibly, than Dad, but she kept finding ways to stick close to Adira: suggesting long walks, bringing out photo albums and asking whether Adira would like to leaf through them with her. Adira was happy to be persuaded. It gave her a reason to put off the host of questions waiting to be confronted.

Adira was still sleeping in, and when she got up on the fifth day after Mom's return, she texted and asked whether Mom felt like going out for brunch. She had not yet sunk back into the complacency of assuming she could go out for a meal, could choose what to eat, could eat at all . . . could walk down the street and see growing things and feel the sun's warmth, could go exactly where she wanted to go . . . .

She was startled, and her breath grew short, when Mom texted back, *Sounds good! Would you meet me at the office?* Mom hadn't been pushing her. Had the respite ended? But she replied, *Sure*, and got dressed more quickly than she had so far. Driving would be faster, so she walked, making herself keep to a brisk pace.

She had somehow expected the office to look ominous, but it stood innocuous in the late morning sun, the front steps freshly swept. She climbed the steps and gave a quick rap on the door in case anyone was standing near it on the other side. Going on in, she called out,

"Mom? Are you here yet?" She smiled wryly to hear the touch of anxiety in her own voice. Mom was clearly not the only one craving more closeness and reassurance than usual.

It was Dad's voice that answered, from some distance. "We're out back!"

Adira trotted through the front room, past the conference room and kitchenette, and out to the back, where the portal's shimmer somehow persisted undimmed despite the sunshine. But next to it, her parents stood in animated discussion with . . . a stag?

Adira's jaw dropped. She hauled it back up and walked slowly over, feeling an impulse to kneel before the visitor and refraining only because her parents' warm and familiar manner made too much of a contrast to such a gesture. She bowed her head to the stag and stammered, "What . . . you said you'd met them. Had you come here for something, brought my father a case?"

The stag shrank down into its fawn shape, and then, suddenly, became a seemingly human child, a toddler with straight silver hair, standing on its feet and laughing a ringing laugh. She knew that laugh, somehow. And the child had black eyes – no, silver, and then filled with a light she had never seen in any eyes, mortal or fae. But she had seen such lights in the forest realm.

"You're the changeling, and also the fawn who helped me?? But how . . . ?"

The child became the fawn again. "When my first hosts could not cope with my presence, your parents took me into their home. Living with me, they picked up clues that I might have come from the forest realm – which I did not yet know. They brought me back." Its eyes sparkled and then faded back into brown. "I, and my people, are grateful to all of you."

Mom knelt down and asked the fawn, in a hushed voice, "May I touch you?"

The fawn arched its neck and moved toward Mom, as if pleading for her touch. She beamed and stroked it. Dad looked on, smiling and bouncing on his toes a little, as if enjoying what he had wrought. Adira looked away to hide her own smile, then turned back to the fawn and said, "If I may ask, how did you learn to speak so well at your age? Or were you, as a changeling, older than you looked?"

The fawn lowered its head, stepped back from Mom's hand, and became the stag again. "In a way. My people have no fixed age, any more than we have a fixed form. We first grow as saplings, like the fae who remain trees, but within a short time we learn the form you called fireflies. In your years, I am older than any of you three."

Dad's eyes went wide, his somewhat smug manner lost in wonder, while Mom seemed lost in thought, as if searching her memory for similar stories. The stag went on, its voice deep and rumbling. "The glamours we assume can affect how we think and feel, so once I was induced –" It stamped its foot and shook its antlers. " – induced to take the form of a changeling, I was not very much unlike an infant. I was not equipped to explain my situation, and therefore dependent on the knowledge and insight your parents brought to the question of my origin."

Dad glanced at Adira before saying, "So if your, ah, hosts hadn't hired 'Valentina' and me, what would have become of you?"

The stag became a fawn once more and edged toward Mom as if seeking comfort. She started stroking it again as it said, its voice now higher, with a sweetness much like the changeling's laugh, "I can hardly know. I might have been trapped in your realm, or the fae of the Autumn Court might have taken me back to use in whatever way amused them. Only if they entirely lost interest in me and then bothered to send me back to my forest, or if they released me from the changeling form and allowed me to assume one with broader capacities, might I have returned home."

Dad bowed and said gravely, "Then I am happy your hosts chose to contact us. And that we were there to come to your aid." He gave Adira another quick look, just long enough to – assess her reaction? What was in his mind?

She thought she knew. But she was nowhere near ready to follow where that thought led.

* * * * *

Since Adira had been restored to him, Abe had talked to her about many things – their recent cases, contact with former clients, the logistical frustrations Mom had overcome to return home, books he had started reading and finished or failed to finish, even the prospects for a hotter than usual summer. They had talked about almost everything except what most concerned them both.

What now?

They were still getting inquiries, requests to represent humans in the usual sorts of cases, and one Abe found particularly intriguing – a human author whose book the Library Realm had refused, and who wanted to appeal that decision. And they had received a missive from the viscount, an oversized envelope dropped through the office mail slot and sending the same tingle up the spine as a visit in person would have done. Inside, Abe found a greeting card showing a small town scene and the ambiguous text inside *Thinking of you*, along with a folded sheet of handcrafted paper. In elaborate and barely legible text, the viscount had written: *Their Imperial Majesties remain pleased with the new addition to their realm, and would be interested in acquiring more. If you and your charming associate are available to serve as – shall we say middle-mortals? – you have permission to visit us on Tuesday next.*

And then, below the even more elaborate signature, a scrawled postscript:

> *Now that you have educated us in the deficiencies of our previous negotiations, you may be sure the contract conditions will be more extensive.*

What would it be like, to revisit that realm? Or any of the other realms he had passed through during the recent ordeal? Could he even perform his professional duties in those settings, or would he be looking over his shoulder and starting at shadows, too distracted to apply his intellect properly to his clients' interests?

And would Adira ever set foot in any realm that reminded her of her captivity? Or any fae realm? She might even want to move somewhere that had no winter. Images flashed through his mind: eleven-year-old Adira throwing a snowball at him with wicked accuracy, seven-year-old Adira's pride in her first solo snowman. . . . What would those memories mean to her now?

Abe could still draft and negotiate contracts, any of the many sorts of contracts that people like himself made with each other. There was a whole world of human endeavor, business of every kind, dealing with anything from the construction of skyscrapers to the staging of musicals to the marketing of new and allegedly better cookware.

And Adira had not gone to law school with the sole ambition of joining his practice. True, the idea of meeting Fair Folk and visiting fae realms had been the earliest root of her desire, but she would never have followed through with that plan if the law's blend of logic and language and psychology had not appealed to her. And given that they had never engaged in trial work – negotiating over Tom's fate had been the closest Adira had ever come – she might find it intriguing to try such work on for size.

But could this be where it all ended, the excitement, the adventures? And the unique services they provided? When he'd first started to hear about human-fae dealings gone awry, he'd been shocked and sorry, but also exasperated. It was bad enough when one human being, or business, signed a normal contract without having a lawyer look it over. How much more they needed protection when trying to bargain with the Fair Folk! Not that he'd ever heard of a lawyer who would take on such an assignment.

And then it had struck him, like a blow, like lightning, that he could be that lawyer, and protect his fellow mortals from the consequences of carelessness and ignorance, or even from naiveté.

As he and Adira had done, time and time again, even to the moment they saved Tom from an eternity under the ice. Saved him, at such cost.

Adira had, after he dropped a few hints, assented to start coming to the office again, and to glance at one of the messages they had received, but she seemed to do it only to oblige him. And when she saw the viscount's card, she shied away like a panicked horse before she collected herself and passed it by.

The only way for Abe to know her plans, if she had made or contemplated any, would be for her to tell him, unless he stumbled on some clue like a letter to a conventional law firm or a bill from a signage company. She hadn't volunteered any such information, or even much conversation, though she made a point of being more affectionate than usual, dropping a kiss on his cheek in passing or giving him a quick hug whenever she came and went.

If he wanted to know her intentions, he would probably have to ask her. And he was stalling, because he hadn't decided his own, and soldiering on in his current field without her seemed a somehow barren prospect.

As he sat unproductively at his desk, Abe was just as glad to be distracted by the spine-shivering sign of a fae visitor. He almost called out the news to Adira, but thought better of it: what if it was the viscount, with some ominous tidings? He dragged himself out of his chair and went into the entry. At first he saw no one, until he remembered to look in all directions for a small fae or a flying one. The visitor, or rather visitors, proved to be the former, and he smiled, his heart lifting, to see the sandpiper forms of the ocean realm rulers. He bowed low, though even his best effort didn't place him eye to eye with them, and said as he straightened up, "Welcome! Have we any pending business I've forgotten, or do you come for another purpose?"

The larger bird said in its high peeping voice, "We wanted to see for ourselves that Valentina was safely home again. And here she is!" it added, at an even higher pitch, as Adira came running in and dropped to her knees to welcome them at ground level. Abe had the impression that Adira would have liked to hug them – and they must have sensed it, as they transformed into their seal pup forms and wriggled closer to her. She picked them up in both arms and squeezed them gently.

It was an adorable scene, taken out of context. Given the actual nature and status of these visitors, it boggled the mind. Adira must have belatedly realized as much, putting the pups back down and curtsying as she rose to her feet.

The pups looked at her with big, mournful eyes, so briefly that Abe wondered if he had imagined it. Then they took their adult seal forms and said, "If it would not inconvenience you, we would like you both to accompany us to our realm."

Was that all they intended to say? Why would they want to defer their explanation? But whatever the reason, Abe, at least, had no doubts as to his answer. He glanced at Adira to confirm that they were of one mind and then said, "Of course."

Abe stepped through onto the familiar cliff. He looked toward the horizon for oncoming large waves, expecting the rulers to appear in their awe-inspiring wave glamours, but saw nothing of the kind. A bump against his shin made him look down to see the seal pups once again. They were nudging Adira and himself toward the path to the beach. Bemused, he followed the suggestion, Adira on his heels. The pups tumbled and frolicked, ahead of them and then behind, as if they were as young and playful as their very misleading glamours made them appear.

Why were they making such an effort to amuse and disarm? He could think of no reason they would take such an approach with him – which meant they must be doing it for Adira's sake.

* * * * *

Adira didn't know what was going on and didn't care. It was such a welcome relief from contemplating the future, feeling guilty because the normal problems of normal people should seem as important to her as to them. Or else sitting in her and Dad's office, stomach clenching at the thought of a Fair Folk visitor, wondering whether this would be the case where some error would finally condemn her beyond forbearance or rescue.

She hadn't felt so young and silly and carefree since some dimly remembered days in college, and that had probably involved alcohol, not the incongruous momentary innocence of roly-poly seal pups, the warmth of sunshine mingled with a cooling ocean breeze that tugged her hair one moment and patted her face the next. It felt like more of the same when she tripped on a ledge at the bottom of the path and fell laughing on all fours in the sand.

The pups, however, had vanished. Sighing for the end of the interlude, she looked around and saw the rulers in their guise of Poseidon and Amphitrite, standing near her feet. But the next moment, they had plopped down on the sand, sitting cross-legged and, to her amazement, wearing cutoffs and rolled-up tee shirts. His read "King of the Waves," hers "Surf Siren."

And beside them lay two identical and magnificent surfboards, glossy, gleaming, swirling together every ocean color from dark and light grays to brightest emerald and jade to turquoise and sapphire.

Adira had never surfed, nor attempted to. But looking at the two fae across from her, still majestic and yet projecting unmistakable friendly intent, she understood the invitation, and knew that they would hold her upright if she wished, or let her try to stand on her own if she chose.

Dad knelt down at her side, his forehead wrinkled and his eyes darting back and forth between Adira and the fae. Hesitantly, he asked, "When my oceanographer client entered your waters, she wore a suit. What would . . . Valentina do instead?"

So he, too, saw this as an invitation addressed particularly to her. One meant to heal her, to make her welcome in a faerie world, a world whose waters were endlessly in motion, not frozen or meant to entrap.

The ocean king said gravely, "She might return to your realm to obtain a similar suit. Or, if she is willing, we will protect her with an enchantment that would prevent the water from touching her, though she would still feel its touch. And if she should fall, the enchantment would obviate the need for breathing until she reached the air again."

A chill ran through her, almost as if a wind from the ice realm had somehow reached her here. An enchantment, such as the one that had kept Tom alive and able to suffer while imprisoned beneath the ice.

Could she let an enchantment change her, touch her very skin?

She let her gaze move over the sand, past the foam at its edge, past the breakers, out to where the waves gathered height and strength before spilling over and rushing to shore.

It wasn't so much a question of whether she could. The question was, rather: could she reject this challenge, and this gift, and yet remain the woman she wanted to be? Remain the Adira who explored new lands and welcomed challenges and overcame fears?

Adira leapt to her feet. She bowed and then said, a smile taking over her face, "I would be honored and thrilled to ride your waters." At her side, Dad exhaled in such relief that his breath brushed her arm – her bare arm, for she found herself wearing an outfit like those of their hosts. She looked down at her shirt and read aloud, "Ready to Ride!"

And yet, the moment somehow felt incomplete. Running the last few minutes over in her mind, she realized where the problem lay. But the solution would require her to take yet another step into the unknown, accept yet another risk.

She took a deep breath, her heart pounding, and said, "I wish you to know, my lords, that my true name is Adira."

Dad gasped. Then there was no sound except the sough of the waves and the calls of distant birds, until the king replied, "We are honored by your trust, and will avail ourselves of this privilege only where no other being but your father may hear us."

Dissipating the solemnity of the moment, a surfboard appeared at her feet, deep purple with extravagant swirls of gold glitter. She hoisted it into her arms, grinning. The queen turned to Dad and asked, "Will you join us, sir?"

He looked at Adira and hesitated. "I would take great pleasure in watching my daughter ride your waves."

Adira dropped to her knees in the sand beside him. "Does that have to be enough? Don't you deserve to celebrate more fully?" It was, she realized almost at once, a question disguising a deeper one. How could they better commit to embracing the uncertain future than by bodily plunging into it?

Adira reached for Dad's hands, and he reached out for hers. They stood up, and another surfboard rose out of the sand next to him, green and gold and silver. As he grasped it, his clothes transformed into deep green swim trunks and a matching sleeveless tee shirt with the words "Never Too Soon, Never Too Late!" emblazoned on it in bright silver script.

The royal fae were on their feet as well. The king pointed to the water and called, "The ocean summons us. Let us answer!"

All four of them picked up their surfboards. Laughing, kicking up sand, Adira raced beside her father, following the king and queen into the waves.

ACKNOWLEDGMENTS

My deep gratitude goes to my beta readers this time around: Margaret DeVere, Steven Karel, Brianna Prislipsky, Wil Scott, Fred Smith, Wendy Teller, and Elisabeth Zguta. Please assume that any aspect of this book you find annoying persists despite their advice.

Various Fair Folk realms in this book were inspired directly or indirectly by photographs by the following contributors to Shutterstock (in no particular order): "Dr._Flash," "Miiisha," Gert Lavsen, Graeme Shannon, "Real Window Creative," "Gwoeii," "andreiuc88," Carlos Castilla, Matt Gibson, Rafael Cichawa, and other contributors whose work was no longer available when I tried to find out who created it. Another photograph, by Darragh Gorman of Lighthouse Industries, inspired my conception of the ocean rulers.

ABOUT THE AUTHOR

Karen A. Wyle was born a Connecticut Yankee, but eventually settled in Bloomington, Indiana, home of Indiana University. She now considers herself a Hoosier. She and her husband have two wildly creative adult offspring.

In addition to writing novels (science fiction, afterlife fantasy, general fantasy, and historical romance) and picture books, Wyle is an appellate attorney (though quasi-retired) and photographer. Her voice is the product of almost five decades of reading both literary and genre fiction. It is no doubt also influenced, although she hopes not fatally tainted, by her years of law practice. Her personal history has led her to focus on often-intertwined themes of family, communication, personal identity, the impossibility of controlling events, and the persistence of unfinished business.

CONNECT WITH THE AUTHOR

Learn more about Karen A. Wyle by looking her up on:
— her author website, http://www.KarenAWyle.com
— Twitter, where her handle is @KarenAWyle
— Facebook, at
   https://www.facebook.com/KarenAWyle
— Goodreads, at
   https://www.goodreads.com/KarenAWyle
— her blog, *Looking Around*, at
   https://looking-around.blogspot.com.

You can also follow the author on Bookbub, which will send you alerts about new releases.

(https://www.bookbub.com/authors/karen-a-wyle)

Like the book? Please tell readers! Online book reviews are enormously helpful – and old-fashioned word of mouth is terrific as well! (The author particularly appreciates Amazon reviews, if you're able to leave such.)

You can sign up for Wyle's monthly newsletter, including news of upcoming releases as well as looks at her writing process and extras like excerpts and cover reveals, via Wyle's newsletter signup link, on the home page of her author website (lower righthand corner).

www.ingramcontent.com/pod-product-compliance
Lightning Source LLC
Chambersburg PA
CBHW060759190726
48285CB00002B/490